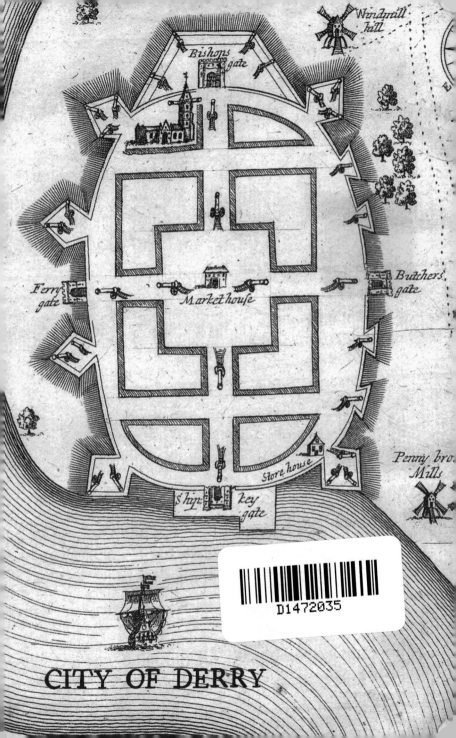

Windmill hill

Bishops gate

Ferry gate

Market house

Butchers gate

Store house

Penny bro Mills

Ship key gate

D1472035

CITY OF DERRY

Tallaght-born Nicola Pierce lives in Drogheda. Following her many successful ghostwritten books for adults, Nicola published her first book for children, *Spirit of the Titanic*. The book received rave reviews, and ran to five printings within its first twelve months. *City of Fate* was her second book for children and transported the reader deep into the Russian city of Stalingrad during World War II. The novel was shortlisted for the Warwickshire School Library Service Award, 2014.

Reviews of *Spirit of the Titanic*

'Gripping, exciting and unimaginably shattering'
Guardian Children's Books

'Captivating'
Sunday Business Post

'Intriguing'
Belfast Telegraph

'I absolutely adored this book. It makes you feel like you were there'
Finty, reader review

Reviews of *City of Fate*

'Compelling novel, combining rich characterisation with a powerfully evoked sense of time and place'
Robert Dunbar, *The Irish Times*

'Utterly brilliant with believable characters and a fantastic story line, this is historical fiction at its best'
theguardian.com

'Excellent ... vivid and moving'
BooksforKeeps.co.uk

BEHIND
the
WALLS
1689

NICOLA PIERCE

THE O'BRIEN PRESS
DUBLIN

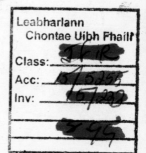

First published 2015 by The O'Brien Press Ltd,
12 Terenure Road East, Rathgar, Dublin 6, Ireland.
Tel: +353 1 4923333; Fax: +353 1 4922777
E-mail: books@obrien.ie
Website: www.obrien.ie

ISBN: 978-1-84717-646-2

1 2 3 4 5 6 7 8 9 10

15 16 17 18 19 20

Cover image: Shutterstock

Printed and bound by CPI Group (UK) Ltd, Croydon, CR0 4YY

The paper in this book is produced using pulp from managed forests.

For my parents

Acknowledgements

Firstly, can I start by encouraging readers to visit the wonderful city of Derry. Her walls are still intact and I especially recommend the walking tours and do not forget St Columb's Cathedral. This compact building provided the city's starving population with comfort and shelter. Go inside and take a right into a humble room that contains Adam Murray's sword, pocket watch and snuff box. They are there for all to see, including an original copy of George Walker's book of the siege.

Secondly, I wish to thank Peter Heaney for being my tour guide on my visit to his city. Apart from taking an entire day to lead me around, and find me every available pamphlet on the siege, he asked the cathedral's caretakers if I could hold Adam's possessions in my trembling hand. I didn't even think to have a photograph taken as I was too enthralled by the sword and watch; it simply never occurred to me.

Peter was also one of the manuscript's earliest readers and I wish to thank him for his sound advice and suggestions.

Other readers include Robert Dunbar, Niall Carney, Damian Keenan and Jack Maguire, and all opinions and suggestions were greatly appreciated.

This is my third novel and it was the hardest one to write yet. I'm not sure if this is a good or a bad thing, but there you have it.

Susan Houlden, my editor, pushed me to expand and explain, and expand and explain some more. This would not be the book it is today if it weren't for her tireless efforts and passion. Any mistakes are entirely my fault!

Emma Byrne's gorgeous art gave me the boost that I needed on a grey, wet afternoon when I felt I would never finish it. If for no other reason I had to keep going because her cover deserved a story.

And, finally, I want to acknowledge everyone who played a part in my writer's life in the last few years: to the librarians, teachers, booksellers and children who read my books or come to hear me talk about them … thank you!

PROLOGUE

I t is the winter of 1688 and bloody conflict rages across Europe. King Louis XIV, the Catholic king of France, wants to rule over the entire continent but cannot defeat his most hated enemy, the Dutch Protestant Prince William of Orange. Meanwhile, the mostly Protestant population of England bristle beneath the reign of the Catholic King James. Telling themselves not to worry, they reason that he is an old man, without an heir, and will be gone soon enough. On his death, his Protestant daughter Princess Mary, who is married to the Dutch William, will take her father's crown and all will be well again.

However, the heir to the throne changes when James and his much younger Catholic wife have a son, a male heir who will bow to the Pope in Rome. This proves too much for the English Parliament. They invite the fiery Prince of Orange to 'invade' and thus challenge James for the throne. William, anxious to rid France of another Catholic ally, accepts the invitation.

James flees to France, to be welcomed with open arms by his cousin, King Louis. There, they scheme to win back his English crown and decide to aim for a foothold in neighbouring Ireland.

It is a good plan except for the fact that not everybody on the island is Catholic or a devotee of King James. Take, for instance, the small walled city up north, founded by a saint and home to proud descendants of Protestant English and Scottish families, and the king's army. Who would have believed that the city of Derry was about to take centre stage for the first of three battles in the war of three kings, James, William and Louis XIV – a war which would change Europe forever.

CHAPTER ONE

A full-blown row had broken out, ruining what had otherwise been a peaceful afternoon, in this part of Derry at least. Horace had strayed again, breaking the rules and showing utter disregard for his surroundings, only these streets weren't *his* actual surroundings, which was the problem. He stood his ground, trying to make himself appear larger and taller than the others. A mischievous twinkle in his eye was the only proof that he knew exactly what he was doing and was more than ready for the circumstances.

In fact he was bigger than his opponents. The difficulty lay in the fact that there was only him while his opponents were a proper gang with a designated leader, followers and some sort of unspoken pact that they would not tolerate strangers on their street.

In baring his teeth, Horace declared his challenge while refusing to retreat. The high-pitched barking and snarling was fierce. There was no mistaking the sound of rage but the casual onlookers were unimpressed. Eyes rolled and heads were shaken at the clamouring uproar. A young girl who was scrubbing hard at a front door with a brushful of sudsy water let out a snarl of her own, 'Oh shut up, the lot of ye!' Horace blinked at her, his expression suggesting that he had no idea what the fuss was all about. However the girl ignored Horace's attempt at innocence and pointed rudely at him, 'You're the cause of all this trouble. Go back to wherever you came from or, by God, I'll give you a swift kick up the ...'

'Horace!' Daniel Sherrard had finally caught up with his rebel of a dog. Smiling nervously at the girl, Daniel beckoned his friend to his side. 'Come over here, Horace. Good boy!'

Horace hesitated; after all, a fight was a fight.

But the others decided that it was no longer worth the hassle; there were too many around now. So they made do with a few threats and curses, wanting to suggest to the invader that he had narrowly escaped the most ferocious violence. Really, it would be best for everyone if he could just have stayed out of their area, back where he belonged in the Protestant quarters.

Daniel called him again. 'Horace!' This time the large dog licked his lips, sneezed and turned to nuzzle his owner's shins. Daniel patted him on the head.

The girl also quietened down though she felt obliged to offer some haughty advice. 'Maybe you shouldn't walk him around here.' She stopped scrubbing to check that the hem of her apron had not dipped into the bucket of water beside her feet.

Daniel shook his head. 'I don't! He runs off on me.'

Horace scratched himself a little and then found it necessary to plop down so that he could scratch himself a lot harder. Daniel watched him and offered the girl an embarrassed shrug. She almost smiled at him but was mindful of her father inside the house who would not be pleased with her talking to a boy, particularly a strange one. She knew all the boys in her tight-knit community which meant that the 'foreigner' had to be a Protestant. He certainly looked unsure of himself. He was far from home.

The other dogs had removed themselves to the far end of the street where they seemed to be having a good sulk together. Gesturing at them, the girl said, 'Best you be getting him home before they decide to make another run at him … and you.'

Both dog and boy were strangers here.

Daniel experienced a tremor of annoyance. This was his city and he was allowed to go wherever he liked. Nevertheless there was no denying it. He didn't choose to come to this street. He was only here because of his disobedient pet. Tapping his leg, he said, 'Come on, boy. Let's go.' Horace gave the dogs a last cheeky bark and bounded ahead of Daniel.

As they neared the Diamond, the centre of the city,

the streets got busier and dirtier. Daniel stepped over the stinking piles left behind by horses and cattle, his mother's warning against dirtying his new boots ringing in his ears. He took hold of Horace by the scruff of his neck in case the dog took off after the livestock.

There seemed to be a gathering in front of the Market-house which usually meant that there was some sort of news pinned up on the wall of the building. Daniel could barely hear whatever was being read aloud over the clucking of the hens and the bleating of the skittish lambs. Carts rolled noisily over the paved stones, competing against the clip-clopping of the horses. Everywhere Daniel looked someone was either busy buying or selling something: candles, milk, animals, fish, eggs and shoes. Whatever a person fancied could be got here.

A beggar caught his eye. There were plenty of them. This one looked to be his father's age. His clothes were filthy and torn, just like his face. Daniel quickly looked away from him, judging the man to be a drunk, and one who was apt to get himself beaten up regularly.

Derry was a garrison city, meaning that she provided bread and board for the army of the king of England. However, two weeks earlier the city's soldiers and their commander, Lord Mountjoy, had left for Dublin, answering the summons of Sir Richard Talbot, the new lord lieutenant of Ireland. The ambitious Talbot was a loyal friend to the Catholic King James, and revelled in his prestigious appointment. Almost the first thing he did was to insist on a meeting with Derry's army of Protestants. Daniel found it peculiar not to see the uniform of the battalion standing out from amongst the crowd.

The previous evening his parents had discussed the turn of events, anxiously wondering what it could all mean. 'Soldiers keep the peace,' his mother had said; to which his father had muttered, 'It depends on the soldier.'

Robert, Daniel's older brother, immediately asked, 'What do you mean, Father?' He had his mother's dark eyes and high cheek bones while Daniel shared his father's features, clear blue eyes and a softness about the cheeks and chin.

Mr Sherrard sighed, 'Lord Mountjoy's regiment are mostly Protestant.'

Robert thought for a moment. 'You mean you think they will send us a Catholic regiment instead of allowing Mountjoy's men to return?'

His father nodded. 'Oh, I think that is a strong possibility, don't you? This city, along with Enniskillen, is one of the last Protestant strongholds, and I suspect that the Catholic lord lieutenant would much prefer us to be policed by his own.'

Daniel was suddenly returned to his surroundings by the sound of a commotion nearby. 'Thief! Thief!' A woman screamed and pretended to break into a run, but whoever it was that snatched her purse was already gone, disappearing into the throng of people who were drifting towards the Markethouse. Daniel shrugged his disapproval. It was the second robbery he had witnessed today.

The city needs her soldiers. That was his opinion. Even he could not help feeling the growing tension on the streets as the rumours raced throughout about marauding, murderous armies representing the Catholic king of England, James II.

A Catholic on the throne of England? How could this be?

Ordinarily Daniel did not concern himself with such worldly affairs but he simply could not ignore the worry in his parents' eyes. It felt sensible to accept that there might be trouble ahead, though how he could not yet imagine.

I wish I was clever like Robert. If his brother had been present, Robert would have playfully punched Daniel in the arm, reminding him that there were three long years between them – nearly a thousand days. It was a huge difference between any fourteen- and seventeen-year-old boy. *Well, that's just it,* he thought. *Robert is no longer a boy, he is almost a man.*

Horace yawned. Daniel glanced down at him. 'Sorry, boy, but I want to hear what's going on and then we'll go straight home. I promise!' Daniel believed that his dog understood every word he said. Since Horace made no move to voice his disagreement, Daniel was free to pat him as thanks for his cooperation. They joined the surging crowd. Daniel was putting his new plan into action, to keep himself informed of whatever was happening in his city and beyond. *After all*, he reasoned to himself, *I'm no longer a child either.*

A man called out, 'Please repeat yourself, sir. We didn't hear you!'

Several people around Daniel cried out, 'Speak up! Speak up!' The new additions to the crowd seemed anxious about what they might be missing. As far as Daniel was concerned their nervousness was thanks to the rumours of Catholic, or Papist, invaders.

The speaker, one of the townsmen, held up his hand and shouted as politely as he could, 'Alright, alright. Quieten down.' He waited for silence. 'This here,' he began, pointing to the pamphlet in his hand, 'was issued by Prince William of Orange.' Some clapping dutifully greeted the prince's name. People craned their necks to be sure to catch every word uttered. In fact the speaker was gearing himself up for his big moment and thus roared his next line, 'The Dutch Prince has declared the infant Prince of Wales to be an imposter!'

Well!

The word 'imposter' was taken up and repeated several times over, first in hushed tones but then as more people joined in it became louder and angrier: '"Imposter"? "Imposter"? Yes! "IMPOSTER"!'

A chorus of 'Hear! Hear!' rang out from the ones who had already heard the news. They'd had time to digest the information and agree that the newborn son of Catholic King James had no right to, what must only ever be, the Protestant throne of England. Anxious to hear the rest of the pamphlet they began shushing in earnest. There was no time to waste just yet.

'Let me continue!' called the speaker. 'Prince William says he doesn't wish to seize the throne for himself but he does believe that his father-in-law, King James, is being ill advised by the worst sort of people.'

Daniel assumed that both William and the speaker meant Catholics when they referred to the 'worst sort of people'. King James had surrounded himself with Catholic friends and servants, losing the love of his two Protestant daughters Mary and Ann and a lot else besides.

Two elderly women beside Daniel accepted this, one of them declaring, 'Well, William is not going to bring violence against his own father-in-law, is he?'

Her friend nodded and then thought of something. 'And he's a foreigner. So, he can't very well go and make war on the English throne, now can he?'

The first one sniffed her agreement. 'You're right, Doris. Sure the English wouldn't stand for that!'

Daniel wished they'd both shut up. The man was now reading out a list of things – bad things – that had been done in James's name, but Daniel couldn't hear a blessed word.

Horace whimpered his impatience to leave which, unfortunately for Daniel, set the women off on another topic.

'That dog smells!' pronounced the one called Doris.

Her friend giggled, 'Almost as bad as your Harold!'

The two women burst out laughing, annoying the ones behind them. Daniel was grateful when the others shushed them. There was no way he would have done it himself; they would have boxed his ears.

There was silence just in time to hear the man finish off by saying, 'William suggests a free parliament, one that can fix all the wrongdoing.'

There was a sober applause to this and then, when there seemed to be nothing else to read or hear, the crowd slowly, almost reluctantly, began to disperse.

Horace licked Daniel's hand as if to remind him of his promise that they would go now. Daniel paused to be absolutely sure that the meeting was at an end, before allowing himself to be pulled along in the direction of home.

CHAPTER TWO

Over the coming weeks changes tiptoed into the city. When Daniel accompanied Horace on his meanderings he saw more and more new faces, whole families with their belongings squashed up on carts, coming in from the hinterland beyond Derry's walls.

One day he, Horace and his father were walking by Bishop's Gate when they spied a young man on a tall, white horse who seemed to be escorting one such family into the city. Mr Sherrard hailed him, 'Why it's Adam Murray! Good day to you!'

The dark haired man, who wore a wide brimmed hat and a long frock coat, turned and smiled warmly, taking the time to nod graciously at Daniel. He addressed the family of refugees, 'If you follow this street around to the right, the lady of the third house said she could take you.'

The woman had a baby in her arms; two more children – boys no more than four or five years of age – were tugging at her skirts, wanting something or other. Their father stretched up his arm and shook Adam by the hand. 'Thanks for your help, Mr Murray.'

Adam rushed to assure him that there was no need for thanks. 'Don't worry. Your family will be safe here.'

The Sherrards waited for the family to leave before approaching. Daniel kept a firm grip on Horace, to prevent him from getting any ideas. Adam jumped down from his horse and embraced Mr Sherrard who asked, 'Is your father here too? I've not seen him in such a long time.'

Adam shook his head and grinned. 'You know how stubborn he is. I tried to get him to move into the city, even for a month or two, but he won't hear of it.'

Mr Sherrard exclaimed, 'So have you now set up home here in Derry?'

Adam shrugged. 'Ach, I'm here and there.' Giving Daniel a sidelong glance, he added, 'Actually, I'm looking to set up a regiment of like-minded souls who are prepared to fight a Catholic army, should it be necessary.'

Daniel stared openly at him. This was thrilling talk indeed.

Adam's horse, a shade of smudged white, nudged the boy in the shoulder, pushing him forward. Neither his father nor Adam took any notice of this as they discussed the latest stories that were spreading through the neighbourhood.

Mr Sherrard asked, 'You think they're coming for us?'

Adam glanced around them before saying, 'Yes, I suppose I do.'

Daniel's father wasn't prone to exaggeration or undue

excitement. He put a hand on Adam's arm. 'You know, a Catholic regiment does not have to mean terror. A city this size, this busy, needs her guards to keep order.'

Adam silently refused to agree with the first part and as to the second he offered, 'But we have soldiers. There are plenty of men here who want to protect everything that Derry stands for.'

Daniel watched the two men stare at one another before his father sighed, quickly following it up with a tight smile. 'Well, in any case, it's good to see you, Adam. Tell your father I was asking for him.'

The younger man returned the smile, though his was easier. 'Thank you, sir. I'll tell him.'

The horse only stopped butting Daniel when his master was back in the saddle again. Horace began to strain beneath his grip; the dog sensed that four legs were about to leap forward and he wanted to be free to play with them. One look from Mr Sherrard, however, put an end to that plan. Horace stood meekly beside his family and watched the horse take off, making no attempt to chase it.

There was a strange expression on Mr Sherrard's face. Daniel thought his father looked disappointed. Maybe he hadn't wanted the conversation to end so soon, or end how it had.

'Father,' ventured Daniel, 'is there going to be fighting? Are we in danger?' These ideas had only occurred to him as soon as he opened his mouth. His father didn't answer immediately. Daniel wanted him to know that he could take it, whatever his father was toying with not saying. 'I see all these people moving into the city. They're afraid, aren't they?'

Mr Sherrard gestured that they should continue walking. 'I don't know, son, and that's the truth. There's no point in my making up something for you because I just don't know what's going to happen.'

Later that same day, Robert Sherrard was much more forthcoming when Daniel asked him the same question. 'Something has to happen and soon!'

Daniel waited patiently for further explanation. His brother was preparing to join his friends at the wall. Working in shifts, they were helping to keep look-out for any sign of trouble, both inside and outside the city.

'Look, Dan, William isn't going to back down. Any decent Englishman wants that old Papist off the throne and William is the one to do it.' Robert had little of his father's discretion.

Daniel nodded to show he was listening hard. 'But, what does that mean for us ... exactly?'

His brother challenged him. 'Come on, what do you think it means?'

Daniel quickly ran through all the bits of information he had collected, glad for the opportunity to have his brother's ear. 'Um ...' he hedged. 'If William takes over from James – which is what we want him to do?' Here he looked at Robert to check he was correct in his assessment thus far.

Robert was pushed for time and decided to shorten the lesson. 'Yes, it's what *we* want here in Derry but down in Dublin, James's friend, the lord lieutenant, Richard Talbot, is far from happy. He will surely rustle up a Catholic army to take over this garrison which, as he knows, fully supports a Protestant king taking back the throne. Actually …' Robert pushed in the last of the buttons on his tunic, 'that's probably what he's doing this very minute. And then they'll be coming for us.'

Daniel hid his panic, or so he thought.

As Robert made to leave, he punched Daniel in the arm. 'Don't worry! This city can hold her own against James, Richard Talbot and whoever else comes looking for trouble.'

Daniel couldn't stop himself from asking, 'Are you sure?'

Robert merely winked as he slammed the door behind him.

Horace looked at Daniel expectantly: weren't they going out too? Just then, Mrs Sherrard, her hands covered in flour, called out, 'Stay right where you are, Daniel Sherrard. I need water fetched from the well.'

Daniel made a face that only his pet could see. 'Yes, Ma'am!'

Robert smirked in the darkness as he heard his mother's shrill voice. These days he was much too busy for household chores. How different his life was now. A few months ago his most pressing concern was to kiss as many girls as he could. Meanwhile, his father wanted him to study something, anything really. However, Robert did not feel that his future was paved between the pages of text books. He would leave those to his baby brother. Mr Sherrard was a hardworking physician who naturally expected one of his sons to take up his profession. It was unfortunate that his eldest son displayed little interest for dealing with sick people. But Robert wanted something different, something more than his father had done. He just hadn't quite worked out what it would be. His mother seemed equally put out that he showed no inclination to become a pastor. Robert was bewildered that she ever imagined he'd want to do that. Church talk was best left to those who liked the sound of their own voice.

The house seemed to have shrunk as his parents' expectations of him poured out into every room until, some evenings, he felt unable to breathe. It was like the walls were pressing against his chest.

But, now! Well, now things were happening beyond his parents' control. Exciting things! Freedom beckoned. That's how he felt anyway, though he couldn't explain why. Maybe he just sensed that a change was coming and that was surely better than nothing at all.

He knocked on the Campsies' door. Henry, his best friend, opened it, his coat on, ready to leave immediately. The two friends fell into step together. From a distance they looked alike, the same height and slenderness, the only difference being that Henry was broader in the shoulders which made him seem older and more capable somehow. He was also more dramatic in style, from the way he flicked dust from his coat to how he walked, ready for whatever was around the corner. 'Any news?' asked Henry.

Robert turned his head to spit. 'Not really, other than my father bumping into Adam Murray earlier. He says he's recruiting fellows to patrol the fields beyond the walls.'

Henry was intrigued. 'Really? Are you going to join him?'

Robert refused to commit himself, knowing that his parents would have something to say. 'Maybe … I'm just waiting to see what's going to happen.'

Henry pretended to believe that the decision was completely Robert's to make. 'Yes, me too!'

The only light in the long, narrow street came from the candles in some of the windows, throwing flickering shadows before and after them. As they passed one murky alleyway the sounds of a fierce battle didn't distract them from their walk. There was a lot of scrambling and scraping of feet accompanied by high pitched shrieks of rage. 'Rats!' said Henry cheerfully. 'I saw one yesterday and I swear it was almost as big as your dog.' Robert didn't believe him.

A cat bawled nearby followed by a few seconds of startling silence until it was answered by a second cat. Some sort of challenge had been thrown down: one animal warily announcing the boundaries of its territory to the other, a rude intruder. Suddenly, the air was punctured by a flurry of barks. If there was to be any fight over boundaries, the dogs insisted on being involved.

On any other night Robert might not have noticed any of this. Fighting rats, quarrelling cats and enraged dogs were the most ordinary and least important sounds of any city. Tonight, though, things were different. Robert sighed and said, 'It's almost like they sense that something is about to happen.'

Henry was puzzled. 'Huh?'

Robert flicked his wrist, gesturing at the assorted chorus on the night air. 'All this noise?'

Henry thought for a moment and then shrugged.

Robert confided in him, 'You know there is a little part of me that longs for something to happen, something big too.' When Henry said nothing to this Robert added, 'I mean … I hope, that is, I want to be able to do something important. Ach! I'm not explaining myself properly.'

Henry did his best to understand. 'You want to do something special or heroic?' That didn't sound right either.

Robert tried again. 'Do you believe or do you even want a future beyond these walls?'

Henry was not an imaginative sort of person nor did he spend time wondering about the future. What was the point in that? He accepted that his life was going to be more or less like his father's. He hoped that one day, he too would be Mayor of Derry. Mr Campsie was an important man in the city. Why wouldn't his son want to be just like him? 'You think too much!' were Henry's final words on the subject.

Robert wasn't prepared to allow him the last word. 'No, it's not that. I just get bored sometimes. A bit of excitement is surely not too much to ask for.'

They arrived at the section of the wall that they would be watching from, for the next six hours or so. Henry gave his friend a playful shove. 'Be careful what you wish for, Robert Sherrard!'

CHAPTER THREE

Mrs Sherrard's day usually began before six in the morning. During the summer months she relished being the first one up in the house. Not even Horace had the energy to get under her feet until well after seven o'clock.

On a cold morning, such as this one, she had to fight the urge to go back to bed. The rain spluttered off the roof, camouflaging her own movements from her sleeping husband and sons. Had the day been warmer she would have waited for Daniel to get up and have him do the fire but she preferred to get it going now, as quickly as she could. *Brr! It's a chilly one.* As soon as the flames began to stir, she wagged a finger at Horace in case he had any ideas about moving closer to the fireplace. He wasn't stupid though. Horace knew that if he annoyed her too early it would result in his eviction outside onto the wet, dark streets.

In her head she had a list of chores to be done: things like repairing Mr Sherrard's Sunday shirt; washing the boys' underclothes; salting the fish she had bought yesterday; peeling the potatoes; boiling up the oats to make porridge and the rye for Mr Sherrard's beer. Except for eating her breakfast and dinner, she was looking at a full day of maybe fourteen hours or so.

Another woman, especially one in her condition, might have strained against the constant chain of chores but Mrs Sherrard didn't. She believed that God meant his people to keep themselves busy, obedient and productive. She was never sick. As she herself said, 'I simply wouldn't have the time for it.'

When Daniel gets up he can empty the chamber pots. At least the rain will wash most of it away.

Unfortunately that meant that it would also wash her neighbours' waste right past her door too. This is why she preferred that if it had to rain, it should come down in a raging torrent that had the strength to sweep everything off the paths.

In the tiny kitchen she checked how much water was in the bucket. She also checked if the mice had been at her bread. To her dismay their dots of droppings were everywhere. 'Maybe we should get a cat!' She had said the words to Horace without thinking. He stared back at her as if she had asked his opinion on the gravest of matters.

A sudden noise in the corner brought him to his feet. She left him to his work: to stand perfectly still until there was another noise, one too small for Mrs Sherrard's ears. He crashed through whatever was in his way, snarling ferociously until the rodent was upside down and swinging lifelessly between his grinning jaws.

Mrs Sherrard told him, 'At least you get to eat meat every day. That's more than most people have.'

Horace unashamedly ignored her as he gulped down his breakfast, crunching thread-like bones and spitting out hairs. He returned to where he had found the mouse. Any dog with his experience knew rightly that where there was one mouse, there was bound to be another.

Mrs Sherrard walked through the front of the house and opened the door for no particular reason at all. Horace, fearing that she meant to send him outside, crept under the table to play dead. She tipped herself over the threshold. Rain streaked her face and drops fell upon her hair, causing it to glisten in the candlelight. Without realising it, she was checking that all was as it should be. The thick walls loomed in the darkness. Of course they were still there. *Why wouldn't they be?*

'My dear, what on earth are you doing?' Mrs Sherrard's husband's expression was one of bafflement.

Flustered to have been caught out like this, his wife snapped at him, 'Really, Edward, I do wish you wouldn't sneak up on me!'

Closing the door smartly, she went to fetch some bread that the mice hadn't touched along with a small glass of milk.

Mr Sherrard watched her, wishing he had waited before opening his mouth, particularly since he knew exactly what she had been doing. Sitting at the table, he said quietly, 'It may all come to nothing.'

His wife busied herself cutting the bread. Mr Sherrard sipped his milk and the rain continued to fall. They were both thinking of the same thing, not that either of them were aware of this. No matter what was going to happen or not happen at all, the baby in her belly would be here very soon. That much was fact.

House by house, street by street, the city stirred to wakefulness as daylight strove to push its way through navy clouds that appeared to be puffed out with rain. They looked as if one could burst them open, only needing to reach up and prod them with something sharp like a knife or a scythe.

The walls gave nothing away. It was they who the wind battered on its travels from miles away. The wind whispered its secret to the birds, the trees and whoever would listen. It carried the sound of a thousand feet or a thousand more, marching north over virgin forest floor, through streams of the purest water and bogs full of ancient history. The land did its best to impede the approach but it wasn't enough. Nothing could stop this coming; it was a storm and it was man-made.

A few short miles south-east of Derry, at Ling, eighty-nine-year-old Gabriel Murray watched the horizon change from black to grey and felt the shift around him. Looking towards the walled city in the distance, he saw the clouds thicken and fold into one another. He had seen many things throughout his long life and had learned how to read signs that would never be written down. His few animals, a handful of cows and an aging horse, were uneasy. To be sure, they continued to graze but they constantly lifted their heads to glance here and there, pawing the ground as if to reassure themselves that it was still there beneath their feet. Gabriel nodded to himself: *it seems we're all waiting for something.*

CHAPTER FOUR

A few weeks after Mrs Sherrard had given birth to baby Alice, Robert arrived home in the early afternoon. Daniel was reading aloud to his father. They looked up, startled, as Robert burst through the door in a state. 'Quick! Everyone is being summoned to the Markethouse.'

His mother had just managed to get Alice off to sleep and was much annoyed with the noise. 'Hush! You'll wake the baby.'

Robert, however, had no interest in sleeping babies. Why were his family just staring at him as if he were a dragon or some wild beast? He gulped a short breath and said, 'You don't understand. You must come *immediately*. The townsmen and church elders have called an emergency meeting.'

Daniel – good old Daniel – leapt from his stool and dropped the book on the table, ready to leave this very minute. Mr Sherrard was less eager to move for Robert's approval. He needed more information. 'What is this all about?'

His father's flat tone made Robert want to push the furniture over. He had kept the front door open, assuming that his parents would be exiting the house as soon as he bid them to. Now he pointed to the neighbours passing by, men, women and children, on their way to the Diamond. Mr Sherrard glanced at the doorway and then back at his son whose impatience was growing. Nevertheless, Robert knew his father would not budge until he was provided with a good enough reason. It didn't matter what anyone else was doing.

Actually, if Robert was honest with himself, this was a quality he admired in his father except that, right now, Robert had no time. Right now, his father's stubbornness was only frustrating him. However, he was forced to give in and take the time to say, 'A letter has been found. I'm not sure of the exact contents but it's something about a Catholic army. That's why they want everyone at the Markethouse. They're going to read it out and decide then what to do about it.'

Daniel looked at his father; surely he was going to move now. To Robert's immense relief, Mr Sherrard did get up and straighten his clothes. 'Alright, boys, let's go then.' This was followed by Mrs Sherrard declaring, 'I'm coming too! Just let me get Alice.'

Robert longed to be back at the Markethouse, but it wouldn't do to run off on his parents, now that he finally had their attention. Daniel stood at his brother's hip in his eagerness to be part of whatever was consuming him.

Horace seemed ready to sacrifice his afternoon nap, but Daniel told him to stay where he was. 'You'll only get trampled on in the crowd.' The dog pouted but knew there was no point in arguing. Nevertheless, he did sound out a few whimpers of protest that were completely ignored. Horace sighed and stared at the wall until it suddenly occurred to him that an empty house meant he could go upstairs and lie on the boys' bed. This cheered him up in no time and he managed a husky woof of fond farewell when the family finally headed out the door.

The streets were thronged with people of all ages and class. Daniel could hear the word 'letter' reverberate throughout. It was a rather cool December afternoon. The sky threatened rain. Indeed that's what Daniel felt hung heavy in the air, a threat, both from the sky above and from whatever they were about to hear.

Robert walked ahead of his parents, politely dipping his head as his friends and their parents greeted him. Daniel watched him with pride. *He knows just about everyone.* Mr

Sherrard gave the barest nod of his head, leaving his wife to do the smiling and hello-ing. He was not what one might call sociable. Daniel once heard him tell his mother that he had no real need for friends; he had enough with his family. His only social excursion was to the cathedral on Sundays. Even then, when the men gathered outside after the service, to talk business and politics, Mr Sherrard would only wish them a cordial good day as he passed them by.

At the Markethouse Alderman Tomkins was waiting to start. The letter was in his hand; he kept his head down as if he were re-reading it over and over again. His face was grave; whatever was in the letter was serious. A large semi-circle formed in front of him, thus allowing as many people as possible to see and hear him. A group of church leaders and elders stood in silence behind him. They watched the crowd with the same grave expression.

When it was judged that the community at large was before him, Alderman Tomkins raised a hand, signifying that the chatter must cease because he was about to unveil the reason for the meeting. A great deal of shushing and hushing ensued with some individuals bent on shushing more people than anyone else. The volume of their shushing made the younger children giggle. They thought they were witnessing a new game and some even joined in, roaring 'HUSH' in delight until their red-faced mothers swiped at them in embarrassment.

Finally there was silence. The crowd waited for the alderman to begin, but the good man, relishing the attention, would not be rushed into speaking. As he perused the sheet in his hand, one more time, his index finger pushed against his lips, one cheeky five-year-old demanded of his mother, 'What are we waiting for, Mama?'

Pretending not to hear the question, Alderman Tomkins was set to stand there a little while longer but a short 'ahem!' from one of his colleagues had the desired effect.

He peered at the faces in front of him as if it had only just now come to his attention that hundreds of people were impatiently waiting to hear him speak. 'Yes, yes!' he said, stretching out the page in his hand. 'We, that is, my esteemed colleagues and I, have brought you here today because a matter of the utmost importance has come to our attention.' He paused, feeling a break was appropriate here. This time the silence was broken by the mother of the five-year-old, who was already weary of waiting. 'But what is it? What's happening?'

Alderman Tomkins sniffed in his most pompous manner, 'In fact, madam, I am about to read it if you would be so kind as to allow me to continue.' Someone somewhere groaned. 'Before I read this,' he said, holding up the sheet, 'I should tell you that this is a copy of a letter that was found on a street in Comber, County Down. The writer does not provide his name but it is addressed to a Lord Mount Alexander.'

At this point one of the church leaders, Reverend James Gordon, a Presbyterian minister, longed to take the letter himself and read it out. All of this time-wasting was, in his opinion, absolutely scurrilous. He gave another brief cough, hoping to accelerate the proceedings. However, it wasn't necessary. At long last Alderman Tomkins opened his mouth and read out the following words:

'Good my lord, I have written to you to let you know that all our Irishmen through Ireland is sworn that on the ninth day of this month they are to fall on to kill and murder (every Protestant) man, wife and child.'

The letter was longer than that but nobody wanted to hear anything else after that awful first line. A gasp rapidly became a roar as the alderman's audience quickly digested its meaning. Daniel saw his mother take his father's arm and, instinctively, he moved closer too. All around them panic was fluttering. One man called out, 'What are you saying? What are you telling us?'

Alderman Tomkins raised his hands to try to settle the crowd while saying, 'Surely the meaning is obvious – the Irish supporters of King James want to wipe us out!' He pleaded with them for confirmation. 'Wouldn't you agree? That much seems to be clear from what I have read.'

The next question to surface was chanted from the back

of the crowd. 'What is today's date?'

Reverend Gordon felt obliged to step forward and answer, 'The seventh of December.'

A few women screamed.

Daniel heard his father mutter, 'Ridiculous!' Mr Sherrard freed his arm from his wife's grasp and moved forward. Robert looked surprised but followed him.

'Could it not be a hoax?' Mr Sherrard called out. 'Is it not strange that the letter is unsigned?'

Some of his neighbours nodded gratefully; this was a much more attractive explanation. Others, like Henry's father, Mayor Campsie, refused to be comforted. Instead, he offered his own theory. 'Perhaps the writer is protecting his own skin. He might well be a Catholic who is risking his life to pass on this warning to his Protestant friend. He could hardly provide his name then.'

The community took a moment to consider this, allowing Mayor Campsie to underline his point. 'Either way, do we really have the luxury of not accepting this as a real threat? It's only us and Enniskillen that are the two main Protestant garrison cities, and that scoundrel Richard Talbot wants us to support his Catholic king … or else!'

From the moment of his appointment by King James, Lord Lieutenant Talbot had made his presence, that is, his religion, felt. His changes were many and made fast. He rid the Irish army of Protestant soldiers and ousted well-to-do Protestants from the best of the government jobs. Catholics poured in from everywhere to fill up the vacancies.

Robert found himself agreeing with the mayor. What he said made perfect sense and didn't it echo what his father had said himself only a few weeks ago?

Reverend Gordon spoke. 'We believe that there is a Catholic army on its way to Derry.'

Someone shouted, 'Evacuate the city!'

The reverend shook his head. 'No, wait.' He had more to say, but the noise was tremendous as people voiced their own concerns, no matter who else was speaking.

However, as his sons noted, once Mr Sherrard started to speak, the crowd quietened down to hear him. 'Are we really to believe that there is going to be an all-out massacre? From what I hear of James, he is not a man to prompt unnecessary bloodshed.'

Mayor Campsie shook his head at this. 'How can we be sure?' Sensing that more than a few of his neighbours felt he was correct, he declared with pride, 'I, for one, could never trust a man who gives up his father's faith. An English king who chooses the Pope over his family and country? I'll tell you what that it is, it's an insult to all of us!'

This was an opinion that he had shared many times since James II took the throne. Daniel heard a whispered groan. 'Oh don't get him started or we'll be here all day!'

His mother heard it too but hid her smile behind Alice's head.

Alderman Tomkins did his best to take charge again. Clapping his hands, he said, 'The question is, dear neighbours, do we allow the army in? They're coming to take up residency here, like any army of the English king.' Not many people were listening to him. He clapped his hands some more. 'That's why we're here today, to decide what to do.' The poor man looked hurt that so few were paying him attention.

It was the Anglican bishop of Derry, Dr Ezekiel Hopkins, who patted him on the arm. 'I was afraid of this. Perhaps we should have a meeting with only the most prominent citizens.'

The alderman refused to agree or disagree with this, only pleading with the bishop, 'But why don't they listen? They should be demanding to hear what we think.'

Dr Hopkins said as quietly as he could, 'That, my dear sir, is mostly a mob with a blind will of its own. But don't give up yet, they just might come to their senses.'

Daniel felt bound to stick by his mother. He could see Robert and his father arguing with the people nearest him and longed to join them. However, he couldn't leave her alone. She already looked bothered by the people pressing in around her, fearing that the baby would be distressed. As if she could read his mind – and she claimed that she could – she said to him, 'You stay right here!'

He widened his eyes. 'Of course!'

She wasn't fooled; she could see he wanted to follow his brother.

The two of them observed their neighbours, feeling slightly distant from the debating. Mrs Sherrard kissed the baby's head. 'Oh, I wish your father would come back to me. There'll be no one answer that will please everyone.'

A man walked by them. Something in his manner made them watch him as he worked his way purposefully through the crowd until he reached the group of elders and churchmen. A circle was formed and heads were bowed as the man said his piece. Gradually the arguing between everyone came to halt. The man was a messenger sent by a Colonel George Phillips of Newtown Limavady. Whatever he said, it certainly caused something of a stir amongst his listeners.

A second alderman moved to the front and addressed the square. 'Colonel Phillips has seen the army himself. And it is a Catholic army. His advice is to lock the city gates against them.' There was probably no need for him to add, 'He says we should prevent them from coming into Derry.'

There was a roar of 'Hear! Hear!' from some. Bishop Hopkins didn't look too pleased. The noise threatened to escalate again. Waving his arms, and doing his best to hide his irritation, he called out, 'Let me just remind you – this army represents King James, the king of England.' Despite the cool temperature, the bishop was obliged to wipe away sweat that was beading his forehead.

He continued, 'As citizens of this city, we are servants to the throne.' He waited for agreement to this and spied a few heads nodding. 'Well?' he asked. 'Who are we to refuse entrance to the king's army? Would that not be treason?'

Both Daniel and his mother made sure not to lose sight of Mr Sherrard. What did he make of this?

Reverend James Gordon, the Presbyterian minister, had made up his mind. 'Lock the gates!' He repeated himself to make sure. 'Lock the gates!'

Dr Ezekiel Hopkins repeated his disagreement immediately. 'No! It is the duty of a subject to obey his sovereign. No matter what, King James is still our sovereign.'

A row broke out again. Mrs Sherrard was not surprised to see her husband shrug his shoulders and make his way back to her. Mayor Campsie took up a new cry. 'But what about the letter? If we let them in, we may be slaughtered!' Ha! That surely put an obstacle in the plan to play polite hosts to James's Jacobite army. Daniel noted with dismay that even his father began to look confused.

Who knows how much longer the debate might have continued if a second messenger had not arrived, this time from the Ferry Quay Gate that overlooked the river Foyle.

There was a brief whispered discussion before Reverend Gordon, looking slightly dazed, informed the city, 'They're here! There are Jacobite soldiers standing on the banks of the Foyle.'

In the resulting chaos, Daniel dived forward to be with his brother. His father would take care of his mother and Alice. Women began screaming for their children, who were standing right next to them. The younger ones were bewildered by the terror on the faces of their mothers. Daniel saw one woman pick up two small boys while their siblings did their utmost to climb up her body, to the safety of her arms.

The crowd began to disintegrate, taking off in all directions but all heading for the same destination: home. One husband bellowed at his wife, 'Pack what you can, as fast as you can!' So, this was it. They were going to make a run for it, not bothering to check what exactly they were running from.

However, not everyone was leaving. Robert saw several of his friends in the crowd. Over and between the figures of their fellow citizens, they signalled to one another to make their way to the Ferry Quay Gate. 'Coming?' Robert asked his brother. Daniel didn't bother to answer such a silly question, though he did check on his parents. They seemed to be heading towards the gate too, no doubt his father refusing to react until he inspected the danger for himself.

Mr Campsie encouraged Henry, 'Go on, son. You lead the way.'

On reaching the gate, several men and boys climbed the ramparts, to confirm to the tense onlookers that, yes, there was definitely an army approaching the city. One of the boys on the ramparts was a former classmate of Robert's. He shouted up to him, 'Hi James, what can you see?'

James Morrison's face was dark with rage. 'They're all wearing kilts, the whole stinking lot of them!'

Another man cooed, 'And they're all bloody giants. Look at them! Did you ever see anything like it?'

William Cairnes, another of Robert's friends, spat, 'They're Redshanks, bloody Scots from the Highlands!' The boys faced him. 'How do you know that?' asked Henry. William couldn't help sound smug. 'My Uncle David is a lawyer and he heard rumours about Talbot's army only taking on men over six feet tall.'

Robert was furious. 'Do they imagine that height will scare us?'

Daniel, feeling scared, said nothing, although he did wonder why William had kept such an important piece of information to himself.

'Look!' said one of the watchers on the wall. 'They're sending someone over.'

Sure enough, two men were making their way to the

gate. Robert guessed the man to be a lieutenant and the companion was probably his assistant. They were met by John Buchanan, the deputy mayor of Derry, and Horace Kennedy, one of the city's sheriffs. Silence fell upon the crowd; no one wanted to miss a word. Mr Kennedy greeted the men coolly. 'You need to show your warrants, gentlemen.'

The lieutenant, noting how many pairs of eyes were on him, nodded amiably and said, 'We have them right here.' The sheriff took his time checking the two documents while the lieutenant and his man stood patiently, their arms relaxed at their sides. It bothered fussy Mr Kennedy that he had to look up at them; they were so much taller than him and his colleagues. He also felt that they looked more confident than they had a right to: *Cheeky dogs!*

In his own good time, Mr Kennedy handed the warrants back to them. The lieutenant smiled, took out another sheet of paper and said, 'On behalf of King James II, I request entrance to the garrison of Derry. I require billets for my men and forage for our horses.'

Mr Kennedy grinned to himself. *We have them now.* One of his fellow sheriffs winked at him. Mr Kennedy asked, 'Who is to be billeted within *our* walls?'

The two men heard the emphasis on the word 'our'. The lieutenant raised his eyebrows. 'Why, our soldiers. Of course!' He hadn't meant to add the last two words but the sheriff's pompousness was beginning to grate on him.

'Oh!' parroted the sheriff. 'Of course, is it? Well, I'm afraid there is a problem with your warrants. Your request for billets must be accompanied by a list of the names of each soldier.'

Doing his best not to show dismay, the lieutenant said slowly, 'We have travelled a long way on behalf of King James. It is he who wishes us to take up quarters in Derry.'

Mr Kennedy beamed at the men. 'I am sorry, gentlemen, but rules are rules. We need a list of names or else we must turn you away.'

In the background, the rest of the army, ignorant of dodgy paperwork, were preparing to cross the Foyle. No doubt they were looking forward to a decent meal and the chance to rest after their journey.

The stand-off at the gate continued, with voices being raised on both sides. Daniel wondered why the lieutenant didn't just go and fetch a list of the names. It seemed the most sensible thing to do.

Meanwhile, the tramping of the soldiers and the neighing of their horses made the residents jumpy. They were still coming and Daniel fancied that the self-important sheriffs were shrinking in size.

The crowd turned inwards to consider the question of letting the army in or not. Daniel heard his father's voice. 'They don't seem violent, or they would have rushed the gate instead of producing warrants.'

However, he was immediately contradicted by Mayor Campsie. 'Are you willing to risk the lives of your wife and children because they don't seem to want to kill us just yet?'

Heads turned this way and that as neighbours and friends were torn between wanting to stand strong together and, at the same time, make the right and the best decision. It was the same dilemma that the church leaders and town elders were in. Bishop Hopkins was still adamant that the army be allowed in while folk like William Cairnes's uncle, David, the lawyer, were equally adamant that the gates be locked against them immediately.

It took Daniel a while to realise that his group – Robert and his friends – had reached their own conclusion. They were indignant boys who hated to waste time on talk. For them, there was only one option. Henry Campsie scanned his friends and muttered, 'Are we all in agreement?' Eleven boys, including Robert Sherrard, nodded in unison.

Robert gripped Daniel's arm. 'Do you want to come with us or go back to Father?'

Daniel reddened under the rude gaze of the others. He stammered, 'C-come with you', hardly knowing what he was agreeing to.

'Well done!' said Henry, who turned and headed for the guards who were standing inside the gate, confident in the fact that twelve boys were following him.

The two men watched the boys approach with some trepidation.

'It's alright,' said Henry. 'We just need the keys for a few moments and then we'll give them back to you. You have my word.'

The guards exchanged a glance and then a shrug as it seemed they simultaneously grasped what might be about to happen. Nevertheless, the first one felt duty-bound to ask, 'What do you want with them?'

It was Robert who chuckled and said, 'Guess!'

The more cautious of the two shook his head and muttered, 'Oh, I don't know about this.'

Henry had no time for caution and informed the man, 'If there is any bloodshed today, it will be on your head.'

The two men, who were both husbands and fathers, did not want such a responsibility. They handed over the keys, deciding to trust in these young fellows who seemed unafraid of the approaching army.

Robert was relieved; he was worried that Henry might have physically threatened the guards and God knows what that would have led to.

All this while, the arguments continued around them. The two Redshank officers were still in the same place, the lieutenant's expression contorted in anger and disbelief. Yes, he had expected resistance but this was ridiculous.

Mr Kennedy, the sheriff, discovered he had a gift for obstinacy. He thought that if he could only keep the army outside the walls then no decision would have to be made just yet, about letting them in or not. He silently thanked whoever had drawn up the documents and forgotten to add in the list of names – even if they were a Papist.

The army was drawing nearer and nearer.

The keys were big. Henry led his own little army to the Ferry Quay Gate and issued instructions. 'Sherrards, pull up the drawbridge!'

Robert and Daniel ran to do just that, winding up the coiled wheel clock-wise. The people on the streets were too distracted to hear the squeaks and grunts of the bridge. As soon as it was up, the boys slammed the gate shut and locked it, staring at one another in heady delight. There was no time to lose now especially as they could hear cries from outside the walls. 'Hurry! Hurry! They're closing the gates.' Daniel felt deliciously light-headed, and his heart galloped against his chest.

The lieutenant swung away from Mr Kennedy. 'What are you doing?' he cried.

No one answered him. The boys were already in full sprint to the next gate.

Within minutes all of the gates were locked: Ferry Quay Gate; Ship Quay Gate; Butchers' Gate and Bishop's Gate. The thirteen boys returned to their starting position at

Ferry Quay Gate. The Jacobite officers, the town sheriffs, Reverend Gordon, the other churchmen and the citizens who had stuck around to see what was going to happen watched their approach in silence. Daniel wondered if Henry or even Robert were going to make a speech of some sort. However, neither boy said a word. They were bold enough to do something but they knew their place. The speech-making would be left to their elders.

Bishop Hopkins seemed as confused as the army outside, who were making their indignation known at the top of their voices. The lieutenant demanded the boys' attention. 'Do you realise that you are locking the king's army out of its own garrison?'

Henry Campsie, out of breath, from nervousness and running, ignored the angry man. Instead he wordlessly searched the crowd for support. And he found it. Bewilderment and ambiguity melted away, for the most part, as the blacksmiths, the tailors, the servant girls, the housewives, the masons, the guards, the candle-makers, the shopkeepers and the sheriffs suddenly understood what the boys had done and why they had done it.

Mayor Campsie, sensing the crowd's mood, punched the air with his fist and announced to the lieutenant, 'Sir, this is our city and it is our duty – as her proud citizens – to keep her safe!'

Daniel heard a baby bawling and saw his parents making

their way through to where he and the others stood. He felt his belly plunge. Was his father displeased? Daniel had never caused his parents trouble before. He had never done anything out of the ordinary. This clearly was a first for them all.

Of course the brash Mr Campsie had been the first to react. No surprise there.

Mr Sherrard stared at his sons, not really knowing what to think. Robert struck a pose between delight and guilt, while Daniel, the child who was most like himself, looked a little terrified. Mr Sherrard could only wonder, *What on earth do I say?*

In the end, his wife took the matter out of his hands, saying, 'Husband, dear, I'm taking Alice home to feed her.' Sensing his uncertainty, she suggested, 'Perhaps you could escort us back?' He looked at her and she nodded, as if he had said something.

And just like that, they turned and headed for home, but not before Mr Sherrard gave Daniel a brief nod of his head to ease the boy's mind.

CHAPTER FIVE

There was some clapping at Mayor Campsie's fiery words, no more than a few pairs of hands but it was a start. Heads swivelled left and right as individuals checked with their companions that they wouldn't be alone if they began to clap too. Smiles were registered and passed along. A few shy cheers were even released.

Henry beamed and shrugged to his friends. 'It's alright. We did the right thing!'

Robert was surprised at the relief on his friend's face. He must not have been as sure of himself as he thought.

His own father's reaction was a disappointment, but his mother had flashed him a look of pride. At least he had managed to impress one of his parents. It had been like this for as long as he could remember; his mother took his side while his father doted on Daniel. *I wonder what Father thinks now, after watching his pet lock out a king's army.*

There was a shout from above. James Morrison roared, 'Here they come!'

A group of soldiers reached the city wall and demanded to be let in. James made a rude gesture to them. Daniel marvelled at his cheekiness but worried that he was taking quite a risk. All it needed was one soldier with either a rifle or a perfectly thrown rock. James seemed oblivious to the danger of annoying the men outside.

Daniel watched the lieutenant beseech the church leaders to have the gates reopened. *Maybe they should tell him about the letter, about the killing on the ninth of December?*

Reverend Gordon, the aldermen, the bishop and the others stood close together and appeared to be arguing amongst themselves before uniting to argue with the lieutenant. Mr Kennedy, for one, was pleased with the outcome. He didn't like the cut of the lieutenant, feeling sure he couldn't be trusted. *They're a shifty lot*, he thought, meaning Catholics, Scots and – quite possibly – anyone taller than him.

Henry returned the keys to the two guards. Now that the deal was done, the guards relaxed into agreement. It was the cautious one who sighed, 'It had to be done. It just needed someone to take charge.' Henry shook his hand.

Reverend Gordon disengaged himself from his peers and strode purposely towards the group of lads. The people parted to let him through, curious about his reaction. 'So,' he said to the line of boys, 'you decided to act without us.'

A smattering of tentative 'Yes, sirs' was the muted reply.

Reverend Gordon nodded, glancing at all thirteen faces in turn, finally saying himself, 'Yes, sir!'

Alderman Tomkins joined him and asked, 'Well, Reverend, what do you make of this?'

Daniel held his breath.

'I think,' said the reverend, 'that I might be so bold as to make a prediction.'

The alderman laughed, saying, 'That's not your usual style.'

'No, indeed,' smiled the reverend. 'However, I find myself moved by the courage of these young fellows. I have a feeling this day will long be remembered.'

Daniel allowed himself to relax.

This time a definite cheer went up from the citizens of Derry. Outside, the would-be visitors tried to work out what was going on. They heard the cheering and still hadn't come to terms with the fact that entrance to the city was being denied to them. After all, their lieutenant was still inside. That was a good sign, wasn't it? How much longer would they have stood there, scratching their heads, if cheeky James Morrison had not decided to put them right?

James's confidence, fuelled by Reverend Gordon's blessing of the closing of the gates, prompted him to yell, 'Clear off! The lot of you!'

Naturally, these six-foot warriors were not about to take orders from a scrawny, ill-mannered fool. They remained where they were and just maybe a few imagined the size of the rock that would knock the loudmouth from his stage.

Furious at what he felt was their misguided arrogance, James took the matter further … much further. Knowing that the soldiers could not see beyond his head and shoulders, James pretended to be calling back to soldiers of his own, 'Hey, you there, bring that gun over here!' At this, the Scottish soldiers decided that it was probably best to move away. Heads down, they shuffled back to join the rest of the forces. James was immensely pleased with himself, a feeling not shared by everyone present.

Robert heard Alderman Tomkins exclaim to Reverend Gordon, 'That little fool! Get him down from there.' The reverend beckoned Robert to him. 'Do you know that boy?'

Robert reluctantly said he did. He too had been alarmed at James threatening to fire on the soldiers, even if he was only pretending. Locking them out was one thing, firing a cannonball – real or imaginary – was something else entirely.

Reverend Gordon said quietly, 'You might tell your friend …'

Robert interrupted him, 'He's not really a friend, sir. We just played together as children.'

'In any case,' said the reverend, 'tell him that if he ever endangers his city like that again, he shall be locked up for the rest of his days. I'll see to it personally.'

Robert bowed his head. 'Yes, sir, I'll tell him.'

Meanwhile, another party was making itself known. Derry's resident Catholics were naturally quite shaken by the afternoon's events. The Presbyterian and Anglican Church leaders merely stood and stared at the dozen or so Catholic neighbours who introduced themselves to the lieutenant. Their spokesman talked quietly. He didn't want to attract attention; he just wanted to inform the officer that their wishes matched his. 'We are a friend to King James and truly sorry for how you and your men are being treated.'

Not surprisingly, the lieutenant had been far from impressed with James Morrison's antics and let the spokesman know as much. 'I know the boy was bluffing but is that the way things are headed?'

The spokesman sighed, 'A letter was found containing a warning that all Protestants are to be murdered on 9 December.'

The lieutenant baulked. 'That's preposterous. Who wrote it?'

One of the other Catholic men said, 'It wasn't signed. Just somebody wanting to stir up trouble, I should imagine.'

The lieutenant thought aloud, 'I need to contain the situation.'

The first man nodded. 'What can we do to help?'

Glancing around them, the lieutenant asked, 'Do you know where the weapons are kept? I presume the garrison is fully stocked. I need you all to go there right now and take command of it, until I can get my men into the city.'

Without a moment's hesitation, the group of Catholic citizens turned and headed away to do his bidding. There was hope yet that everything would work out peacefully. Most of their wives had begged them to leave Derry that very day, but they had held out, wanting to do what they could to help. Derry was their city too, their home. It was a brave decision, especially when so many of their friends were busy packing up to leave. Also, they had heard that most, if not all, of the Dominican friars had already gone. It was probably just as well since their Protestant neighbours seemed to believe that all Catholics were about to turn into murderers the following night. 'Aye,' one of them had said, 'probably on the stroke of midnight!'

Unfortunately, the lieutenant's instructions had been heard by more than the group of Catholic men. A rush of whispers floated through the crowd.

Robert heard it first. 'He's sent the Papists to seize the weapons!' Slapping Henry's arm, he called out, 'Come on!'

The thirteen boys broke into a run, even though some of them had no idea why.

Samuel Hunt, who clearly enjoyed his mother's baking,

wheezed after Daniel, 'What's going on now?'

Daniel, doing his best not to smash into anyone or trip himself up, replied, 'We're going after the guns!'

Samuel wished he had a horse or that his friends would slow down a bit.

'Short cut!' yelled Robert and led the way. Some skill was required; the street was narrow with plenty of people milling about in the most useless fashion. Robert longed to push his foot up the backside of a woman who had suddenly spotted a friend. She stopped sharply, blocking his way, and was not impressed with how clumsily he slid by her. He gritted his teeth as she exclaimed, 'Well, I never. You rude, rude boy!'

There was also the delicate matter of not skidding into the smelly splotches of all shapes and sizes that had been left behind by horses, cows and dogs. The street was littered with them. Daniel was forced to quickly tiptoe through a particularly large blob of greenish brown mess. It was the size of a brick, a soft, squidgy brick that did not want to let go of his boot. His mother would have something to say about that.

Robert glanced back a couple of times to check his brother was still behind him. He and Henry were the front runners and kept pace with one another. Robert warned his friend, 'This could get dangerous.'

Henry winked back. 'Yes, I know.'

Officer Linegar was not having a good day. His rotten tooth was throbbing with pain, so much so that it felt like it had its own heartbeat in his gum. Because he was on duty he couldn't do the two things he longed to: cradle, in his hands, the part of his jaw that was aflame with pain and take a drop of whiskey for it. No, he had to stand upright and do his job which was to guard the garrison's store of guns and artillery. Today it was of the utmost importance that he carry out his duty to the king. Toothache or not, James's army needed all the help they could get. When he saw a group of boys heading his way, their expressions grim and determined, he suddenly realised that he too was in need of help. In a way he had been waiting for this moment. Surely it had only been a matter of time before a raid of some sort was attempted.

The first two boys hollered their intention. 'We are taking command of the magazine. Stand down!'

Officer Linegar shook his head, his tooth in agony at the sudden movement. The pain was so bad, he decided against opening his mouth to make a reply. In any case it should be obvious what he would have said, *As if I'd take orders from the likes of you*! He quickly counted the boys, and understood that they meant to do as they said. His only option was to raise his rifle and force four words out: 'Halt or I'll fire!'

The boys didn't exactly halt but they slowed their pace

to a trot. Not one of them had ever had a gun pointed at them before. The guard's stance was solid and it looked like he would make good on his threat. Nevertheless, Robert was not convinced. 'There's too many of us,' he said. 'He can't shoot us all, not that he'd have the guts to!' He listened behind him for the Catholic men, but they had fallen far behind.

Henry agreed with Robert. 'He's right. Stay together. Let's go!'

The boys broke into a run once more, the ones at the back whooping, 'Get him!'

This was too much for Officer Linegar. He released the trigger and let fly a musket ball which tore into Henry's left arm, just above the elbow. Henry howled in pain and fright as his limp arm was flung backwards on impact.

Some of the boys faltered, but Robert urged them on. The guard had no time to reload his rifle and he did not want to kill any of the boys. That would only make things worse. Within seconds he was surrounded and pummelled to the ground. As the kicks rained down he hoped that one of them would be decent enough to dislodge his tooth. As far as he was concerned, the beating was proving to be less painful than the evil in his gums.

Robert took the guard's gun and brought the one-sided fight to an end. He ordered two boys – Alexander Irwin and Alexander Cunningham – to take Henry, who was cradling his wounded arm, to the physician. The rest of them frogmarched the bruised guard to a cell. Robert told him, 'You should have stood aside.'

Officer Linegar, realising he had done all he could, was philosophical. 'Maybe so but a man has to do his own particular duty at the end of the day.' Raising his hand to his cheek, he groaned, 'Toothache!'

Robert wasn't interested. The guard felt he had nothing to lose at this stage. 'You would be doing a fellow a tremendous favour if you procured me some whiskey, you know, should you happen to come across it.'

Daniel couldn't help feeling sorry for the man. One eye was thickening up while his top lip was covered in blood. At the same time, the boy was shocked that Henry had been hurt. Not for one moment did he believe that the guard would actually shoot at them.

Shouting outside indicated that the Catholic residents had finally arrived. Robert laughed. 'Did they really think we'd allow them to take our weapons?'

The guard sniffed. 'Your weapons?' He tried to laugh too but he couldn't.

Robert ran his fingers over the rifle. 'Forgive me. Of course they're not *my* weapons as such; they belong to Prince William – now.'

Officer Linegar wasn't done yet. 'How much time do you think you have?' he asked.

Robert looked puzzled, so the guard explained, 'James's army is right outside the gates. Do you even know where William's is?'

Robert grinned. 'As it happens I do.' Gesturing to his friends, he proudly declared, 'It's right here!'

CHAPTER SIX

When Daniel woke up on the ninth of December, the day that was set for the massacre of Protestants throughout the land, he was relieved to discover that he had not been butchered in his sleep. Robert had told him there was no need to worry but it was impossible not to worry just a little bit.

Robert was still asleep. He had spent most of the night on the wall, keeping watch. William Cairnes's uncle, the lawyer, had taken charge. He doubled the numbers of guards, wanting to show the civilian population that they were safe thanks to their brave men and impenetrable city walls.

Daniel had promised his mother that he'd fetch the day's water before he went to the walls to do his shift. Horace greeted him as he reached the foot of the stairs, demanding that the boy spend a couple of minutes scratching behind his ears before he would allow him to pass. Daniel asked him quietly, 'You would have barked if anybody tried to attack us, wouldn't you, boy?' Horace replied with a sloppy kiss. 'Ugh!' Daniel protested, 'Your breath is horrible!' He sat down on a stool to put on his boots, aware that he did not feel quite himself. When could he be absolutely and definitely sure that he, his family and neighbours would not die today?

Robert had assured him that an invasion would be noisy. There would have to be shouting, screaming and horses thundering over the paved stones. Dogs would bark manically no matter whose side they were on. Right now, all he could hear were the usual sounds. Birds were singing, though not too many on this cold December morning. One dog was barking morosely in the distance. Not even Horace could be bothered to feign interest in that. Cart wheels were rumbling somewhere but that just meant that supplies were being delivered to the market place. These ordinary sounds were a source of real comfort for Daniel. Really, he couldn't imagine any of this coming to an end.

He had a fleeting wish to own a gun, just in case. However, there was no gun in the Sherrard house; there weren't enough to go around. Daniel was there to see the magazine unlocked and the disappointment on the lawyer Cairnes's face. 'Is that it?'

Daniel, not knowing any better, was struck by how many guns were there. He whispered to Robert, 'There must be over a hundred!'

Robert knew enough to realise that there were a lot more Papist soldiers outside the walls than there were guns to defend the city against them.

A count was done. There were a hundred and fifty musket rifles. Mr Cairnes called for all able-bodied men to present themselves to him, those who were not already soldiers. Three hundred men placed themselves at their city's beck and call. Daniel knew then that there weren't enough rifles.

Mr Sherrard was one of the three hundred, although he still had a living to make and a family to feed. Mr Cairnes took down all the names and made out a time-table. The watching from the walls would be split into shifts, with the three hundred new part-timers sharing the burden.

Daniel voiced his concerns to his father. 'We don't have enough men or guns.'

His father asked him a question in turn, 'Have you heard about the noble Spartan warriors?'

Daniel nodded his head, remembering his history. Sparta was sometimes a trustworthy ally of Ancient Greece and sometimes her deadliest enemy. Nevertheless, when Persia attacked Greece, it was Sparta who leapt to her defence. Daniel smiled, guessing where his father was going with this.

'That's right,' said Mr Sherrard. 'Three hundred brave warriors held off the monstrous Persian army, thanks to a decision to make their stand in a narrow pass between two steep mountains.'

His son nodded. 'There were too many Persians for the narrow pass so it didn't matter what size the army was, the three hundred held them off.'

'Exactly,' said his father. 'They had the mountains and we have our walls.'

Daniel knew that the three hundred Spartans had died in the end but only because they had been deceived by a 'friend' who showed the Persians how to surround the defenders. Neither Sherrard mentioned this part of the story; it was more important to remember the noble and courageous battle of the Spartan warriors. They had never faltered in their belief about their combined strength.

By the time Daniel returned with the buckets of water his mother was up, preparing the breakfast. Alice was in her crib, finally fast asleep, and his mother placed a finger to her lips, warning him not to make a sound. The water sloshed merrily as he edged himself around the furniture, taking care not to knock over a stool.

Mrs Sherrard shared her younger son's nervousness, despite her husband's unshakeable belief that no massacre would take place today. The previous evening when he had sought once more to reassure her, she had asked, 'Are you saying that the Comber letter was a forgery then?'

Her husband had never lied to her. 'Well, I don't know for sure, but I would be surprised if it wasn't.'

This had not been good enough for his wife. 'So, you

don't know for sure that our lives aren't in mortal danger come the morrow?'

All Mr Sherrard had been able to do was sigh and shrug his shoulders. He knew he did not believe in a massacre but he also knew he had no sure evidence to offer his wife. Therefore he lacked the means and maybe even the confidence to attempt to convince her. Because what if ... what if he was wrong?

Not surprisingly, neither of them had slept too deeply though Mr Sherrard had told her that the bells of St Columb's would ring out if the walls were in any danger of being breached.

As Daniel took his place at the breakfast table, Mrs Sherrard enquired, 'Was there many about?'

Daniel shook his head. His mother went to check on the bread she had baked the night before. The smell of it lingered in the air.

Sunday mornings were usually quiet but this one had come with its own brand of stillness. Daniel had been glad of Horace's company to the well and back. Hearing his and Horace's every footstep was unnerving in a way he had never noticed before. Horace's overgrown nails noisily struck the cobbled stones and then, on hearing rats or cats, he would dash off down a dark alley, leaving Daniel bereft. The boy waited, ill at ease, not wanting to move until Horace was back by his side.

He was actually surprised and even a little hurt that his parents were happy enough for him to go out alone on this particular morning. Although maybe he was to take comfort from this, that there really was nothing to fear from today.

The previous evening, he and the others had attended an open meeting in the Town Hall to discuss, once more, what to do about James's army. Some of the churchmen still advocated allowing them into the city, repeating the same reason over and over, that it was treason to do otherwise.

Deputy Mayor John Buchanan offered, 'We should let the soldiers in because we won't have any peace if we do not.'

Alderman Tomkins was disgusted. 'How dare you! We are a Protestant city, which is why Richard Talbot wants to control Derry and make slaves of the lot of us!'

There was a mixture of 'naying' and 'yeaing' to this until Bishop Hopkins took to the floor. He too believed that one should obey one's king even if one disagreed with what he was saying. The boys shook their heads in disbelief, with William Cairnes going so far as to murmur, 'What rot!'

However, the bishop had a second point to make. He paused, taking the time to peer into the faces of his audience as he set his scene. 'My friends, consider this. What if it doesn't go William's way? What if James wins? I mean, what if he regains control of his throne, this time after triumphing over William's army?' The boys scowled; they had not thought of this. Bishop Hopkins continued, 'Won't James have every right to be enraged by our behaviour? Who's to say that he won't make an example of us, to show other Protestant towns like Enniskillen and Dungannon that he means business? He may order his army – the very army we are shunning – to treat us the same way that Oliver Cromwell treated the town of Drogheda.'

Drogheda! This was the garrison town that Cromwell had razed to the ground, years earlier in 1641, bringing death and destruction to soldiers, women and even children. Who knows how many had died? The bishop, realising he had hit a tender spot, went on, 'Women and children were pushed into the river to drown. People, including clergymen, were slain on the streets in daylight, in front of shops, in the doors of their own homes.'

Mr Sherrard shifted in his seat. The noise caused several heads to swivel in his direction. A nod from Reverend Gordon prompted him to speak. 'With all respect, my lord, I don't believe that James is another Cromwell. There is simply no evidence to support what you say.'

Daniel, who was sitting with his brother and their friends, noted relief on some of the faces of the men who were staring at his father. He was also glad to see the tiniest bit of pride in his brother's eyes. He much preferred when his father and brother got along. Mr Sherrard's soft tone and reasonable approach soothed some of his listeners.

Unfortunately, the bishop wasn't one of them. The eyes of the churchman narrowed in annoyance as he glanced around to see who else agreed with the physician. He posed, head cocked to the side, as if in deep reflection over Mr Sherrard's words. The ensuing silence was a tense one, men and boys trying to determine the bishop's reaction.

'Although,' began the bishop, 'I think it is noble to want to defend James like this …' Robert felt a tingle of displeasure; was his father being insulted in some way? 'But,' added the bishop, 'it is, I feel, unhelpful. I mean, the only way to prove your theory is to put James to the test.'

The cocky owner of one of the busiest taverns spoke up. 'And the only way to test him is to open our gates to his army, to see if they wish to kill us or not.'

Some people actually laughed a little. Another man, a popular shopkeeper, offered, 'The city walls protected the Protestants in 1641 when that madman O'Neill went on the attack. I tell you Catholics cannot be trusted, and that goes for the king too.'

The bishop looked to be lagging behind; he had lost his footing somehow and sought to regain it. 'But what about the fact that James might win, as I have said?'

Alexander Irwin had had enough. This normally polite

boy, who lived a couple of streets away from the Sherrards and rarely had a bad word to say about anyone, stood up and actually shouted at Bishop Hopkins, 'You have a way with words, my lord, but I'm afraid I can't listen to you any longer!' There was a lone gasp from someone nearby while the bishop stood in shocked silence, the colour draining from his face. Alexander felt suddenly awkward and looked down at his friends for reassurance. Emboldened, they all jumped to their feet and nodded at him to lead the way, and out they strode without a backward glance, while David Cairnes and Mr Kennedy, the sheriff, smiled after them.

Outside Henry thumped Alexander with his good arm and complimented him on his rude behaviour. 'You surprised me!'

Alexander shrugged to hide his own surprise. Had he really just shouted at the bishop of Derry in front of everyone?

'What now?' asked Robert.

Henry was confident that a decision would be reached and said, 'The gates will remain locked. It's what the majority wants.' The others tended to agree with this. 'But remember,' Henry added, 'It's not just the enemy outside; it's also the enemy inside that we must be wary of.'

Robert nodded. 'We should keep an eye on the Papists who are still here.' He paused before saying, 'Although if they have any thought for their own safety, they should really leave the city now.'

Daniel made a rare contribution to the conversation. 'At least we have the rifles and the gunpowder.'

Robert seemed proud. 'Daniel is right. The advantage is ours!'

At ten o'clock Daniel took his place on the wall. From where he stood, just beyond the Ferry Quay Gate, he had a clear view of the Redshank soldiers who were camped out on the eastern bank of the river Foyle known as the Waterside.

Mr Cairnes had instructed that the city was to be alerted immediately if the watchers saw anything untoward … anything at all. James Morrison passed this information onto Daniel, who suddenly felt breathless. 'Does he mean the massacre for today? Is that what he means?'

James wasn't one for playing down a situation or taking care to tell a younger boy not to worry so much. No, indeed. James merely looked terribly serious as he scanned the Foyle, eventually saying, 'It certainly seems so, doesn't it?' Then he did tell Daniel not to worry but only because, 'I'll be right here with you!'

Daniel offered a slight shake of his head that James interpreted as his being magically cured of any anxiety.

Although, to be fair to James, he did have one of the precious hundred and fifty rifles in his possession. Gunfire was the fastest way to alert the population that they were under attack. Generously, he allowed Daniel to hold it for a second or two. Daniel was surprised at the weight of it. When he handed it back he was obliged to receive a lecture on how to load it and then fire. James was most informative. 'Of course, you need to have a steady hand and a keen eye. No point otherwise. You'd be wasting powder just shooting at fresh air.'

Daniel didn't like to say that he had worked this much out for himself. Instead he said, 'I suppose I should know how to use it, in case you are shot or wounded.'

James was aghast. 'Nothing like that is going to happen to me!'

Daniel rushed to assure James that he agreed.

It was a cold morning. The clouds merged into one large mass of greyness as they glided across the sky. There was nothing much to see. The Jacobite army were completely ignoring the city. Not a single soldier seemed so much as to glance in their direction. They sauntered around their campsite. Some were engaged in lighting fires and making their breakfast while others were taking care of the horses. It was virtually the same occupations currently absorbing the residents of Derry.

Three hours later and Daniel was, much to his surprise, bored. James yawned, 'No massacre then!' The casual observer might be forgiven for thinking that at least one of them seemed slightly disappointed. Their attention naturally wandered until they both found themselves watching a large group of noisy crows.

James sighed. 'I'm glad I'm not a crow!'

Daniel giggled. 'What?'

James had no idea he had said anything strange and he continued on, 'They turn on their own kind, you know.'

Daniel was still puzzled by the topic.

'Imagine,' said James, 'we were all crows in Derry.'

Daniel nodded out of politeness if nothing else.

James continued, 'So, maybe you – Daniel Sherrard – get sick.' He paused to consider his words and changed his mind. 'No, not that. In fact you've never been sick a day in your life and you now find yourself at a good age. It is your fiftieth or even sixtieth birthday.'

Daniel found it easier to imagine Derry populated by crows than to imagine himself as an old man.

James was in his element now. 'You have been a good citizen all your life but now you are aged and weary. So, you make mistakes like dropping things or tripping up over stones in the street.'

Daniel could understand this part. Just yesterday he had overturned a mug of milk, infuriating his mother with the waste of it, though Horace had gratefully lapped it up.

'Nobody says a word to you about dropping things or falling down. Then, one day, you are told to attend a meeting at the Town Hall. You hear that everyone has been asked to attend it.' James's voice was low and thick with barely concealed excitement. 'So, you put on your good coat and you head out onto the street where you see all your neighbours and friends making their way to the Town Hall, just like you. When you get there you feel something strange is going on. Some of your oldest friends don't even return your greeting, while others that you don't know very well are madly hugging you and bellowing "hello" in your face as if you were miles away.'

At this point, both boys glanced towards the army to make sure it hadn't advanced any nearer to the city.

'The doors are closed,' James paused for effect, 'and then locked behind you. This had never happened before. The town leaders announce the commencement of the meeting.'

Daniel leant in to hear him better as James was almost talking in a whisper. He certainly wasn't prepared for James to shout 'Suddenly!' Daniel jumped backwards.

'Suddenly,' James repeated, 'you find yourself in the centre of the crowd. You're completely surrounded by all these folk you have known for years. Their stares are empty but their hands aren't. You notice that they are all carrying daggers and they are pointed at you. Each and every one of them takes their turn to stab you, until you are dead.'

Daniel wasn't sure if he was allowed to say something so he didn't.

James asked, 'Do you understand what happened? They killed you off because you got old and became a burden on the community. Crows do that to one another.'

Daniel nodded. 'Well, I've very, very glad I'm not a crow then!'

James shrugged and said, 'It's worse to be killed by friends and neighbours. At least you know where you stand with your enemies.'

CHAPTER SEVEN

'Long live William of Orange!' Reverend Gordon urged his parishioners and others to show their gratitude for the good news which had just arrived from England, and so they did. They roared their appreciation for the prince of Denmark's decision to support William of Orange and Mary, his wife, as future king and queen of England. Outside the cathedral the reverend ordered for two cannon guns to be made ready to fire. Someone else called out, 'Long live the prince of Denmark!' The crowd roared again.

Daniel, James and some of the others climbed the walls, to see whether the Jacobites had heard any of the fun yet. Such good news for Protestants would have to affect the Catholics on the banks of the Foyle. Robert and Henry positioned themselves beside one of the cannons, warning everyone else to stand well back. Actual cannonballs would not be used because all artillery needed to be saved, just in case. A captain of the guards waited for Reverend Gordon's say so before dropping his arms, the signal for Henry to light the fuse. The cannons belted out their own version of joy and determination while the crowd roared once more: 'Long live William of Orange; long live Protestants everywhere!'

The Redshanks were understandably startled. Daniel could make out men jumping to their feet, naturally wondering if they were under attack. However, they seemed even more confused when the sound of a cannon firing was not followed up by an explosion of some sort, with a cannonball smashing into a tree or landing somewhere in the middle of them, to wound or kill. But there was nothing of the sort. Could they hear the cheering from the city? Daniel couldn't believe that the tumultuous noise was not being flown across the river by the choppy breeze.

James got carried away, as he was wont to do. He did his best to hide what he was doing but Daniel was standing right next to him and could plainly see he was loading his rifle. 'Er …?' mumbled Daniel but James was too caught up to hear him. Daniel shrugged to himself. *He won't dare fire it.* He was wrong. James had been waiting a long time to do this; that was how he explained it to himself. Besides, he couldn't actually inflict any damage on anyone; they were too far away. Really, the gunshot was simply a nice accompaniment to the cannon fire.

Below them the butcher, Mr Cook, was assembling his own version of an army. Boys, about fifty of them, surrounded him and then followed him to the gate. People were laughing and pointing. 'Let's go tell those scallywags that they can bugger off back to wherever they came from!' The butcher raised his hairy fist in the air, and his boys cheered in delight. The gate was unlocked and out they poured, not a gun between the lot of them, only heart and comradeship. Mr Cook started the chanting, 'You miserable Papists scoundrels, get going while you still can!' The lads took up the call and repeated it, along with the most flamboyant of insults.

Daniel and James watched the Redshanks begin to stir in earnest. What was going on? Cannon fire, gunfire and now it looked like they were going to be attacked. They couldn't see that the butcher's warriors were young, unarmed and much too giddy to hurt them. Daniel was sure he heard the words 'Run for it!' For a moment he thought it meant that the army was going to run towards the city and Mr Cook's army. However, much to his amazement and relief, it meant run in the opposite direction, away from Derry. It was a while before it sank in, what they were doing: these towering giants were running *away*. And what a magnificent sight it was to behold. James bellowed in his ear, 'We've scared them off!' The two friends hugged one another as Derry rejoiced. There was more cheering, more backslapping, with lots of people who hadn't done anything being lavished with congratulations.

James went to reload his rifle, but Daniel spoke up this time. 'Oh, there's no need for that. You'd be wasting gunpowder!' James was forced to agree with this, especially on spotting Reverend Gordon climb the walls to see the Jacobites in disarray. He didn't doubt that the reverend meant what he said about having him locked up if he ever endangered the city again.

Meanwhile, a couple of miles away, Gabriel Murray heard echoes in the air. *God above*, he thought. *Is the city under attack?* Something told him it wasn't cries of anguish he was hearing. He didn't feel tempted to go and check it out. His horse was as old as he was, in horse years at least. They only made the most necessary of journeys.

Sometime later, his dog began to complain. 'What's the matter with you?' Gabriel asked. These days the dog normally held his peace beyond a guttural growl or two. He was more like a shadow than an animal. Something was up alright. Gabriel watched him stretch his snout up and sniff the wind before emitting a brief torrent of barks that lost their sharpness. Gabriel teased him for not finishing his sentences properly, 'Do you realise you only say "Woo!" instead of "Woof!"?'

His horse was nervous too, shaking its head and stepping one way and the other. Gabriel searched the sky for a clue. To be sure, it wasn't a pretty picture unless you had a preference for grey clouds. However, it didn't seem that a storm was on the horizon. Normally the animals got skittish when thunder and lightning were on their way. In any case the cows were still standing. They usually sat down when rain was due. So, what was it?

He was too old to be scared by most things, he was just curious as to what the animals could sense. He stood against his front door and waited. It was not long before his patience was rewarded when he spotted a group of men in red coats coming over the hill. Although they looked impressive from a distance, Gabriel began to notice a few flaws in their appearance as they drew near. Hats were askew and some of them were in their stocking feet, while only a few wore their regiment's coat and carried weapons. Oh, he knew who they were alright: Jacobites. *Now, are they going to cause me trouble?*

He mused to the dog, 'I wonder if the city scared them off?' Certainly it was all a bit unexpected, but what could he do except wait and see?

The first group passed him by, followed by a second and then a third group of soldiers. None of them showed any interest in the old man though he smiled pleasantly at them, especially the younger ones, boys of sixteen or seventeen years. Of course, he presented no threat, with his stooped, skinny frame and ill-fitting clothes.

He couldn't resisting calling out, 'Are you heading home, boys?'

There were some scowls and eye-rolling, but one older fellow deigned to answer him, 'I hope we are, sir, as I'm sure you do too.'

Gabriel shrugged. 'Ach right, we'll always have hope, if nothing else!'

CHAPTER EIGHT

The days passed as they always do, no matter what is afoot. Life went on behind the walls of the city. After all is said and done, it is the small things that matter most. Chamber pots had to be emptied, bread had to be baked and eaten, candles were lit and extinguished and so on.

Derry was as lively as ever, watching over her swollen population and doing her utmost to keep it safe. In this she was helped when orders were issued to repair all cannon guns and have them placed on wheels so that they could be quickly moved from one place to another. A cannon gun was also positioned on the highest tower in the city, that of St Columb's Cathedral.

When they discovered they were not being pursued, the Jacobites returned to their camps. People took little notice of them. As James Morrison said, 'It's almost like they're part of the landscape now.'

The same argument raged back and forth:

Should we let them in?

No, we bloody well shouldn't!

But they've said that they mean us no harm.

And you believe them, do you?

Oh, I don't know!

One morning a message arrived from Lord Mountjoy, the commander of the regiment that had been summoned to Dublin by Lord Lieutenant Richard Talbot, explaining that he had been sent back to sort out the situation. He asked for a parley with the city's leaders. A Protestant, whose two sons lived in Derry, Lord Mountjoy was anxious to find a solution to the city's predicament.

There was some discussion as to who would go and meet with the returned commander. Bishop Hopkins had left Derry for London, feeling hard done by at the scorn that was poured on his warnings of a Jacobite triumph. John Buchanan had lost the respect of his peers with his gentle pleading for peace at any cost while Mayor Campsie was ill in bed. Eventually, it was agreed that the aldermen would meet him at Mongavlin Castle, eight or so miles from the city, and they had their part of the dialogue worked out beforehand.

Alderman Tomkins said, 'Well it's simple, your lordship. All we – that is, the people – want is, firstly, for Talbot to promise that only Protestant troops will be lodged in our garrison. Secondly, we want our present soldiers, made up from the population, to remain in place, and thirdly we want a general pardon for all that had taken place until this present moment.'

There was nothing complicated about their demands; indeed Lord Mountjoy could have recited them himself without any help. However, and this was the sticking point, as he informed the delegation, 'You know as well as I do that there is no way that the lord lieutenant will agree to the first point and perhaps not to the second one either and most definitely not to the third.' He sighed heavily when the only responses to this were cold, uncomprehending stares. They reminded him of the man he had just left in Dublin, the lord lieutenant himself.

Lord Mountjoy was a superb soldier, for whom an order was an order. Therefore, he hadn't questioned his boss when, three days after reaching Dublin with his tired men, he had been ordered to head back to Derry to sort things out. Before he had left he had heard, with some amount of glee, that such was Richard Talbot's anger at the gates being closed to the Redshanks, he had actually ripped his expensive wig off his head and flung it into the fire. How he would have enjoyed seeing that.

However, with his superior's wrath still ringing between his ears, despite spending the last few days marching from Dublin in cold, unforgiving weather, Lord Mountjoy did not indulge his former townsmen unnecessarily. And so he told them, 'I'm afraid, gentlemen, there are few options.' The ensuing silence was only broken when he added, 'Go home and think over your position. Tomorrow morning I will present myself at Bishop's Gate and ask to be allowed through.' He stood to indicate that the meeting was at an end. 'Good day, sirs!'

The following morning was 12 December and, as promised, Lord Mountjoy turned up at Bishop's Gate and asked for the gate to be unlocked. Henry Campsie and Robert Sherrard were on duty and refused. It caused a bit of a stir amongst the crowd who had gathered to watch the goings-on.

Because his lordship was a former resident of the town and not shy when it came to spending money, some of the traders wondered if the rules should be relaxed. 'Surely,' said Mr Dobbs, the owner of the coffee house, 'we could just let Lord Mountjoy through. He might like a beer or a coffee after all his marching.' The cobbler, Mr Sanderson, couldn't help wondering what state the men's boots were in after walking to and fro from Dublin. Those selling food and snuff nodded their heads in complete agreement with Mr Dobbs.

This line of reasoning was bludgeoned by the scorn that poured forth from Henry and Robert.

Robert rolled his eyes. 'For God's sake, he's Talbot's man. Allowing him in is the same as giving in to the Catholic king.'

Henry declared, 'Now is not the time to make a mistake!'

Mr Sanderson asked, 'Well, what are we going to do then? Just leave him standing out there?'

The usual merry-go-round of 'yeses' and 'noes' began all over again. More people arrived on the scene, the boys' fathers included.

Mr Sherrard suggested it might be wise to reopen negotiations. 'Don't forget that this man is also the Master of Ordnance.'

Someone rather cheekily called out, 'So what?'

It was the mayor who answered him, 'So … he knows how little ammunition we have and the poor condition it's in.'

Mr Sherrard smiled at this unexpected but welcome show of support. 'Exactly!'

With the appearance of Reverend Gordon and a few others, it was decided that a party of ten men should go out to talk to Lord Mountjoy. The men were chosen and in due course the gates were unlocked, but not to allow his lordship inside, only to allow the ten men out to meet with him.

It was a cold and dry morning. People waited about to hear how the meeting went but, as one hour passed into the next, they got restless. Some headed home or back to work. Finally an agreement of sorts was reached. The town elders agreed to allow Lord Mounjoy's most trusted man – Lieutenant-Colonel Robert Lundy – into the city with two companies of Protestant soldiers, about one hundred and twenty men in all. Lord Mountjoy gave his word that no other troops would enter Derry and should Lundy be called away, for any reason, he would hand the city back to its elders, just as he found it.

It was a start in the right direction, at least this is how Lord Mountjoy described it in his report for Lord Lieutenant Talbot.

The following evening, there was a welcome reminder that Derry wasn't the only obstacle to King James and Richard Talbot's plans for a Jacobite Ireland. Robert brought the latest news home in great excitement. His face was flushed, and his alarmed mother called for her husband while asking, 'Goodness, Robert! What has happened now?'

With his family gathered around him, Robert let fly. 'A force at Enniskillen attacked a Jacobite regiment and sent them on the run all the way back to Cavan!'

His family breathed together, taking in the news. 'Who attacked first?' asked his mother.

Robert was oblivious to her anxious expression. 'Why, they did, Mother. They heard that two regiments were coming to take up residence in the town and decided not to stand about waiting for their arrival.' He laughed. 'Much to the Jacobites' surprise!'

Mrs Sherrard pulled her shawl tightly around her

shoulders. 'I wonder if they have not acted hastily.'

Robert was patient with her. 'They had little choice, Mother. Enniskillen doesn't have walls like ours.'

His father stayed quiet, so Daniel asked him what he thought, noticing how Robert bristled, obviously expecting to hear something negative.

Mr Sherrard glanced at his wife and sons, saying, 'This is quite an achievement for Enniskillen.'

Robert exhaled and felt confident enough to say, 'It is a beginning.'

His father nodded carefully. 'Well, yes. That's what it is – all it is – a beginning.'

Daniel watched his brother deflate just a little. Sometimes it was hard to interpret their father. Was he now belittling Enniskillen's worthy triumph?

Robert managed to ask, 'What are you saying, Father?'

Mr Sherrard patted his wife on the arm and asked for a mug of beer. She understood that he wanted her out of the way so that he could discuss matters more freely with his sons. No husband wants his wife to worry needlessly about matters she has no control over. It was only right that Mr Sherrard confide in his sons, who were almost full-grown but still had so much to learn. It was only right that they learn from their father. Off she went with Horace behind her, hoping she'd throw him a morsel of something.

Robert tried not to be sulky. 'You don't think we can win. Do you?'

'Win what?' Mr Sherrard's question surprised his boys. They exchanged looks, checking whether the other had the answer to this. As the youngest, Daniel didn't mind being tripped up so he tried, 'Win Derry for us?' Robert gave him his support with a solid nod.

Their father smiled. 'Alright. But I have to warn you both that this situation could go on for a long, long time. Closing the gates against James's men has started a chain of events and not one of us knows where it's going to end or when.'

Robert, assuming he was being criticised, grew prickly. 'We had to close them or else risk the city being invaded by murderers!'

Mr Sherrard thought for a moment before asking, 'My boy, did you truly believe we were going to be massacred?'

Robert puffed up. 'It has happened before!'

'Yes,' agreed his father. 'Many things have happened before, but it doesn't mean that they will happen again.'

This was confusing. Robert shook his head to clear it.

'Look,' said his father, 'all I am saying is beware of the more excitable sort. Closing the gates was rather flamboyant. Perhaps fear of invasion wasn't the only reason for doing it; some people enjoy drama and attention.'

Robert breathed heavily. 'Are you talking about the

Campsies and my friends?'

Mr Sherrard welcomed the return of his wife. She had been eavesdropping in order to barge in at the appropriate moment. Ignoring the tension and the fact that her eldest was struggling to contain his emotions, she handed her husband his beer and smiled brightly at everyone.

Robert turned away and made for the door. 'Just remember,' his father called, 'no matter what happens, form your own opinion. Calmness is strength.'

It was only Daniel who said, 'Yes, Father!'

There was a curt nod from Robert as he opened the door and dived out onto the street.

It occurred to Robert that he was beginning to feel more at home outside the house. He was heading to take his place on the wall, where he'd be sure of decent conversation and of being treated with respect. *That's the trouble with Mother and Father*, he thought. *They still think of us as children.* He thundered along, hardly noticing the greetings that were being thrown to him. He was too caught up with his silent monologue. *If it was left to Father, these streets would be covered in our blood.*

His battle for independence with his unimaginative parents was proving to be more demanding on him than the one brewing between James II and William of Orange. *Well, at least I realise now that nothing I do will ever be good enough for them*, he thought, meaning his mother and father.

Back at the house, the air still sparked with Robert's anger. Daniel wished he had made his excuses and followed his brother, but he had missed his cue and so found his parents staring at him quizzically. *What do they want me to say?*

Finally his father said, 'You know that we only want the best for you and Robert, don't you?'

Daniel squeaked out a 'Yes, of course!'

His mother sighed. 'There is enough rage in this city without it being brought into our home.'

Mr Sherrard sat down on a stool and sipped his beer. 'Very nice!' he said to his wife. There was silence again until he said, 'This city is like a cauldron that has been sitting on a pile of dry twigs. Only one person is needed to set the twigs alight. The soup in the cauldron gets hotter and hotter as more twigs are added. If there is no proper care, too much firewood will be added and the contents will bubble up and be ruined.'

Daniel found his voice. 'But we have to stand up for what we believe in, Father.'

Mr Sherrard swirled the beer in his mug. 'Yes, we do. I think maybe I just don't fully trust who is building the fire.'

Baby Alice began to wail, letting the whole street know that her nap was over and she was hungry.

'Time to get back to work,' said Mr Sherrard with a

smile. 'Come on, son, I want to show you my new book.' They both went into the workroom while Mrs Sherrard headed upstairs to her daughter.

Alice's face was scrunched up like her fists, and tears streamed down her cheeks. Mrs Sherrard peeled off the small hill of blankets that she had piled on top of the infant. Next she did something she always did. She lifted up the baby, placed her nose in the crux of her daughter's neck and sniffed. She felt better immediately: *Nothing – not even freshly baked bread –smells half as nice as a newborn.*

A few miles away Gabriel Murray was sitting in front of his fire, watching the flames flicker and strain, marvelling at the multitudes of oranges and reds. Adam, his son, had just left after a brief visit, during which he had updated Gabriel on the recent goings-on: Enniskillen fighting back and the skirmishes that Adam was currently organising against Jacobites who strayed too far from their camp. Gabriel had listened but said little.

His son was passionate and intelligent with plenty of courage. Apart from his animals, Adam and this house were all the old man had in the world. His wife had died when Adam was two years old. Gabriel had to bring him up alone; he made it up as he went along. These days he felt his wife around him and her pride in their son. If he closed his eyes, he could hear her remind him, 'A home and a family. It was all we ever wanted.'

So what if he sensed peril approaching? Gabriel wasn't scared of death. After a lifetime being the best man he could, he had no fear of meeting God. 'Aye,' he sighed, as he stretched his legs closer to the heat, 'what will be, will be!'

CHAPTER NINE

On 22 December, Lieutenant-Colonel Robert Lundy entered Derry and took control of the garrison. He had been promoted by his commander, Lord Mountjoy, in recognition of his obedience and hard work. Not that it felt like a reward.

Hours upon hours of talks with the town's elders had yet to produce a final solution. However, thanks to Lord Mountjoy, there had been some agreement in the form of the 'Articles of Agreement': no other troops, apart from Lundy's, could enter the city before 1 March 1689; the citizens could continue to guard the walls just as they had been doing; strangers to the city could not carry arms or stay overnight unless they had permission from Lundy or Horace Kennedy, the sheriff.

The articles had only been achieved by the fact that Lord Mountjoy had chosen not to ask his superior, Richard Talbot, for his opinion or his permission regarding them. But surely the lord lieutenant would agree with the fact that he was carrying out his order to 'sort out' the situation.

On top of that, Enniskillen's triumph had breathed fresh confidence behind the walls.

Lundy's position was not an easy one. He was no stranger to the city. Originally from Scotland, he had been a member of Derry's garrison since 1685. However, not too many residents would have recognised him since his foremost allegiance and devotion was to his job and, consequently, he was not the type of man to be found drinking ale in the local taverns. Certainly, he shared the Protestant faith, though his was of the Episcopalian strand which set him slightly apart from the Anglicans and the Presbyterians.

Yet, for all his knowledge of the city and his Protestantism, his position was not going to be easy because of who he and his superior, Lord Mountjoy, took their orders from ... the Catholic lord lieutenant, friend and supporter of King James. It was confusing for everyone.

A delegation of town elders arrived from Enniskillen to ask him what their next move should be. To their utter disgust the lieutenant-colonel advised them to cease their opposition to King James. But really, what had they expected an army man to say? *I'm not a rebel! I cannot be seen to encourage resistance to His Majesty.*

Like Lord Mountjoy, he was duty bound to be a loyal servant to the throne and, therefore, to the lord lieutenant in Dublin.

Yet, precisely because he was an army man, he began to draw up plans on how best to fortify Derry, should she come under attack. The state of the artillery store and the walls could not be ignored no matter who was king. The city needed improvements, anyway, regarding its military defences, and as such the lieutenant-colonel felt it was his duty to improve them. He was not a man to stand idle and only God knew how long this stand-off between Derry and the Jacobite Army would continue. At best it would keep his men busy.

It was a peculiar situation but both the lieutenant-colonel and Lord Mountjoy agreed that because they were professional soldiers they had no business taking sides. As far as they were concerned whoever sat on the throne was king and that was that. They also worried that if Derry continued to keep her gates locked against the army outside it was only a matter of time before the city would be invaded.

Neither man was surprised when Lord Mountjoy received a summons from Richard Talbot to report back to him in Dublin. They knew that the lord lieutenant would be bewildered if not absolutely outraged to hear of Lundy helping the city to improve its defences. All Lord Mountjoy could offer was that having his man, Lundy, installed as governor of Derry was better than having him stuck outside the walls along with everyone else. Surely, it was better than nothing at all.

Of course he knew the lord lieutenant would have wanted a Catholic in charge or, at the very least, Catholic soldiers strewn throughout Lundy's two companies of men. But, as Lord Mountjoy told himself, *I'm only human. What Talbot needs is some sort of miracle worker.*

Lord Mountjoy told the lieutenant-colonel that some of his friends had advised him to stay in Derry. However, Lundy understood that his commander could not refuse to obey an order; it was what made him such a good soldier. They had a sombre goodbye, with Robert Lundy wondering if he would ever see his lordship again.

When the bell of St Columb's Cathedral rang out its goodbye to 1688 and welcomed 1689 in its stead, the lieutenant-colonel was not alone in wondering what the new year would bring.

The bell sounded jubilant as its clanging punctured the quiet that had fallen over the population. Cold weather and the lack of anything definite happening, one way or the other, made it feel like a sort of hibernation was taking place both behind and outside the walls. A silent agreement was reached in that the best thing was not to dwell on the past nor think too far ahead. Just concentrate on each day as it fell, on each moment at hand.

Of course there were those who refused to be dulled by weeks of inactivity. Just as Lieutenant-Colonel Robert

Lundy was discreetly readying the city, for what he wasn't sure, others were making their own preparations.

The news from England had warranted celebration. James II, along with his wife and baby son, had left for France. *Well, that was good news, wasn't it?* Most people in Derry certainly agreed that it was. James had done the sensible, no, the right thing in vacating the throne and country, making way for his Protestant daughter, Mary Stuart, and her husband, Prince William of Orange. Hurrah!

Only it wasn't as simple as that.

The less impressionable of the population didn't miss the important part of the story. James II had fled to France, to King Louis XIV, the war-mongering Catholic who wanted to rule all of Europe, especially the parts favoured by the Dutch Prince of Orange. 'Mark my words,' said the likes of the Reverend Gordon and Mr Sherrard, 'a ferocious clash of arms is on the horizon!'

Robert Lundy attended city council meetings throughout January. Money was the big concern. Gunpowder and ammunition could be brought from England but it had to be bought first. William Cairnes's uncle, the lawyer, was despatched to London to present a plea for material help to the soon-to-be-crowned king and queen.

Meanwhile, most of the city's Catholic residents finally decided to pack up and leave their homes behind.

Daniel and Horace still walked the streets together,

though not as often now.

One day, as usual, Horace was ignoring Daniel's pleas to stay by his side. The town was so packed and busy that Daniel worried Horace would be lost or run over by a cart. Suddenly Horace's head snapped upwards and his ears stood up as he let out an exultant bark. Daniel heard the mischief in it and, once more, hollered for his dog to return to heel. He was not the least bit surprised when he was thoroughly ignored and instead obliged to break into a run as Horace led them down a long, narrow street that was already too full without a large, over-excited dog bounding through it.

Daniel lost sight of Horace as the dog charged around yet another corner. Then he heard barking, only it wasn't his dog, but it sounded familiar all the same. *Oh no! Trust him!*

Out of an entire city that was crammed with thousands of extra people, Horace had managed to find one of 'those' dogs from 'that' particular street. Daniel made it just in time to witness the two animals trading insults from about three feet away from one another.

It turned out that the other dog was part of a procession. Daniel recognised the young girl who had been scrubbing the door. He felt his cheeks redden and hoped she wouldn't notice him, which given the size of the street, would have been impossible. Most of the people in the procession trudged by, too depressed and worried to be interested in barking dogs. Daniel took a step against the wall of a house to give them room to pass. Both men and women carried bundles of clothes, pots, plates and children.

Daniel was mortified, though he wasn't exactly sure why. However, a man, who Daniel assumed to be the girl's father, soon put him right. Pointing at the boy, he said, 'I know you!'

Reaching for Horace, who kept trying to dodge his grasp, Daniel decided it was best to come clean. 'Well, yes. I've sometimes walked my dog around ... er ... your street.'

The girl glanced at Daniel and looked away again. Daniel felt she was afraid he would act like they knew one another. In any case, he was immediately distracted by her father who was demanding, 'Aren't you one of *them* that locked the gates against the Redshanks?'

Daniel saw deep anxiety in the girl's eyes. She had a baby in her arms, no bigger than Alice, and a jumble of clothes were strapped to her back. At her side were two, no three young children who watched Horace with great interest. Doing her best to bring this uncomfortable interview to an end, the girl said quietly, 'Papa dear, we're holding up everyone behind us.'

Her father was determined however to have his answer

and asked again, 'Well?'

Daniel felt dizzy as he said yes, though he couldn't resist playing down his own contribution by adding, 'There were thirteen of us in all!'

'Pah!' spat the man. 'That makes no difference to us now. And I'll tell you why, shall I?'

Daniel hadn't asked for an explanation nor did he want one. He made a mistake by trying to escape. 'I have to get home ...'

It was as if he had lit a fuse on one of the cannons.

'"Home" did you say?'

Daniel was helpless to make a response. The man spat again, narrowly missing Daniel's foot.

'Let me tell you about *home*! My *home*!' He pointed at his daughter. 'Her *home*!' And at the younger children. 'Their *home*!'

The dogs had stopped their barking, their attention on the man who was shouting at Daniel.

'I have lived in this city all my life. All my life! I was born here and my parents were born here. It's all I've known, all I ever wanted to know. And that's what a *home* is, boy!'

Daniel nodded fast, hoping his cooperation might calm the man somewhat.

'But today I've had to empty my home into sacks, only as many as we can carry, and tell my children that we have to leave Derry.'

It was only now that the younger ones understood what was going on. The littlest girl, who was maybe five or six years old, was horrified. 'But I don't want to leave Derry!'

Her father asked her, 'Well, my love, where do you want to go?'

She replied, 'I want to go back to our house.'

'See that!' said her father to Daniel. 'My little girl just wants to go home!'

Her two siblings chimed in, 'Me too! Me too!'

To everyone's surprise, the man's rage disappeared and tears sprang instead. He wiped them away but there were too many of them. It was nothing short of a miracle that his daughter managed to retrieve a handkerchief from one of her bundles. It floated out of her hand and Daniel, glad to do something, dived to pick it from the ground. To his relief, the man accepted it from him.

The girl spoke neither unkindly nor kindly, 'My mother is buried here. We've to leave her behind too.'

Why did she feel she had to explain this awfulness to him? Daniel could think of nothing to say, only wanting to beg her forgiveness but not even sure how to go about doing that.

As if to help him out, she added, 'We should have left ages ago. Derry stopped being our home the moment the gates were closed.'

With that, the girl ordered the children to move, patted

her father on the arm and bid him to lead the way. Not another word was said. The family resumed their journey while Daniel put his head down and continued up the street, keeping a firm grip on Horace. Rightly or wrongly, the Sherrard boy felt thoroughly ashamed of himself.

CHAPTER TEN

Reverend Gordon was once again the bearer of good news. From the pulpit of St Columb's Cathedral, he bellowed, 'My dear brothers and sisters, today is a wonderful day for us, for today William of Orange and his lady wife, Mary, have been crowned king and queen of England!'

All in all, 1689 was shaping up to be a very good year indeed.

After the sermon, people stood outside to chew over this latest piece of information. Henry Campsie, whose father had recently been named Mayor of Derry once more, shook the hands of his friends. Robert couldn't help thinking that Henry would make a fine politician one day. His arm was just about healed yet Henry found it necessary to keep it bandaged. Daniel suspected that the bandage was like a badge of honour and Henry didn't want it to be forgotten that he had been shot for protecting the city.

'King William! Ha! Doesn't it sound much better than King James?' Henry must have said this line twelve times now, but each time he repeated it his audience heartily agreed.

William Cairnes didn't like to boast but had to add, 'Of course, my uncle met him in London!'

Just before William had been named king, he wrote a letter to the elders of Derry, thanking them for their loyalty to his wife and himself. He also promised to furnish the towns with supplies. As soon as the weather improved, a ship called *Deliverance* was going to live up to her name and deliver food and ammunition to the city.

Robert said, 'I suppose there is no rush now that William is king. Richard Talbot will surely call off his soldiers.'

He gave Henry a quizzical look and was relieved when his friend nodded and said, 'Yes, I was just thinking that. He'll probably offer his services to William now.'

Samuel Hunt crossed his arms over his stomach and scoffed, 'I hope that King Billy tells him to take himself and his services elsewhere! You couldn't trust a man like *that*.'

He scowled as he pronounced the last word and Daniel assumed 'that' to mean Papist.

'King Billy?' repeated Robert. He winked at Samuel, saying, 'I like that!'

William Cairnes looked dubious. He pushed his unruly hair out of his eyes and said, far too quickly, 'Hmm … I think I prefer William.'

He should have kept his mouth shut. A chorus immediately sang out: 'Alright, Billy? What did you say, Billy? Billy, Billy!'

William pouted, but really he was delighted to be the centre of their attention. 'You're worse than children!'

Henry raised his eyebrows, indicating that they should be careful. They fell quiet immediately while Daniel was one of a few who swung their heads about to see what Henry meant. Lieutenant–Colonel Lundy was nearby. The boys decided to move away from the cathedral.

Henry said what most of them were thinking. 'There is something about that man that makes me uneasy.'

Robert was first to agree. 'I don't trust him!'

This was followed by a smattering of 'Nor I!'

Only Daniel held his peace, feeling slightly out of his depth. The others seemed to know so much more than he did. Henry was lucky his father was mayor. He and William Cairnes usually heard the news before the rest of them, although Daniel couldn't help feeling that their opinions sometimes sounded rehearsed.

As the group prepared to break up and return to their various chores and houses, Henry said, 'I wonder whose side he's on now.'

This line carried more weight when it was immediately followed by Henry bidding everyone farewell. When asked for an explanation, he only winked and said he had to go.

Robert and Daniel said their goodbyes too and left with him.

As if the three of them were already engaged in a discussion, Robert said, 'Lundy surely follows whoever is sitting on the throne.'

Daniel thought this sounded right and felt a shiver of impatience when Henry smiled at them as if they were ignorant children. 'Ah, but wasn't it James who gave Lundy the leadership of Derry, through Lord Mountjoy who represents Richard Talbot? Doesn't that make him a Jacobite?'

Daniel refused to be impressed. 'Well then, what does Talbot say about Robert Lundy? Does he call him friend or foe?'

To his intense pleasure, Henry didn't have an answer to this question. All the mayor's son could say, rather vaguely, was, 'I'm sure it's just a matter of time before everything comes out in the wash.'

The rain was getting heavier. They might have stood under one of the various porches only there was no room. Plenty of people were ahead of them, some of them with no roofs to call their own, their houses being elsewhere.

Henry said, 'I don't mind saying it would be better if they all went home. They're a strain on our resources.'

Daniel felt Henry was simply repeating something his father had said.

Robert said, 'Well, now that William has the crown, perhaps they will feel confident to go back to wherever they came from.'

'And the Catholics of Derry could return home too,' added Daniel.

There was a shocked silence.

'What did you say?' asked Henry.

Daniel hadn't meant to say what he thought about the Catholic refugees out loud. He opened his mouth but only to feel the rain drop onto his tongue.

Robert rushed to assure his friend. 'He's only teasing you, Henry. Don't mind him, I don't!'

Daniel sniffed for a response.

On arriving at the Campsies' house, Robert arranged to meet up later that evening, for their shift at the wall. He didn't wait to hear the clip of the Campsies' front door closing before grabbing his brother by the arm. 'What's the matter with you?'

Daniel sighed. 'Henry gets on my nerves sometimes. He can be such a know-it-all!'

Robert argued, 'But he does know more than us.'

Daniel was petulant. 'Only because his father is the mayor.'

Robert held out his hands. 'And what's wrong with that?'

Daniel didn't answer, prompting his brother to marvel, 'I've never seen you in such a bad mood. What is it?'

Daniel felt himself blow hot and cold. It was just a bad mood, no need to fuss. But then he found some words and asked, 'Don't you ever get tired of him constantly airing his opinions?'

Robert stifled a laugh. 'Eh … no!'

Daniel tried again. 'But have you ever noticed that he never has good news? He's always set on worrying us.'

Robert flicked raindrops off his nose. This was all new to him.

They walked on in silence until Daniel spoke again. 'I know you and Father have your problems …'

Robert could not resist mounting a defence. 'That's not my fault!'

Daniel grew impatient with the unnecessary interruption. 'I'm not saying it is. Anyway, that has nothing to do with what I'm saying.'

Robert sighed. 'Which is?'

Daniel continued, 'Well, I like the way Father thinks about things. Some people think in a straight line which must never be broken but Father thinks in circles.'

Robert chuckled. 'That doesn't sound very flattering. You mean he goes around and around, never making any progress? At least a line can get longer.'

Daniel quickly shook his head. 'No, no. That's not what I meant!'

Robert smirked at the sour expression on his little brother's face.

Coming in sight of their house meant an end to their

conversation had to be reached.

Daniel said, 'I meant that Father collects information from more than one source. He looks for options before making his mind up. His thinking is as wide and rounded as a circle.'

Robert appreciated the effort his brother had taken to present his argument. Keeping his mind clear of his various gripes with their father, he generously said, 'Ah, I see what you mean. That's a good way of putting it.'

Daniel accepted the compliment with a weary 'Thank you!'

The door suddenly swung open. Horace filled the entrance as their mother called out, 'What have you two been up to?'

Her sons grinned at one another and replied in unison, 'Just talking!'

On 21 March King William's *Deliverance*, the ship containing men, ammunition and money, finally arrived. It should have meant tidings of joyous relief but, instead, it only brought more trouble for Governor Lundy. He stepped on board and was received by the captain who handed him a letter from King William.

The letter contained his orders and Governor Lundy was obliged to read it aloud to those present: 'His Majesty wishes that I distribute the weapons and ammunition as I see fit and use the money to fortify the city against attack.

He further wishes to be kept informed of our situation and …'

Here, the governor read the next couple of sentences to himself before he continued aloud. He did his best not to sound self-conscious, yet he could not blind himself to the smirks on the faces of those around him. It was mortifying, but he had no option other than to read: 'His Majesty desires that, from now on, any persons taking office either in the army or in the council must first swear allegiance to him.'

It started to drizzle and Lundy was obliged to fold up the royal message to prevent the words being smeared by raindrops.

The hairs stood on the back of his neck as he felt his every movement, every little facial twitch, being closely inspected. He knew exactly what they were waiting for, his swearing his own allegiance to King William, but he grew stubborn with anger. *I will not parade myself like some street performer.*

What about the fact that I have already embarked on the city's fortifications? William cannot seriously think that I needed his say-so before strengthening the walls and building the ravelin to protect Bishop's Gate.

Knowing what was at stake, that quite possibly he would not be allowed any of the ship's bounty until he swore his devotion to William, Governor Lundy demanded a private consultation with the captain, away from prying eyes. It was not a wise decision.

No one from Derry could swear to Lundy's swearing the oath to their new king. Therefore, it was generally assumed that he did not.

CHAPTER ELEVEN

Some weeks later Daniel had cause to feel sorry for Henry Campsie. His father, the mayor, was seriously ill. Mr Sherrard visited the Campsie house every day and returned again in the evening. A fever had taken hold of his patient, and try as he might Mr Sherrard knew he was losing him. He told Mrs Campsie to pray as her husband's life was in God's hands.

Henry felt useless. He was the oldest but had no great yearning to become man of the house just yet. His nights were spent watching over his father as he slept. What else could he do for him now?

Keeping a single stub of candle lit, he watched the flickering shapes over his father's bed, swiping at the flies and moths who were tempted to land on the sheets. He had asked Mr Sherrard, when they were alone, 'How long does he have?'

The physician looked into the eyes of the boy he had delivered eighteen years earlier and said, 'I'm not sure. All I can do is make him as comfortable as I can. I don't think he's in any pain.'

Henry nodded and whispered his thanks.

Before he took his leave, Mr Sherrard told Henry that he would be back the following morning, adding, 'Your father was a good man, Henry. We owe him a lot. You can be proud of him.'

Mr Sherrard let himself out and was glad to be escaping from the heaving sadness of the Campsie household. He breathed deeply and then scrunched his nose as the smell of fresh manure soared up his nostrils. *How long has it been since I've taken a good walk outside the walls? These days the city seems too small and dirty.*

It was easy to forget that there was a whole other world outside. For the first time in ages Mr Sherrard noticed the silvery glow of the moon. There was a time he used to spend hours staring at the night sky, teaching himself the different constellations and experiencing elation at every shooting star. When he was a little boy his mother told him that a shooting star meant a good soul was going straight to Heaven. He sighed; *poor John Campsie will be there soon enough.*

Of course, in his line of profession, Mr Sherrard was well used to dealing with the dying. However, despite all his experience, he desired to know more about what actually happened in death.

He remembered how he had treated his mother on her deathbed. She had outlived his father by a good ten years or so and was fiercely independent until the day she was forced to take to her bed and, in her words, 'wait for the end!'

Whenever her son had stood over her, she had mistaken him for her dead husband. Gently he would tell her, 'No, Mother. It's Edward, your son.' Eventually he'd given up as it had only confused her.

On that last afternoon, he had stepped into the next room to fetch something and had heard her gasp. She hadn't spoken in two days and thinking he had heard her murmur his name, he had run in, knocking over a stool. Reaching her bed, he had stopped in fright. This wizened old woman, who had shrunk in length and breadth, whose skin was as thin as the pages of her bible, had appeared to glow.

'Mother?' He hadn't meant to sound panicked.

She had turned to look at him and had smiled. Her fever had gone and she had appeared younger than ever. All her weariness and sickliness had gone. How happy she had looked. He had felt her farewell as she'd switched her attention to the air in front of her. Then she had bowed her head briefly and said, 'Yes!'

Her son had watched her die then. The last breath had left her body; he swore he saw her soul go with it as her eyes had glazed and her body had wilted in thanks. Her journey was finally over.

Now beneath the Derry night sky Mr Sherrard shivered, realising the mist he had supposed was gathering was only his tears.

A few miles away Adam Murray was updating his father on the latest news. The old man was stirring soup that was simmering in a pot over the fire. Adam scratched his father's old dog behind his ears, saying, 'Lieutenant-Colonel Lundy is flourishing, but as what I can't figure out. Is he a spy or a coward?'

His father didn't seem particularly interested either way. 'Fetch the bowls, lad. This is just about done.'

Adam sighed and did what he was told. He also poured two mugs of beer and brought everything to where the stools were positioned in front of the fire. His father didn't bother with tables anymore, preferring the comfort of sipping his soup while plopped in the warmest part of the house.

As Adam watched Gabriel ladle the soup into the first bowl, he spotted a fresh tear in the seat of his trousers. 'Father, you've ripped your trousers again.'

Gabriel smiled. 'That explains the draught down there.'

Adam laughed. 'I'll mend them for you after we eat.'

As a reward for this, his father prompted him to continue. 'Well, what's this about Lundy?'

Adam took his bowl and stirred the soup with his spoon. As usual Gabriel had waited until it was too hot to eat, to serve it up. Sure enough, the spoon burnt his lip when Adam tested the temperature. Meanwhile, his father took his place beside him and began to eat immediately. Adam could only conclude – *he must have no feelings left in his tongue!* He said, 'He has fortified the city, there's no doubt about that.'

His father looked at him and blinked, obliging Adam to remind him who he was talking about. 'Robert Lundy.'

His father rushed to assure him, 'Oh, yes. Yes!' Then he thought of something. 'How's that horse of yours?'

Used to his father's meandering conversations, Adam replied, 'Pegasus is fine. She'll probably need new shoes in the next month or so but apart from that she's grand.'

'Aye,' said his father, 'you have a good animal there. Take care of her.'

Adam exhaled before saying, 'Yes, Father, I know. I do take very good care of her.'

His father took a mouthful of boiling soup and exclaimed, 'You probably need a wife!'

Adam rolled his eyes at the dog who probably agreed with his father.

Adam returned to the former subject with some determination. 'Colonel Lundy is talking about breaking up the other Protestant garrisons in Dungannon, Monaghan and Cavan. Why would he do that? These towns are full of men eager to fight the Jacobites. From what I can see, he's preparing Derry for attack while also getting rid of our valuable allies. I reckon he's playing a dangerous game.' When Gabriel said not a word to this, his son continued, 'Nobody has accused him of anything yet, but I hear there are a lot of complaints behind his back. For instance, he has been told that more Jacobite soldiers are on their way but doesn't seem to be doing a thing about it. Also, it seems we had a chance of receiving fresh soldiers into the garrison and he turned them away. I cannot prove it yet, but the rumour persists. There was a meeting, but only a select few were present to decide, it would appear, to reject more men. At the very least his behaviour bewilders me.'

Again there was silence at this.

'Father,' said Adam, 'are you listening to me at all?'

Gabriel stopped slurping his soup long enough to say, 'Of course I am, son.'

Adam went to talk again. 'It's just that …'

However, his father interrupted him. 'I hope you find a girl who is even half as lovely as your mother was.'

Adam's smile and tone were tender. 'Yes, Father. I'll do my best to.'

Gabriel waggled a finger in his left ear, trying to clear it so that he could hear better while saying matter-of-factly, 'It sounds like Lundy doesn't believe in himself.'

Ignoring whatever his father had found in his ear, and was now stuck to his finger, Adam asked, 'Do you really think that's what it is, a lack of self-esteem is causing him to make worrying mistakes?'

His father grunted, 'He's just a man after all. And it's contagious too.'

Adam asked, 'What is?'

Having scooped up the last of his soup, Gabriel placed the bowl at his feet and stood up to wriggle himself out of his trousers. Next he went searching for needle and thread. When he sat back down again, he said, 'A few passers-by have told me that Lundy doesn't believe that Derry can be defended.'

'Really, Father? You never mentioned this.'

Gabriel was incredulous. 'But I just have. Lundy doesn't have faith in himself and, consequently, people don't have faith in him.'

Adam put his empty bowl at his feet and pulled the trousers into his lap, taking the needle and thread from his father, saying, 'That seems to be the point alright. They just don't trust him.'

His father gave the old dog a perfunctory rub across his matted spine and sighed. 'You can never truly know what goes on inside another man's head.'

Adam shrugged as he began to sew. 'But if you accept leadership over a city, I think a great deal should be transparent.'

His father took out his box of snuff and stuffed a

thimbleful up his nose before offering it to his son. The old man gave a hearty sniff and asked, 'Will you be staying here tonight?'

Adam shook his head. 'I can't. I'm on patrol. I'll do my best to drop in before the end of the week. Is there anything you need?'

His father, enjoying the warmth of the fire and the tiny snores from the dog, replied, 'No. Thank God!'

CHAPTER TWELVE

There was a new notice on the Markethouse to be read out to the men and boys of the battalion. April showers had created dozens of puddles throughout the Diamond. They sparkled like precious stones as they mirrored any slivers of sunshine that managed to puncture the grey clouds.

Henry Campsie had turned up, much to the Sherrard boys' surprise. His absence would have been understandable since he had buried his father that very morning. The brothers had attended the funeral with their parents but had been unable to get near poor Henry due to the huge number that turned up. The mayor had been a popular man and all his peers lined up to convey their personal sadness to his widow and eldest son. Afterwards Henry imagined he might stay home for the rest of the day. However, once home, he had an abiding need to get away from the room where his father died and away from his mother's tears.

Gervais Squire was the new mayor. His signature, along with the other city elders, adorned the 'Mutual Agreement', the document that was to be read out.

The lawyer David Cairnes had returned from another visit to London, bearing a letter from King William about his appreciation for Derry's efforts on his behalf and his promise to look after them. Mr Cairnes informed Lieutenant-Colonel Lundy and the city councillors that there were preparations taking place this very minute, in London, to help Derry and he strongly felt that nobody should be allowed to leave the city.

With everyone fired up, knowing that King William was following their every move, it was decided to draw up a list of rules – a 'Mutual Agreement' – for the population to keep the city on her best behaviour.

Robert and Daniel lined up with the other soldiers to hear the news. Robert quietly asked Henry how he was and received a half-hearted shrug for an answer, making him feel he should have asked a more sensible question. Daniel thought Henry looked different or strange. There was something about his clothes; they were too big for him. Later he would find out that Henry was wearing his father's old tunic and trousers.

Daniel struggled to concentrate on what was being said. The speaker, one of the aldermen, was making an announcement: 'We will not put up with cowards. To this end, a pair of gallows is to be erected and anybody in the garrison, who commits treachery in its many forms, will be hung by the neck until they are dead.'

Soldiers were smiling and nodding enthusiastically. Daniel could not mimic their response. Instead, he swallowed hard and tried to imagine what it would be like to be swinging from a rope, wishing for death to come quickly.

Daniel felt an unpleasantness steal into the atmosphere, despite the fact that some men were responding so positively to the man's words. *Surely*, he thought, *this means that we are now going to play judge and jury with our neighbours and friends*. Anybody's patriotism could be called into question by anybody else. *Why did this sound familiar?* And then it hit him that he was accidentally remembering James Morrison's story about the crows, about the way they turned on the weakest in the community.

Daniel looked at his brother to see if he shared his thoughts, but his brother cheered heartily when everyone else did. Daniel rushed to cheer himself, especially when Henry gave him a peculiar look. It seemed like the judging was to start immediately.

The speaker continued: 'Nobody is allowed to leave the city unless they have special permission from the newly formed Council of War, made up of our most prominent citizens and headed by Lieutenant-Colonel Lundy.'

It was Robert who experienced a mixture of emotions at this. On the one hand, this was all hugely exciting and couldn't have happened at a better time. Suddenly he was part of something real and important. This was what he had been searching for, the chance for glory. On the other hand, this excitement and newly discovered self-belief made him impatient to see what lay beyond the city he had grown up in. He dreamt of sailing the sea and seeing London. William Cairnes's uncle had told him about the endless streets, the fancy buildings, the pretty girls and the sheer wealth of the aristocracy.

A plan was forming in his head. He believed that a soldier's life would give him all that he wanted: travel, a nice wife and untold riches. The possibilities were endless. Why, he might join King William's army and make his mark in some exotic land he had yet to hear about. The world was finally opening up to him.

But, first things first.

He must help to hold Derry for his king and if that meant seeing nothing but these worn, well-familiar streets for another few months, well, so be it.

Once the threats and proposed punishments for this and that were read out, the speaker moved on to the good news; that is, the rations that would be made available to every soldier in the garrison. As of yet, there was no actual money to pay the men, but this was a temporary situation that would surely be rectified by King William and the parliament in London.

In the meantime, the speaker read: 'Each soldier shall receive a weekly ration of eight quarts of meal, four pounds of meat and three pounds of meal. A daily measure of beer will also be provided.'

The men cheered their gratitude.

Lieutenant-Colonel Robert Lundy studied the faces of the men. *How defiant they seem. Not one of them shows any uncertainty.*

Their belief was solid, God was on their side and therefore Derry would be saved.

Lundy searched the sky above for a sign that they were right. After all, the Jacobites had their God too – the same God, by all accounts. Would He choose between the two kings of England, William and James?

Oh, why can't I just believe like they do? Lundy hoped, however vaguely, that Lord Mountjoy would return from Dublin, but he had had no word on how his commander had fared at the hands of an enraged Richard Talbot. *Blast that man! Why doesn't he come up here and see how things stand for himself?*

A raven landed on the roof of the building in front of him. Robert Lundy stared at the bird who seemed to be listening to the goings-on. Birds were believed to be messengers, so was this his sign? What was the other thing he had heard about ravens? Where had he read it, about them meaning war?

He shivered. What exactly was it that bothered him? He took in the city around him, or at least the part he could see from where he stood. Most of the men in front of him were inexperienced. They were soldiers who had yet to fight a single battle. There weren't nearly enough weapons and, if it came down to it, Derry was on a path of no return. Should the city dig in her heels and attempt to out-wait the Jacobites the lieutenant-colonel knew there wasn't enough food. The population was far too big. Every soldier standing here, who was braced to fight, was local and so had parents, siblings, grandparents or children that would need to be fed. *God help us all!*

It had been his idea to dismantle the old houses near the walls. They took up valuable space that would be needed by a fighting army.

Of course, he had sensed his unpopularity growing day by day and had a brief, grim thought about the new gallows. *I hope I don't end up swinging from them.* He sighed to himself. *I'll do my best for this city but it might not be good enough.*

As he stood there watching the enthusiastic crowd, he was unaware that he was the focus of someone else's attention, someone who already believed that the governor was not good enough for the job in hand.

A recent addition to the city, Reverend George Walker had made his way to Derry after Lundy ordered the break-up of the garrison at Dungannon. He was an Anglican reverend first and a soldier second: *I'm a soldier of the Lord whether I am at the pulpit or on the battlefield.* And so he was. A couple of short months ago, when he was rector at Donoughmore in Armagh, he heard about the Jacobite army position at Derry's walls. This was his moment, he felt, to show his worth to the Lord. So he gathered his own soldiers together and marched to Dungannon, preparing to lay in for whatever came their way.

As far as Reverend Walker and his friends were concerned, Lundy's order to break up the garrison did not make sense. Superior in size to Derry, Dungannon had been ready to fight. Provisions had been gathered for the expected trouble ahead while troops, including Reverend Walker's, were formed and armed. All that was needed was a nod from Lundy to make their move. But he surprised them by telling them to evacuate the town. Naturally this created confusion and dismay. However, orders were orders. The troops fell back, allowing Jacobite soldiers, in turn, to fall upon their provisions. *No, it made no sense whatsoever.*

Taking his bible in hand, the reverend had prayed long and hard over what he should do next. In the end the answer was simple. *I'll go to Derry!* God, he felt, had told him that the city needed him.

He was ambitious, *but only to be all that God wants me to be.*

Judging from the expression on Lundy's face, it would appear that Derry's governor keenly desired to be elsewhere. The reverend found himself disapproving of the man's demeanour; his shoulders were hunched with tension, his chin dipped apologetically while his face had a waxy sheen to it. He looked like a man overly burdened with worry – and with guilt. *No, Lundy did not deserve to govern this city. Not at all.*

The reverend knew another man who would make a far, far better governor.

A spasm of delight passed over him as he gripped his bible and felt anointed by the Lord.

CHAPTER THIRTEEN

James Morrison was humming the same ditty over and over again. Daniel didn't like to ask the older boy to stop but then realised how ridiculous this was. He had signed up to fight Jacobites so why would he feel awkward about something like this? 'James …'

His fellow guard glanced at him. 'What?'

Daniel smiled to show there was no malice behind his words. 'Well, it's just that you've hummed that song about five times now.'

To his relief, James laughed. 'Whoops! Sorry, I'm always doing that. It drives my mother mad.'

Daniel breathed easily. 'Ah, it's alright. So, when do you think we'll get our ammunition?'

The cannons had been repaired, polished and repositioned on the walls, but as of yet, there was nothing to fire them with. James shook his head and said, 'Only the great and wise Lundy knows the answer to that question. He's ordered us to save our gunpowder and muskets.'

Daniel offered, 'I suppose he's right. Isn't he?'

James gawked at him. 'Do you think so? Reverend

Walker has heard that more Jacobites are heading for us and all we can do, all we are allowed to do, is stand here and bloody wait.' James blew his nose into his hands and added, 'And did you hear what the lieutenant-colonel said to the reverend? He told him it was a *false* claim. Can you believe that?'

Daniel hoped that James would leave it at that but he didn't.

James had spent the morning lecturing anyone who would listen on why Lundy's response to the reverend's news was the most stupid thing he had ever heard in his life. He began once more. 'Imagine you're a city that refuses to obey the law of the land …'

Daniel suddenly felt tired but he knew it was only because he was about to spend the next quarter of an hour or so listening to James pontificate. Although he had to admit he preferred listening to James over Henry Campsie.

On the plus side, all that was really required of him was to nod occasionally when not scrunching up his features in pretend disbelief. In fact, he could probably get away without doing any of this as long as he agreed with James. That was the important thing.

Earlier that morning Robert had teased his brother about this blossoming friendship. 'Has he let you fire his gun yet?'

Daniel had made a face in reply. 'Very funny! He doesn't

have any powder!'

Robert had smirked. 'I bet he does have some but it's tucked into his boots and is too damp from his sweaty feet.'

Before Daniel had been able to say anything else their mother had come into the room, carrying Alice. 'Robert Sherrard, you're worse than a gossipy old woman!'

Her sons had laughed.

She had sat down on a stool to rock the baby to sleep and had asked, 'So what is the news in the town? Is there anything your mother should know?'

Daniel had grinned. 'Now you're asking us for gossip.'

Those moments were delicious, when thoughts of defence and war could be forgotten, and they could relax together – two grown boys teasing their mother who wanted to have fun.

On watch, Daniel and James stood and stared out across the Foyle, both lost in thought until Daniel asked, 'Do you think you'll get married?'

James was taken aback by the suddenness of the question. Checking Daniel's expression to see he was serious, he asked, 'Whatever made you think of that?'

Daniel was telling the truth when he shrugged, 'I don't know. It just popped into my head.'

James accepted this as a reasonable explanation. 'I suppose I will, yes. That's what men do, isn't it – find a respectable girl, make her your wife and have a family?'

Daniel asked cheekily, 'Have you found a respectable girl yet?'

James winked. 'I might have!' Then he added, 'But I won't be doing anything about it until I know Derry is safe from harm.'

Daniel nodded and said, 'We're sort of stuck until this is all sorted.'

James's gaze suddenly darted to the ground. A tiny movement had caught his attention, his full attention. He bounded off.

'What are you doing?' asked Daniel.

James put his fingers to his lips and dramatically pointed to a mouse that was minding his own business. Daniel sighed. James frequently boasted he was faster than a cat and, of course, he couldn't resist the chance to show off in front of him. It was tiring having to constantly provide a response.

Mrs Sherrard told Daniel that the reason James was so *needy* – her word – was that he was the only child of a doting mother. His father had died when he was a baby and so he was the only man in his mother's life. 'He missed out having a father,' his mother said. 'I'm sure he envies you and Robert having one another.'

Daniel could understand this and determined to show James more kindness while Robert scoffed at the idea. Daniel wondered if his brother didn't envy James since he didn't have to deal with a parent who stubbornly expected him to be better than he was. *We always want what someone else has.* That's the conclusion that Daniel reached.

To hide his irritation and also to remind James that he should be focused on working, Daniel leant over the cannon as if to inspect it. He polished it a little with his sleeve, noticing how cool it felt even through his tunic. A spider had spun his web in between the spokes of one of the wheels. When was the last time this gun was used? The web was an inappropriate ornament for such a fearsome weapon. Daniel tore it with his index finger and then had to rub his finger against the wall to release it from the sticky strands.

'Daniel?'

Daniel decided against looking up immediately. *Let him come and stand next to* me, *where he should be, keeping watch.*

'Daniel?'

James's tone was low and urgent, but Daniel paid it no heed. *He has to learn not to keep running off.*

And Daniel might have kept this up had not another guard shouted, 'Look, it's them!'

At this, Daniel's head snapped upwards to see James holding a wriggling mouse by the tail in one hand while using his other to point across the river Foyle.

The cool, silent body of the cannon stopped Daniel from stumbling at the sight of a huge army, newly arrived, to flesh out the one that had been camped there for ages.

James called out, 'It's that lot that Reverend Walker was talking about.' He dropped the relieved mouse as he added, 'There's Lundy's false alarm!'

Daniel asked, 'What do we do?'

James spat, 'Nothing. That's his orders. We do nothing except stand here with empty guns and watch.'

Daniel watched and felt that the new arrivals were a great deal superior to the old ones. They had more horses for one thing, while they also appeared more disciplined and professional. Another guard joined himself and Daniel and said, 'They're taking care to be noticed by us. We're meant to be trembling with fear now and unlocking the gates.'

James cursed at them while Daniel suddenly asked, 'Wait! What are they doing?'

The three of them stared and stared until James declared, 'They're loading a cannon!'

That couldn't be right, could it? It was hard to accept this after months of inactivity when the guards at Ferry Quay Gate complained about the boredom of watching the camp do nothing interesting in the least. The fact that Derry might be fired upon had seemed a relevant one back in December but now, five months later, it was hardly considered a possibility – until now.

The older guard muttered, 'They're just bluffing!'

Daniel was too polite and inexperienced to disagree, although it struck him that it was a trifle silly to go to the bother of loading up a cannon and not fire it. If the old soldier was prepared to remain still while the enemy cannon was primed and pointed in their direction, James and Daniel were prepared to look foolish and they cowered down to cover themselves.

They needn't have bothered. Not that the Jacobite cannon wasn't fired; it most definitely was. Those Papists had the cheek, after all this time, to fire one single cannonball which hit the Newgate Bastion, a few feet away from the boys. Daniel and James jumped up, ready to dash off for ammunition, their fear forgotten.

'No,' said the old soldier. 'Stay where you are. They're leaving now. See for yourself.'

The two boys saw the men get back in line and an order was made to resume marching again.

'What is it? What happened?' Reverend Walker was out of breath, his wig askew. The whole city had heard the solitary boom.

The older soldier replied, 'It's alright, Reverend. Just a new battalion saying "hello"!'

The reverend breathed noisily through his nose. 'They're going to Strabane to collect more recruits.' He slapped the cannon, making the boys jump again. 'How dare they! We should have returned fire.'

Daniel was too timid to point out the obvious, but James was happy to do it, 'But, sir, we're not allowed to keep any gunpowder on us … otherwise we surely would have fired.'

The reverend spun around to face them. Keeping an eye on the marching army, he shoved his wig farther up his head. 'What did you say, boy?'

Daniel saw James falter. 'I'm s-sorry, sir. I didn't mean any disrespect.'

'No,' sighed Reverend Walker. 'What you meant was that the individual who thought that they were only a false alarm is the same one who insisted on the gunpowder being hidden away.'

His audience dared not say another word.

'Tell me,' said the reverend to the older soldier. 'Do you think they'll be back?' He calmed visibly when the man replied immediately and honestly, 'Yes, sir. They'll be back.' In fact the churchman began to smile, though Daniel thought it the coldest smile he had ever seen. 'Well, then,' he said. 'Let them come back and this time we'll be ready and waiting.'

CHAPTER FOURTEEN

Adam Murray was having a busy morning. Due to a burst of dissatisfaction with Robert Lundy, he had found himself in charge of approximately fifteen hundred soldiers. How did this happen?

His father had a simple explanation: *they recognise the leader in him and plainly see his courage.* As far as Gabriel was concerned, it was all perfectly natural and no surprise at all. So, he wouldn't be bothering to congratulate his son on his informal promotion. Adam was still expected to visit, burn his mouth on the soup of the day and sew whatever needed mending.

In truth, Adam was taking it all in his stride. Thanks to Robert Lundy's fit of temper one evening, Adam only went into Derry when it was necessary. The lieutenant-colonel had ordered the gates to remain locked against hundreds of Derry soldiers who had been out ambushing the Jacobites. Apparently he thought it was necessary to protect the city's supplies from her own fighting men. It proved too much for some of the men who decided, on that very night, to take the next boat to England. The rest of them were now following Adam Murray, or Colonel Murray as they called him. They pledged to fight until death, believing that death on the battlefield would be infinitely kinder than handing themselves over to the Catholics. They trusted Adam. He never showed fear; he was always in front, sitting on his white horse, leading the way. He made a perfect substitute for the shady Robert Lundy.

Adam did ask his father if he was alright with his son devoting most of his time to warfare. In ordinary times Adam would have helped out with the farm, but these days there just weren't enough hours to allow him to do this.

Gabriel was typically blunt. 'Aren't you really asking me for my blessing?'

Adam shrugged. 'I suppose so.'

His father was cleaning his fingernails with the old bread knife. 'I've never stopped you from doing what you want to do and I'm not about to start now.'

There was silence as Adam dissected his father's words, to find the encouragement in them. Like most sons, he did, on top of everything else, hope to make his father proud.

However, Gabriel, as far as Adam could see, was not like most fathers. Sometimes it seemed that the old man did not have the least bit of interest in what was going on around him. He rarely ventured away from the farm and did not make a particularly good listener when Adam filled him in on the latest news. No doubt it was to do with his fair age. Gabriel was already in his forties by the time Adam arrived, shocking his poor parents to the core. Now he was a stubborn old man who wanted nothing except to see his wife again. Gabriel never actually said this, but Adam understood it all the same.

Hours later, Adam thought of his father's blazing fireplace as the weather turned miserable. Instead of polite April showers, blustering gusts of drenching rain embraced Adam and Pegasus as they led his fifteen hundred men across the plains a few miles from Derry.

As he rode, Adam considered the situation. Confusing rumours were trickling out of the city, mostly to do with Robert Lundy's lack of faith in holding it. And Gabriel was right; this lack of faith was spreading and it was dangerous. Adam heard that a captain and an officer in Derry had been murdered because they had decided that the city was done for and prepared to board a ship that was returning to London.

Adam was shocked by the absence of discipline and loyalty of everyone involved. Lundy's game-playing, if that's what it was, was backfiring on him. The people were running out of patience.

'Sir?'

Adam looked around. Three figures were coming towards them. He recognised two of them to be his own men. The third one was in uniform and looked familiar.

He greeted Adam and introduced himself. 'I'm Captain Neville, sir. We've met before in the city.'

Adam got down from Pegasus and shook his hand.

Captain Neville said, 'Your men thought it best that I tell you myself what is happening.'

'I see,' said Adam, wondering if the captain was fleeing Derry or requesting to join his regiment.

Looking slightly sheepish, Captain Neville admitted, 'I've been locked out since last night, but I'm hoping to get back in. The night guard, a man I dislike, pretended not to recognise me.'

Adam was suspicious. 'Why would he pretend that?'

The captain hesitated, aware of the large number of ears that were attempting to eavesdrop. Spying a large tree to their right, Captain Neville suggested that he and Adam shelter from the rain, hoping that Adam would understand that this was a conversation for his ears only.

Adam did and agreed, electing only to bring Pegasus with him as a neutral observer. He told his men to continue their march to Brookhall, a couple of miles away, where they were to make camp; he would follow them as soon as he could.

Some of the men demurred, one of them asking if

Adam was sure the captain meant him no harm. Adam raised his eyebrows at Captain Neville who rushed to reassure them that he was one of King William's men, just like they were. This satisfied Adam's soldiers who saluted him and moved on.

As Captain Neville, Pegasus and Adam strolled towards the tree, Adam asked, 'Are you carrying any weapons?'

Too polite to point out that Adam really should have asked that question when he was surrounded by his own men, Captain Neville raised his arms, saying, 'You can search me if you like. I'm not armed but I've a good excuse why not.'

Captain Neville reached out to pat Pegasus on the neck. The horse shucked her head in thanks or perhaps it was irritation. Pegasus disliked windy weather; it made her grumpy.

They reached the tree, the rain slapping the leaves in such a way that it sounded like applause. Perhaps neither man noticed the wonderful smell. The tree was so generous in size and coverage that they could have closed their eyes and been fooled into thinking they were in the middle of a forest.

Adam merely glanced at the captain who needed no further persuasion. 'Yesterday,' began Captain Neville, 'I was part of a group of three that was sent to parley with the Jacobite camp.' Adam was not expecting this but didn't interrupt. 'Lieutenant-Colonel Lundy said that the city should be surrendered.' The captain shrugged at the expression of disgust on Adam's face. 'Anyway, three of us were selected to meet with Talbot's man, Colonel Richard Hamilton, to ask about King James's demands and find out what terms he would grant us.' Here, the captain rubbed water off the bridge of his nose. 'It was actually a good meeting, to be honest. We were received with graciousness and told if we surrendered, and handed over all our weapons and horses, not a drop of blood would be shed. Colonel Hamilton was adamant about that.'

Adam stared at Pegasus who stared back. The captain continued, 'Hamilton gave us a day to consider our answer and promised us that no Jacobite troops would approach our gates while the leaders were deliberating their response.'

Adam stayed silent. He did not … that is, he could not … well, he just wasn't sure how he felt. *To be promised clemency if we surrendered? That the city would be allowed to continue in peace if it submitted to James, who — it would appear — didn't want any harm done to her. Does that even make sense?*

Oblivious to Adam's inner turmoil, the captain described how the meeting took no more than a couple of hours. 'But while we were gone there was trouble. I'm not exactly sure what happened, but it seems that fear took hold in the city. Somebody, or bodies, is possibly exaggerating the size

143

of the army that is accompanying James to Derry.'

Adam had heard that James was coming north but wasn't sure whether to believe it or not. It struck him as the act of either a pathetic man or a stupid one.

Captain Neville said, 'Afterwards the three of us presented ourselves at the gate, gave the password but were denied entry without an explanation. I think a little power can be a dangerous thing.' He looked to Adam for agreement, but Adam was saying nothing yet. Undaunted, the captain continued, 'We demanded to see an alderman, any of them, but the guards refused to fetch them. Finally my two companions were allowed inside but Colonel Whitney, who was supervising the nightwatch, abused me shamefully and the gate was shut in my face.'

Adam didn't look particularly sympathetic when Captain Neville said he was forced to spend the night in a stranger's filthy cabin. 'Then, this morning, I heard the most peculiar thing. During the night someone found two of the gates unlocked and the keys were missing. Can you imagine the panic that might have caused?'

Adam's eyes narrowed and he offered, 'Somebody left the gates open for the Papists to sneak in and spy on us?'

His companion gazed at him. 'That's what I thought, only there was no sign that any Jacobites had been inside.'

Adam shook his head, saying, 'That doesn't mean anything. A few of them could have made their way inside, to convince people to surrender. They could have disguised themselves as ordinary folk and done as much damage with words as with guns and swords.'

Captain Neville was struck dumb for a moment. What Adam said made perfect sense. Running his fingers along the trunk of the tree, the captain murmured, 'Hundreds of strangers living on the streets. Yes, it would be all too easy to mingle amongst them and start one little rumour about atrocities that might befall them if Derry doesn't surrender. That's all it would take.'

Nodding in grave agreement, Adam asked, 'When is James expected?'

Captain Neville looked embarrassed and his voice shook as he gulped his reply, 'Today!'

There was no time to lose. Adam heaved himself back up onto Pegasus, who seemed surprised at her master's urgency. The horse had hoped to escape the rain for a while longer.

It was the captain's turn to ask a question. 'What are you going to do, Colonel?'

Adam didn't pretend to have a plan. 'I don't know yet but I have to do something.' With that, he directed Pegasus towards Derry. The city was about four miles away and the ground would be soggy from the rain. He spurred the horse into action, thinking, *how could they just give up like that? Have they no pride?*

As Pegasus thudded against the soft earth, sending clods of mud flying in her wake, Adam ordered himself to stay calm. The first thing he had to do was reach Derry before the Papist king.

CHAPTER FIFTEEN

King James wondered if the atrocious weather was in league with his French advisors in not wanting him to reach his destination. Drops of rain cascaded down his large nose, but he paid no heed to them. From beneath his wide-brimmed hat, a glorious wig, dark in colour, full of bounce and ringlets, generously framed a long pale face that was no longer young. King James had never been handsome but that, one would assume, is not important when one is king.

And surely he deserved to be king if only for the fact he had to put so much effort into being one. He had received a rapturous welcome in Dublin, where the people – indeed, *his* people – lined the streets to cheer him on. These loyal subjects made him feel like a true king, something he hadn't felt for a while.

On the wet and windy journey north, James had had plenty of time to think. He had lost the love and respect of his two daughters. Goodness knows how many enemies he had in England, but still, he was here for the sake of his baby son. This precious infant ensured there would be a Catholic on the throne of England for many years to come. *He's my chance to start over again. I owe it to him!*

The king's plan was a simple one, as the best ones normally are. The difficulties with Derry did not worry him unduly. In truth he was confident that once the Protestants, Presbyterians, and whoever else was behind the stand-off, saw him that they would appreciate the respect he was showing them, by presenting himself in person. He wasn't entirely sure what would happen next but he daydreamed of being shown around the city and meeting its now cheering inhabitants. Of course he would show them how gracious he was, that he could forgive them all for their recent transgressions.

Perhaps the city needed money for new buildings and roads. He determined to give serious consideration to whatever they asked of him, as their king. Perhaps he would throw a banquet; yes, why not, to prove there were no hard feelings. Who could resist a king who was willing to dine and sleep among them? He would befriend the poor, just as Jesus did in Jerusalem.

Really, his French advisors worried too much. It was understandable; they're French after all, and foreign to these lands. *But these people are mine, it is only natural that I understand how best to deal with them.* James nodded his agreement to the thoughts in his head.

The Count of Avaux, his chief advisor, was appalled at

the idea of a king journeying all the way to an obstinate and sulky city. Rubbing his hands together as if he were washing them, he pleaded, 'Sire, I fear this is beneath you. You are submitting yourself to an ungrateful population but it is they who should be submitting to you.'

King James smiled patiently at the little man whose constant expression was a heavy frown as if he was always perplexed by the world he lived in. 'There, there, Avaux, you must trust me. A true king knows when to bend and when to stand strong. Some peoples just need a little more care than others.'

The Frenchman looked gloomier than ever. His sodden moustache drooped, as did his mouth, as if he was displaying a double expression of woe. Always particular about his appearance, Avaux loathed the Irish weather for its dire treatment of his clothes.

His job was proving far more difficult than he had anticipated. He had been tasked by his own king, Louis XIV, to help James in his campaign to take back the English throne. However, it was frustrating when James behaved as if he knew more than anyone else. Furthermore, Avaux was in competition for the king's ear. The Irish lieutenants were filling his head with nonsense, encouraging him to crawl on his knees to a city that Avaux had never even heard of before now.

As if the conversation was not going badly enough, the

king said, 'You know, I actually admire these people. All they are doing is standing up for themselves and their religion.'

'*Mon dieu!*' Avaux muttered beneath his breath.

When they were a couple of miles from the city, King James was told Derry was preparing to surrender. Ah, this must be the sign he had prayed for. *Yes*, he thought, *a banquet is the perfect way to portray myself as a noble monarch and allow the people to benefit too.* The businessmen – the butchers, the shopkeepers, the taverns – would surely appreciate supplying their wares for a generous price.

'Your Majesty, there is the city before us.'

James was intrigued to see at last this place he had heard so much about. In fact, he could hardly believe he was here. The walls were mighty and impressive. Of course it was nowhere near as big and grand as Paris and London; still this was a city, or a fortress to be reckoned with. He could appreciate that, even at this distance.

His advisors moved up to ride alongside him. 'My lord, what do you wish to do now?'

King James was perplexed. 'Why, I want to go there immediately. What else would you have me do?'

There was a tense silence until Avaux said, 'Your Majesty, might I suggest we make camp at the next town so that you can rest? We can send word that you will visit tomorrow morning.'

Nobody was the least bit surprised when James drew himself up and declared, 'Nonsense! I want to go now!'

There was a collective bowing of heads accompanied by a morose chorus of 'Yes, Your Majesty!'

Meanwhile, the French lieutenant-general, de Rosen, had been ordered to take his men to within a mile of the Ship Quay Gate. Didn't anybody alert him and his company to the fact that Colonel Richard Hamilton had promised to keep *all* other Jacobite regiments four miles from the gates? It didn't seem so, although it may have made no difference to the haughty and impatient Lieutenant-General de Rosen. He was one of the most senior of the French officers to accompany King James from King Louis's majestic castle in Versailles, and he much preferred to be feared than respected. It is doubtful that Lieutenant-General de Rosen would have adhered to the 'four miles from the wall' agreement had he known about it.

All in all, this was a serious error, whoever was to blame for it. The people of Derry had allowed Lieutenant-Colonel Lundy and his men inside the walls because they had been promised that *no* other troops would approach any of the gates. It seemed that King James and his men had reached their destination without informing or communicating their whereabouts to Colonel Hamilton.

Oblivious to all this, King James innocently urged his horse to the south-west of the city, towards Bishop's Gate, closely followed by his trumpeter, advisors and secretary. His presence was causing quite a stir amongst the guards on the walls and around the gate, but he hadn't expected anything less. The sight of an actual king was surely a thrilling one for ordinary people so far from London.

His companions looked nervous. Ordinarily, this might have annoyed him. Today, however, was different. Today they would provide a sharp contrast to his own relaxed features. The people of Derry should see that he did not display any doubt about his reception.

The rain got heavier while James waited for Derry to make her move. He expected that whoever was in charge would present themselves and unlock the gate to him. Where was Lord Lieutenant Talbot's man, Lundy? He waited and waited.

Nothing happened, except that a crowd of soldiers and people seemed to be gathering on the other side of the gate.

There was only one thing to do and he knew better than to ask Avaux's opinion at this point. The truth was he needed this city; he needed this island in its entirety in order to strengthen his quest for the whole of England. So, this would be where he'd make his mark and whatever he had to do would be worth it. Tipping his horse gently, he gestured for his trumpeter to accompany him. They went right up to the gate, watched by the rest of the party and battalion.

A voice roared out, 'Halt! Who goes there?'

At last, thought King James, *someone to engage with.* Aloud he said, 'I wish to speak with your governor, Lieutenant-Colonel Lundy.'

The trumpeter, a young lad of nineteen years or so, would not allow his king to humble himself further. He called out, 'His Majesty, King James, wishes to enter your city!'

'Huh!' said one of the guards, 'Robert Lundy is no leader of ours!'

The trumpeter was at a loss. The status of Lundy was not the most pressing matter. Wishing that one of the French advisors would join them, the trumpeter tried again. 'Can one of your other leaders come to the gate, then? His Majesty is tired from his journey.'

A fierce whispered conversation followed. King James stared ahead, trying to hide his bewilderment. Eventually the answer was given. 'No! They're in the council's chamber and can't be disturbed.'

Behind the walls there was quite a fuss. Henry Campsie was slow to believe that King James was outside. 'Are you sure it's him?'

James Morrison winked. 'See for yourself. He's not wearing a crown but he's dressed like a king and his trumpeter says it's him.'

Robert Sherrard asked, 'Should we fetch the churchmen?'

Henry shook his head. 'Absolutely not. From what I

hear they'll surrender to him. I'll wager that's what they're meeting about now.' Henry paused to think. 'No, we'll handle this ourselves.'

Robert was surprised. 'What? Are you going to go and talk to him? I'll come with you; I've never seen a king before.'

Henry snapped, 'What king? It's not William of Orange out there, is it?'

Daniel wanted to box Henry's ears when he saw the embarrassment on his brother's face. He couldn't help himself; he glanced around hoping to see one of the aldermen or Reverend Walker, or even Lieutenant-Colonel Lundy. He felt the situation required one of the elders, even an unpopular one such as Lundy. There was something about the redness of Henry's cheeks and the feverish look in his eyes that made Daniel uneasy. Unfortunately all he could see were guards and young lads like himself, and, of course, the curious who began to throng the gate, wanting to see James in the flesh, as it were. What a spectacle!

Then, to Daniel's immense relief, Henry also cast about for a second opinion. 'Where's Adam Murray?' he asked.

The group brightened up at the mention of Adam's name. *Yes, Adam Murray! He'll know what to do!*

Perhaps it was inevitable that a popularity contest had been brewing between Lieutenant-Colonel Robert Lundy and the local farmer turned soldier Adam Murray.

Unfortunately for the former it was no contest at all. Adam inspired confidence with his fierce resistance to the Jacobite cause. He was not troubled by doubts as to whose side he was on. He was a Derry Protestant and that was that. Nobody was paying him to be there or expecting him to behave in a certain manner. As far as Adam was concerned, the only person he had to answer to was God and – maybe, also – Gabriel, his father.

James Morrison, who had climbed up on top of St Columb's Cathedral's tower, the highest point in Derry, shouted down, 'I think I can see him – I can definitely see a white horse!'

There was a sudden flurry of 'Where? Where is he?' But James only spoke to Henry. 'Pennyburn Mill! I'm sure it's him!'

Of course it was Adam, riding for his life and the life of the city.

Pennyburn Mill was a mile north of the city. Adam had pushed Pegasus hard for the first three miles and then on seeing the fresh armies around Derry knew he was too late.

'DAMN HIM!'

Adam shouted this out to the plains between them. He braced himself to watch. Would they let the Papist in? It was all over if they did. Like James himself, Adam waited and waited, peering hard over Pegasus's head.

But nothing happened. Nothing at all. The different sections of the king's army made no movement, so they must not have been allowed entry to the city.

Filling with a renewed hope that common sense had prevailed, even in the face of this infamous royal visitor, Adam turned Pegasus. He needed his army or even just some of them. Lundy must have lost Derry! This jubilant thought propelled him to keep going and keep calm. It wouldn't do to lose his head now. There was still time but he would have to think and act quickly. Now it was a race between him and those inside the city who wanted to surrender it.

In the city, most of the boys climbed the walls, impatient to see Adam Murray on his white horse. Daniel sent a prayer to Heaven above, *Oh let him come now*!

'Where's he going?' asked Robert as they watched the horse and rider turn away.

Henry grasped the situation immediately. 'I bet he's gone to fetch his men. We need to hold James here until he returns.'

Daniel asked, 'But what if Robert Lundy or some of the others arrive?'

Henry shrugged. 'They won't come if they don't know that James is here!'

Daniel wasn't convinced. He gestured to the crowd below. 'What about them?'

Henry smiled. 'None of that lot want to surrender and, even if they did, none of them would be allowed to interrupt a council meeting!' Henry was adamant about that.

Outside the city gates a voice called, 'Your Excellency!'

James guessed it was Avaux and pretended not to hear him. He wouldn't be thwarted now. God above would reward him for his patience and humility. Raindrops seeped down the front of his cloak but it was of little importance to him. He preferred to think upon this as a test of his belief and strength. He didn't mind getting wet if the good people of Derry just let him inside. *One must decipher which is the greater sacrifice in order to triumph. Jesus was nailed to a cross; this lack of welcome hardly compares to that!*

The young trumpeter wished he was tucked up in bed, back home in Dublin; anywhere else but in this Godforsaken place.

There was a shout from the other rampart, where Lieutenant-General de Rosen's battalion was being watched. Henry Campsie led his friends over to see what was going on.

It was a nasty shock to find so many enemy soldiers standing there, in formation, waiting to make their next move. Rifles were held in both hands and were no doubt loaded and ready to shoot.

Robert exclaimed, 'They're far too close. That's not what Hamilton promised!'

Daniel felt that Henry was delighted at this breach.

Some of the boys started to shout at the Jacobites, 'Get back, you fools!'

The warning shouts were ignored, and Henry was suitably outraged. 'Who do they think they are?'

Robert needed to find an explanation. 'The Papist fools are only feeling confident because their old king is at the gate.'

Daniel felt things were happening too fast but he had no authority to call for calm. His only option was to get his brother's attention. To this end, he moved to his side and muttered, 'We need to alert Reverend Walker.'

Robert shrugged. 'I know but ...'

Henry dashed about, trying to see everything at once. He asked, 'Where's Colonel Whitney?'

Robert answered him, 'He's with Lundy and the others.'

James Morrison added to the panic by exclaiming, 'They're coming closer. My God! Do they mean to storm the gates?'

That was it for Henry. He seized a rifle from one of the guards and, with a growl, made for the part of the wall that was nearest Bishop's Gate, where the ever patient King James was still waiting to be admitted.

Robert and Daniel bumped into one another in their effort to keep up with Henry. The two Sherrards were suddenly alarmed about their friend's intentions. To

Daniel's horror he saw that Henry had gunpowder. Grabbing Robert by the arm, he asked desperately, 'Is he going to shoot the king?'

Robert was aghast. 'No, he's not. He wouldn't do something that stupid!'

He convinced neither of them.

There was a blast of gunfire.

'Oh, no!' gasped the boys together as they raced to look over the wall.

Horses spluttered and neighed in protest, King James was trying to steady his while some of his men ran to help him, taking care not to stamp on the slain body of the trumpeter. A large blood stain was flowering rapidly from the centre of the boy's chest.

Robert sprinted off after Henry, pushing through groups of guards who were reeling from the sound of peace being shattered. Daniel stayed where he was, watching the king finally rein in his horse One of the king's men grabbed the trumpeter's riderless horse. It quivered in fright.

Robert felt sick. What had Henry been thinking? He arrived by Henry's side and shouted the exact same question at his friend. 'What the hell are you thinking?'

Henry was cool, though a fire danced within him and there was a buzzing in his ears. He turned to face Robert and asked, 'Are you with me?'

Robert was confused. 'What do you mean?'

Henry, looking behind and around Robert, beckoned for attention from a bigger audience before declaring, 'This is it! There's only this moment. What we do today will echo through the years to come. No surrender!'

He paused before saying it again, 'No surrender!' Then he shouted it as loud as he could. 'NO SURRENDER!'

The crowd on the ground took up the chant. 'No surrender!'

Henry punched the air and said it back to them. 'No surrender!'

Daniel watched him in grudging admiration. The crowd were dancing and shouting their defiance. This was their city, their home, their religion. No surrender. It was infectious. It gave voice to their pride, their love, their passion – call it what you will. No surrender.

Henry leant over the wall and called for everyone else to take up the cry, and those proud citizens of Derry – men, women and children – flung the words at the head of James, his French advisors, Lieutenant-General de Rosen and every single Jacobite solider who could hear them: 'NO SURRENDER!'

Someone picked up a stone and fired it at the group below. It was the signal for everyone else to do the same. An avalanche of pebbles and rocks rained down upon the royal party. They quickly retreated.

Daniel's stomach lurched at the sorrowful expression on

the king's face. He wanted to call after him: Well, what did you expect? As far as he could make out James was refusing to move out of sight. Daniel was incredulous. *Does he still believe this is all going to work out well?*

Robert was throwing stones too. It was glorious to be able to do something as dramatic as this: pick a stone, push back his arm over his head and then hurl it as hard as he could. He experienced a delicious freedom in releasing the small rock. He was barely aware of his anger. His strongest feelings were not particularly directed at the Catholic king and his followers. No, sir! Robert blamed the church leaders, the aldermen and all the city elders for putting the people in this position. Gritting his teeth, he reasoned that King James had been bold enough to approach the gate because he was under the impression that Derry was about to be his. *Damn Robert Lundy!* He was the real enemy. *Damn his soul to Hell!*

From the walls Daniel could see Adam Murray in the distance but his relief was small. He's too late! Why couldn't he have reached the city earlier?

A figure dashed past Daniel. It was Colonel Whitney, waving his arms and yelling, 'Cease firing! Cease firing!' Nobody saluted him or moved aside to allow him through. He was one of *them*, a council member who wanted to surrender. Only when his passage was well and truly blocked did he realise what was happening. He roared, 'Get out of my way!'

Some of the men smirked openly while others asked him what he was doing.

The colonel's only option was to explain himself. 'Lieutenant-Colonel Lundy and the others want the shooting stopped!'

As if on cue the crowd below shouted once more, 'No surrender!'

Looking for the nearest thing to a friendly face, Colonel Whitney spied Henry Campsie. The colonel had attended Mayor Campsie's funeral and had shaken the boy's hand. Now he asked the former mayor's son, 'Did someone discharge a rifle at King James?'

Henry didn't hesitate. 'Yes, Colonel. I did!'

The colonel was stumped and stared at the boy in front of him.

Henry added, 'I had no choice.'

Colonel Whitney profoundly disagreed. 'But what if you had hit the king? You might have started an all-out war, one we're nowhere near ready for. What were you thinking, lad?'

Henry idled, allowing Robert to speak up and defend his friend's actions. 'Henry did what he felt was necessary. They were coming at us from two sides and there was no one here to tell us any differently.'

The colonel shook his head and turned back towards the

steps. It did not escape his notice that Adam Murray's army was about a mile away and coming fast. The beleaguered officer mumbled something to himself that nobody but Daniel could hear. 'God help us all!' The colonel's words chilled Daniel to the bone.

CHAPTER SIXTEEN

Adam read the note that was handed to him:
You should immediately withdraw your
men to the back of the hill out of sight
of the city!

He asked the messenger, James Murray, a cousin of his from his father's side of the family, 'I don't understand. Why must I move out of sight?

James grinned. 'Because, my dear cousin, your little band of merry men is making Governor Lundy and the elders anxious regarding their desire to surrender. The sight of you lot coming to our rescue might well confuse the Jacobites. And they can't be having that, now, can they?'

Adam blanched. 'Are they that close to unlocking the gates?'

James nodded. 'That's the official message from the War Council. Now let me give you the unofficial message. Ignore all that rubbish about hiding. I can tell you here and now that the people are behind you. You need to get to Derry as fast as your horse can carry you because it's widely believed that you're the man to stand up to both the council and the Jacobites!'

Adam couldn't help asking, 'Really?'

James nodded. 'Your name is on everyone's lips. God-speed!'

Adam, along with forty of his men, was obliged to try to dodge the Jacobites who had been forced back from the gate. As soon as the Jacobites saw them, they fired some musket balls after them but failed to hit anyone. Adam was grateful for the fact that he and his men were on horse-back and could easily sprint out of range of the rifles. He was also inclined to believe that the Catholic soldiers were not allowed to start a war just yet.

Finally, they arrived at Ship Quay Gate, which was locked. Adam rattled it, bringing two guards to ask him his business. This was not the welcome he had expected. Where was his cousin now when he needed him?

Feeling a little awkward, Adam asked to be allowed inside. He didn't know the guards and so did not know that they supported Lieutenant-Colonel Lundy with his fears of a vengeful King James. They refused to unlock the gate, merely stating, 'We have our orders!'

However, one of them did ask if Adam had special per-mission to enter the city. This was frustrating. The only official letter Adam had was the one telling him to stay clear of the city. He said, 'I've been told the people are expecting me. My name is Adam Murray.'

The guards remained unimpressed. 'What people?'

By this stage Adam wasn't entirely sure himself.

Just then, two younger guards appeared. Adam was relieved to see that he recognised them: one of them was James Morrison, the other the physician's son, Daniel Sherrard. 'Colonel Whitney wants you two at Bishop's Gate to report on James and the army there. Give us your keys, we're to replace you.'

Once the two guards were on their way, James unlocked the gates and ushered in Adam and his soldiers. Adam shook his and Daniel's hand and kept moving, although he was unsure as to what he was going to do next.

He got down from Pegasus, telling his men to stow away the horses at one of the stables. 'We don't want to attract attention just yet.' The words had only left his mouth when he heard his name called from all directions: 'Look, it's Adam Murray!' They came and kept coming, men, women and children, wanting to shake his hand and welcome him back. His soldiers stuck closely to him in case of trouble. Adam had never experienced anything like this before. Their trust in him was touching, but it came, he knew, with immense expectations and responsibility.

They all moved together towards the Diamond, Adam and his men enclosed by the crowd of well-wishers. Adam kept a discreet look-out for Lundy, Reverend Walker or any of the council members who would dispute his presence in the city. On reaching the Diamond, he felt he should address the crowd and hoped his voice sounded strong and confident. 'I give you my word that I will fight for you, this city and the Protestant faith!'

How they cheered! Adam was relieved; he had never spoken to so many people at once before. Their belief in him moved him to add, 'I also pledge my assistance to suppressing the War Council and their talks of surrendering to the Catholic king!'

The people roared in gratitude and relief. Adam was exactly what they needed, a bright light in the fog of confusion that had recently descended on the city.

He needed to know who was with him. From now on he could afford to take nothing or no one for granted. Thinking fast, he spoke again, 'My friends, I must ask you to show your colours. Any man or woman who is prepared to fight with me must wear a white cloth on your arm. We need to know who is on our side.'

He had no problem warning them, 'What I'm asking isn't easy. You'll be wearing your defiance of the elders on your sleeve for all to see.'

Not one person faltered in their enthusiasm for him. Soldiers amongst the crowd showed their support with the brilliance of their smiles and their swords raised over their heads. Daniel and the others added their voices to the cheering, although Daniel fancied that Henry looked a little put out. His moment of glory was over now that Adam Murray was here.

Daniel breathed in the happiness around him and studied Adam as a leader, silently concluding, *they like him because he's not afraid and doesn't care what anyone thinks of him.*

A soldier pushed through to Adam and told him that he was to make his way to the Council Chamber. 'Lieutenant-Colonel Lundy and the others are waiting to speak to you.'

Adam nodded as if he had been expecting the invitation. As he entered the Chamber, all heads turned at the sound of his footsteps. There was no time for small talk or introductions.

Lundy accosted him immediately. 'Why are you here? What grievance has brought you here?'

Slightly overawed at having so many eyes upon him, along with the richness of the council members' clothes and the fact they were all seated, leaving him alone to stand as if he were on trial like a common thief, Adam found himself confronting Lundy with the people's accusations. 'You must know, sir, the suspicions about you and your attentions; suspicions that have been raised by your own behaviour.'

Lieutenant-Colonel Lundy opened his mouth to say something, but Adam rushed to continue, 'I'm here at the invitation of the people. They do not want the city surrendered!'

He allowed Lundy his chance to reply, but it was a wasted opportunity as the lieutenant-colonel chose to focus on being insulted. 'Suspicions?' he asked. Obviously unable to get past this he repeated it again. 'Suspicions?'

Adam felt his insides burn. Was he really meant to soothe Lundy's feelings while the Jacobites were just outside the gate? 'Do I have to point it out for you, sir, that decisions like refusing to allow ammunition to be given to our soldiers or refusing to lead a willing army into battle encourages people to question your allegiance? Are you truly that naïve?'

Adam was obliged to take a moment to steady himself. It would not do to be thrown into jail for insubordination. When he was ready to speak again, he tried for a more respectful tone. 'Sir, please, I would beg of you: take to the fields and fight the enemy. Your soldiers are more than ready to follow you.'

The lieutenant-colonel did not seem the least bit troubled. Adam could see that the man's mind was already made up and long before his arrival.

'Mr Murray,' Lundy heaved out a deep breath, 'you are not thinking clearly. No doubt, the mob outside see things as simply as fighting the army, easily winning and then we and the Prince of Orange will live happily ever after.'

Getting to his feet, the lieutenant-colonel approached Adam, man to man, wanting to reason with him. By all accounts this was the young officer he had to win over in order to gain the crowd's trust. 'What if we win this battle, Mr Murray? What if we all go out right now and confront the king and his army? What if we trounce them good and solid, maybe send King James running for his life?'

Adam stared coldly while silently wondering what on earth Lundy was getting at.

The lieutenant-colonel understood that Adam was biding his time, so he continued, 'But what if Williams loses – in the long run? Think about that. James may well lose today's battle but might still win the war for the throne. What do you suppose happens to us then?'

Again there was silence from Adam to this.

'I know what the Jacobites are capable of. They would butcher us in victory; make us pay for every harmed hair on every Catholic head. Don't you see what we are trying to do here? We are the ones who must think ahead and work out how to keep two potential kings happy with us.'

Of course Adam understood what Lundy was saying and it might have served to confuse him if he had been a different sort of person.

A clock ticked somewhere behind him as these prim old men waited for the young soldier to fall into line and agree. The lieutenant-colonel held up a piece of paper. 'These are the terms that we are going to suggest to King James. All of us here are going to sign it. Perhaps you would like to sign it too?'

From where he stood, Adam could plainly see the day's date on the document – 18 April 1689 – but he made no move towards it.

Lundy went on to let Adam know that he was aware of the mood outside. 'You are popular with the people. They will listen to you.'

Adam stiffened as if he had been accused of something, he just wasn't sure what.

The lieutenant-colonel explained the young man's situation as he saw it. 'Whether or not you know it, you are in possession of power. However, with power comes responsibility. You understand that, don't you?'

Adam longed to be back outside, away from this grand room with its heavy curtains and ornate furniture. It was high time he made a response. Glancing around in order to address them all, not just Lundy, he finally spoke. 'Thank you but I won't be needing your pen. I will not sign my name to that document, or any like it.'

Lieutenant-Colonel Lundy blinked to cover his surprise and irritation, while a hint of a smile plucked at Reverend Walker's features. One of the aldermen asked, 'Can you tell us why?'

This time Adam replied immediately, 'Because I'm a soldier. I don't sign terms of surrender. I fight on the battlefield. Now if that is all gentlemen, I will take my leave of you!'

Half expecting to be told that, no, he would not be permitted to take his leave, Adam briefly bowed his head and made for the door, relieved that he was allowed to do so.

He found his soldiers at the Diamond. The crowd were milling around, most of them wearing white armbands. A shout went up, 'Here he is!' Adam quickly told his listeners about the council's document. Silence greeted this revelation, making Adam wonder if he had agreed to help Lundy, would the crowd have been converted to surrendering. Leaving his listeners in no doubt as to his intentions, he declared, 'But I refused to sign it. I told them that I preferred my sword and rifle to their pen!'

With that, a large woman came out of nowhere and flung herself upon him, all heaving bosoms and tree-trunk arms. 'Oooh, God bless you, sir!' His friends gently wrestled him out of her embrace.

It was easy for Adam to believe that the whole city was on his side. While he had been with Governor Lundy the crowd seemed to have doubled in size, all proudly bearing their white cloths, including the soldiers.

Of course not every single resident stood before him. There were still quite a few who felt that Lundy was right, that James could win, and it could only mean dire consequences that the city had dared to fire upon a king.

Not fifty years ago the rebel Sir Phelim O'Neill led his

Catholic soldiers to rise up against the Protestant population, killing men, women and children in their hundreds.
*Well, wasn't it the fear of another wholesale slaughter that
locked the gates in the first place? And now it's this same fear
that prompts the likes of Lundy and Walker to reopen them to
James.*

Robert and Daniel's father stood at the side of the
square to watch the proceedings. When the rain thickened,
he moved closer to the wall. *Adam is a good man; he's not led
by vanity. He isn't wealthy and has no ambition beyond wanting
to keep Derry free.* That was something to be thankful for.
Mr Sherrard shrugged to himself, wanting to throw off
his nervousness at what was happening. *Thank goodness it's
not Henry Campsie that the crowd are cheering.* Since losing
his father the boy, as far as the physician was concerned,
had taken on a desperate look. *God only knows what lengths
he might go to, both to make a name for himself and to distract
himself from grief.*

Later, when he heard how Henry had fired upon King
James, Mr Sherrard was to wish anew that he had been
able to prevent Mayor Campsie from dying. His death was
proving to be too soon for Derry.

Still, thought Mr Sherrard, *this stalemate situation cannot
be allowed to continue forever. Now that we are practically surrounded on all sides, it is surely only a matter of time before our
hand is forced. They must find someone to surrender the city,*

someone who is foolhardy enough to pass this crowd. Who would volunteer for such a task? Though really I think it's far too late for that now.

Outside Derry, a mile or so away, a disheartened and deeply disappointed king sat astride his tired horse, drenched through and bleak in figure. His advisors stood by, whispering. Blissfully ignorant of the bewilderment and pity surrounding him, James stared at the walled city in silence. *How had it come to this?* His body ached from the damp and the cold – and, yes, from the shock too. That young lad, the trumpeter, how proud he had been when his king beckoned him to his side. James felt genuine sorrow. *It was the most important moment of the boy's short life. He had died for his king.*

It didn't occur to James that the people of Derry might be afraid of him, his soldiers and his religion. Instead, he dwelt on the personal attack. *How they hate me. Why couldn't they have let me in and hear what I had to say? Well, I can do nothing more for them now. If they refuse to listen, that is that.*

A gentle voice called to him, 'Sire?'

James gazed around, past Avaux, the owner of the voice, at the army of men behind him, all soaking wet and wondering why they were still there, neither making camp nor moving on. He closed his eyes for a moment and knew in his heart that it was time to go. Both the lord lieutenant and his cousin, the French king, had warned him it might come to this, but he had not wanted to listen to them. *How naïve I have been*. But, now, it was different; he was different. After listening to Derry's population screaming their chorus of 'No surrender!' and dodging their bullets, his limit had been reached. Those proud citizens had left him no choice. *Now* he was bound to act like royalty. Giving the city a last, lingering look, he quietly asked, 'How far is it to our camp at St Johnston?'

Avaux replied, 'I believe it is about five miles from here, Your Majesty, in Donegal.'

King James sighed to himself and then said aloud, 'Have the cannon brought to us there … and anything else that will be needed for the forming of a siege.'

Avaux barely hid his relief. 'As you wish, Your Majesty!'

A few miles away, in his small, homely cottage, Gabriel Murray sniffed the air and informed his elderly dog, 'Well, now, old friend. I think that something has finally begun! I just hope that Adam knows what he's doing.'

Back in Derry, amid tentative celebrations for having seen off the Papist king, the governor had also reached his limits. Within hours of Adam walking out on him, Lieutenant-Colonel Lundy informed the council that he no longer wanted to be governor. Having seen himself through Adam's eyes, he recognised that he would never make a difference to what was happening. He had no friends and no supporters, aside from the dutiful but cool politeness shown to him by the politically ambitious old men of Derry.

The following day, and much to his surprise, Adam was invited back to the chamber to take part in the election for the new governor. As far as he was concerned, stepping down as governor was the first sensible thing that Lundy had done since his arrival. However, before he could make his vote Adam had to decline the governorship himself.

Reverend Walker smiled at the shocked expression on the young man's face. 'You have the crowd at your heel and your own soldiers who call you colonel. Surely you realise you are the obvious choice.'

Adam shook his head. 'With respect, Reverend, I have no interest in politics. I'm just a soldier.' He pretended not to notice that his response was met with barely contained relief by those who fancied themselves as leader of Derry. *Well, let them have it if it means so much to them.*

For himself he could only vote for those men who, as far as he knew, had not loudly clamoured to surrender the city nor tried to forge a close relationship with Lundy. And it seemed that others shared his opinion. The two most popular councillors proved to be Reverend George Walker and Major Henry Baker. Accordingly, the duo was elected as co-governors of the city, effective immediately. The two were fighting men who had not been favourites of the former governor and this was their reward.

Governors Walker and Baker welcomed a challenge and surely this was not going to be easy, to take over the running of a little city that was in constant danger of being squashed like an insect beneath one's boot. Governor Walker was still very much an Anglican reverend, who in considering Derry's position compared it to the Israelites standing in front of the Red Sea.

At God's bidding, the prophet Moses led the Israelites out of Egypt, where they had been enslaved. The journey was treacherous and, it seemed, had come to an abrupt end when the refugees found themselves between their hot-tempered pursuers and the Red Sea. Naturally, they panicked, believing that they were well and truly caught. However, Moses begged them not to lose faith, telling them, 'Be brave. God will save you. He'll fight for you. Just wait and see!'

CHAPTER SEVENTEEN

Two days after Governors Walker and Baker were sworn into office, Daniel woke up in confusion, unsure if the noise which had disturbed him had been part of a dream. Horace's frantic barking soon convinced him that it wasn't. Then a second crash sounded in the distance followed by a third.

The sight of Robert's empty bed produced an awful shock until Daniel remembered he had the night shift on the wall. Pulling on his clothes, Daniel charged downstairs, where a trembling Horace was mightily relieved to see him.

The house shook with the next explosion. His parents were behind him, Alice still miraculously asleep in her mother's arms.

'What is it?' Mrs Sherrard fought an urge to scream.

Her husband and son opened the front door and stood in silence until Mr Sherrard said, 'It sounds like Ship Quay Street?'

Daniel nodded and said to his mother, 'It's alright. We're safe here.'

They could hear screaming in the distance. Then the quiet street burst into action as neighbours piled outside to check that their houses weren't in danger. There was a pause, so it seemed, when the sounds of many footsteps and shouts grew louder and louder. Mr Sherrard touched Daniel on the arm and they slid back inside the house, quietly shutting the door. Most of their neighbours copied them. Seconds later, their street was full again, this time with women, children, dogs, old men and women, half-trotting, half-running down the narrow street. Daniel and his parents watched from the small window. Panic distorted the already strange faces, the dogs barking madly as if the fires of Hell were upon them.

Horace started up again only to be smacked on the nose by Mrs Sherrard.

Mr Sherrard felt obliged to find out what was happening. Opening the front door, he called out, 'What's going on? What are you running from?'

An old man, who, for all his fright, seemed glad to ease himself to a temporary stop, gasped, 'The Jacobites. They're firing on the old houses on Ship Quay; the cannonballs are smashing right through the roofs all the way down to the ground floor.'

At this Mr Sherrard opened his door a little more, to call up the street, 'Is anybody hurt?' The man, doing his best to control his breathing, replied, 'Don't know, sir. None of us hung around long enough to see.' He felt the need to explain further, 'We sleep on the street, you see. No room for us anywhere else!'

'Of course, of course!' said Mr Sherrard. What else could he say? He turned to his family and said, 'I'm going to run over to see if anybody needs me!'

Daniel took his father's place at the front door while the physician ran for his bag and coat.

In the street the old man nodded. 'It's a fine start to a Sunday morning, isn't it? And it's only the beginning.'

Daniel was curious. 'The beginning? What do you mean?'

'Aye, indeed,' said the man. 'Most folk around here have no idea what's about to happen.'

Pulling the door closed behind him so his mother couldn't hear, Daniel wished the old man would hurry up and say whatever he was about to.

'You mark my words, young man; these explosions are nothing. The next time we hear them will be in the middle of the night and the next night and the night after that. The truth of the matter is we won't be allowed to rest until this is all over. They are going to terrorise us with noise and bombardment.'

Of all people, Henry Campsie appeared at the man's side. Daniel was somewhat shocked when Henry roughly pushed the man, causing him to cry out, 'Oy, what's the meaning of this?'

Henry bared his teeth in a chilly grin. 'I think, old man, that you are trying to scare us.'

Daniel blushed though he didn't know why. Neighbours reappeared at their doors to watch. Henry's fiery expression reminded Daniel of how Henry had looked just before he shot at King James. What was the sense in trying to intimidate a harmless old man? Daniel wanted to shout at Henry to leave the poor fellow alone but could not find the courage.

In confusion the man stepped away from Henry and turned to continue his journey to wherever he was going. However Henry had not finished with him yet and, instead, persisted, 'Are you for King James, then?'

The man faltered. Was he bewildered to be asked such a question or was he terrified because he had been found out? He began to stammer, 'What? No ... I ... I'm not!'

It was Mr Sherrard who saved him, urging him to keep walking the road. 'Go on, Old Timer, best you go join your family and friends.'

Reeling from the glaring attention of Henry's roughness and aggressive accusation, the man stumbled away, no doubt wishing he had never opened his mouth in the first place.

Henry watched the man's retreat carefully in order to hide his annoyance at Daniel's father. However, he felt it was his duty to both explain his actions and warn Mr Sherrard, 'We need to be aware that the city is infested with Jacobite sympathisers.'

Mr Sherrard fixed his coat and said lightly, 'And perhaps he was just an old man who likes to talk!'

Henry's expression was tight. 'Yes, sir'. He tipped his hat in false agreement.

Daniel longed to say something to bridge the gap between his father and Henry but could think of nothing. Meanwhile, Mr Sherrard's mind was on more important matters; he bid the boys farewell and headed off in the direction of the city's broken houses.

Henry bit his lip and appeared deep in thought.

Finally, Daniel offered, 'So, they have fired upon us?'

Henry snapped back into action. 'Adam Murray is looking for men to join him in an attack on the army.'

Daniel murmured cautiously, 'You mean, Colonel Murray.'

Henry answered impatiently, 'That's what I just said!'

Daniel didn't bother to argue.

Across the river Foyle, to the north of Derry, the newly arrived lines of Jacobite tents straddled Pennyburn Hill. Apart from being an irritating eyesore, the tents represented the Jacobite army laying stake to good foraging territory. Standing on the part of the wall between Ship Quay and Butchers' Gate, Colonel Adam Murray recognised that, at the very least, this would cause a problem for Derry's horses who needed to graze on the fresh grass outside the city's walls.

Of course the situation was made infinitely worse due to the orders of the Jacobite French commander, Lieutenant-General Maumont. Adam clenched his jaw as he took in the acres of ruined land. The Frenchman had instigated what was called a 'scorched earth' policy to make sure that the people and animals of Derry had no hope of living off the land outside Derry. The smell of smoke had lingered for days and the guards on the wall could only watch in frustration as the Jacobites went about their work, burning crops and every piece of decent grass.

Adam also recognised that the Jacobites must be prevented from going into the nearby little village at Penny-burn. At present it was unoccupied by either side, but those tents blatantly signalled that the Jacobites were planning to do just that.

If the enemy took Pennyburn it would give them a useful vantage point over the city, not to mention it would be far too close for comfort. Adam knew he had to do something and that something would involve a fight. He sent out a call, asking for soldiers and horsemen to join him in the city's first offensive.

The young officer could not overlook the fact that most of the soldiers available to him were recent recruits who had never stood in battle. However, he reasoned that all they needed was experience, and as soon as possible. *We could lose a minor battle if needs be, if only we win the war.*

'Colonel Murray, they're on the march.' Robert Sherrard delivered this message, adding, 'And they're heading for Pennyburn village!'

It was the news Adam had been expecting and dreading. He scrunched up his features in annoyance until Robert gave him something to cheer him up. 'About a thousand or so have answered your call to arms.'

'That many?' asked Adam, unable to keep the gratitude out of his voice.

Robert grinned. 'Yes, sir, including myself. They are gathered at the Diamond awaiting further orders.'

Adam clapped the boy on the arm. 'Come on, then. Let's get to work!'

At the Diamond, Adam was warmed by the sight of so many volunteers and relieved to note the presence of quite a few horses too. A decent cavalry, he felt, was required for what he had in mind. Most of the men and boys were also carrying weapons of one sort or another. Someone must have managed to get rifles from the artillery store. He put up his hand for silence. 'We need to be quiet and look as innocent as we can. What I mean is, once we go through the gate, we don't want to worry the Jacobite lookout. Let them wonder where we are going and what we are doing.

It will give us time to reach them.

'I need five hundred men with rifles to head out in small groups, and hide yourselves behind the bushes and trees that line both sides of the road to Pennyburn. Those with horses will come with me. We'll lead the confrontation at the foot of the hill. Our task is to dominate the enemy's attention for as long as we can. Meanwhile, the remaining infantry will wait until we are underway, to discreetly make your way to the high ground overlooking Pennyburn village.'

The men raised their rifles in quiet agreement, and Adam finished by saying to the foot soldiers, 'Remember, do your best to look as if you have no special purpose in mind. We need to surprise them.'

And so it was that the first five hundred snuck out in little groups, making for the road to Pennyburn, quickly diving behind the bushes and trees. Those with horses followed Adam; they boldly took the path to Pennyburn, just a small party. Then, in their own good time, the second lot of five hundred sauntered out, vaguely heading for Pennyburn Hill, or so it seemed.

This was the guts of Derry's defending army proudly watched over by those who stayed behind to man the walls. James Morrison was not impressed with being left behind.

On seeing the knotted lines in his friend's forehead,

Daniel offered, 'Our job is just as important.'

James pouted until Daniel remembered, 'At least we have our own ammunition now!' Well, that was certainly something. The soldiers and volunteers were finally allowed to defend their city properly, with bullets and cannon.

As the boys stood together, with the rest of the guards, they were joined by many civilians. This expedition – the first attempt to push back the Jacobites – was of huge interest to everyone living in Derry. Daniel found it necessary to plant his feet squarely on the ground so that he could not be pushed off his lookout spot. A group of fearsome-looking women were trying to nudge both him and James out of the way.

One of the women suddenly pointed and shouted, 'They've seen them!'

James and Daniel watched as a band of Jacobite soldiers on horseback pounded down hard towards Adam and his cavalry.

Daniel was grateful that his family had never been able to afford a horse and that Robert had been one of those sent to hide behind bushes.

Just as Adam had assumed, the Jacobite soldiers on the hill spied the approach of the Williamite cavalry and quickly sent word for help.

There was a scuffle of footsteps to Daniel's right which the boy determined to ignore until a man's voice snarled,

'Out of my way there!' Governor Walker made the women shift over to give him enough room to stand beside Daniel. The young man couldn't help the spurt of pride he felt in the governor's choice of position.

'Ah,' sighed Walker. 'Now let us see how our young colonel fares.'

Was this a compliment or a slight? Daniel didn't have time to decide as just then the two Jacobite and Williamite horsemen came together in a sudden blend of red and black, and clumps of earth that were kicked up by so many hooves.

Muskets were raised and fired, causing inexperienced Derry horses to jolt and leap about, knocking into one another as their riders worked to steady them enough to remain within the fight. Swords swung out and, much to the onlookers' delight, a couple of Jacobite red jackets toppled to the ground.

Adam chose his man after driving Pegasus through the ranks of the enemy, slashing at them with his sword. The rider in the centre of the Jacobite cavalry was obviously a high-ranking officer. His sleek black horse was better looking than the others while the man's armour and bearing, including the crest on his wide-brimmed hat, pointed to his elevated position. On top of that, a grim-faced trumpeter rode alongside him, ready to issue orders with a tuneless blast.

When Adam heard the officer roar words unknown to him, he suddenly realised that he was facing Lieutenant-General Maumont, the man who had implemented the 'scorched earth' policy. If Adam had had time, he might have allowed himself to be impressed by the French commander presenting himself in battle instead of sending his men out to do his bidding. Well, it would be his duty to show the commander that he had made a dreadful mistake.

The lieutenant-general did Adam the honour of recognising him as the leader of the Williamites. With pointed swords both men simultaneously made their decision to charge at one another. Once the head of a monster is removed the body no longer knows what it is doing. Deafened by the sound of his own blood thundering in his ears, Adam hardly heard the sickening thud as the two horses crashed against one another.

The Frenchman's sword was longer and wider but it failed to hit its mark. Adam was too fast and sharp to be caught as he twisted and turned in the saddle, avoiding the deadly blade, all the while waiting for the opening, that tiny gap in time and space that can change the course of any fight, depending on the fighter. Everything around him was a blur as he watched for his advantage. And here it was: Maumont's horse took a sudden step forwards, obliging its rider to overreach himself in his impatience to kill the dark-haired Williamite. There! Adam plunged his sword beneath the outstretched arm into the commander's armpit, the part of him that was not covered by the expensive breastplate. Adam left his sword there and watched the man's sleeve bleed dark red.

It was over for the Frenchman. Adam felt nothing as he watched the man recognise, with a silent gasp, that he had been fatally wounded. His naïve trumpeter rushed to help his superior while Adam instinctively snatched up the French commander's better sword. *An eye for an eye, a tooth for a tooth and a sword for a sword!*

Who knows, maybe Maumont understood his victor as Adam informed him, 'Sir, I am taking this since you will not need it again.'

Daniel gripped the wall in front of him. 'We're winning!' *What must it be like to be smack in the centre of life and death?* He found it somewhat eerie to be watching such dreadful action from a safe distance. On the wall, those watching could hardly hear a thing.

For a few precious minutes it seemed that Adam and his men were indeed the winning side, but they were up against experienced soldiers. Even Daniel and James could see that the Williamite men had no time to reload their rifles for a second shot or they risked being run through by a Jacobite sword. But, of course, this was all part of Adam's plan. Wasn't it?

Adam began to draw his men back, slicing the air with

his sword and roaring, 'Fall back! Fall back!'

His men obeyed and clapped their spurs against their horses' ribs for the sprint towards Derry. Naturally, the Jacobites followed, taking care not to trample their fallen comrades.

So, back, all the way back to the road they fled – a road that was attractively lined with those trees and untidy clusters of brambles and bushes that hid would-be warriors. Robert Sherrard and Henry Campsie clenched their rifles and longed to flex their tensed-up limbs. They heard the thuds of the horses' feet digging into the ground and heard the roars of the riders alongside the rattle of their swords.

Eventually, when it seemed it could be much too late, the order was given and out they leapt, to fling themselves upon their attackers. A roar from the walls of Derry goaded them to do their worst. Those with rifles knelt down, with shaking hands, to take aim, doing their damnedest not to injure their friends and neighbours.

Robert found himself assaulted by the smell of sweat, of both men and animals. He had never noticed the sheer hugeness of horses before. Surely they were as big as some of the poorer houses in Derry. It was hard not to worry about being stood upon in all the confusion. He had fired his rifle but knew not what had happened after that. Instinctively he got to his feet as he fumbled about for more powder and a fresh musket ball, hardly looking down to check on his progress. There was too much going on at the same time. It was difficult to concentrate. Men shouted, some screamed in pain, while horses spluttered and whinnied hysterically, especially the Derry-bred animals who had only known about ploughing silent fields. And what was that other smell, apart from sweat and smoking rifles? It was all around him, so sweet and sickly. Blood! Of course it was. This was a battle after all and the wounded and dead lay side by side.

Adam, alone, took the time to read the situation and note the flaws. For all their passion and desire to win, his men were flailing in the face of hardened soldiers. The Jacobites knew how to manoeuvre, to coerce their enemy into place and also how to defend each other. Furthermore, they knew how to spare their gunpowder.

The Williamite men leaping out from behind the bushes should have staggered their shooting, ensuring that guns were always being fired while others reloaded. All Adam could see were his volunteers bent over empty rifles or else too distracted by swinging swords to think about firing again. He blamed himself. *I should have prepared them better. I forgot to tell them not to fire all at once!*

He had to do something because he couldn't afford to lose men. There was only one option and, though it wasn't particularly noble, he had no choice. 'Back to the walls!'

he roared, dodging enemy swords as he worked Pegasus in and around the fighters. 'Everyone back to the walls!'

Governor Walker heard him and knew what was required. He ordered the cannons to be loaded and bellowed at his parishioners and the others, 'Fetch stones, rocks and anything else you can let fly!'

Daniel saw the reluctance to move in the faces of the women; they didn't want to miss a single moment of the action. No doubt many of them had sons, husbands and brothers out there and they wanted the luxury of being able to concentrate on them alone. But that is exactly what it was, a luxury and one the army could ill afford.

When there was nothing more than a sluggish attempt to move away, Walker raged, 'Anyone who doesn't do as I say will be hanged as a traitor!'

Well, that sent them sprinting alright, clamouring down the steps to grab rocks and boulders in a variety of shapes and sizes.

To the armed guards the governor said, 'Keep your rifles ready and wait for my word!'

Daniel felt his heart shudder against his ribs as he struggled to master his breathing which was coming out in uncomfortable, harsh bursts.

James whispered, 'Don't worry, you'll be fine!'

But Daniel was starting to panic. 'What if they come into the city?'

James, who hadn't thought of anything except what was happening in front of them, was puzzled. 'Who? The Jacobites?'

However, Governor Walker overheard them. He had just been thinking the very same thing but could not betray his anxiety. With a stern expression, he loudly declared, 'They will not get inside because we will not let them. Is that understood?'

Feeling mortified, Daniel wanted to fling himself on the ground and beg the governor's forgiveness. He swallowed hard and, as confidently as he could, answered, 'Yes, sir. Right, sir!'

James repeated Daniel's words and then the boys turned back to see what was happening, not noticing the governor's strained posture as he briefly looked about, wondering if this bunch of badly dressed and ill-armed boys, old men and women could possibly be enough.

Are we about to prove Lundy right? The governor sent a silent prayer heavenwards. *Dear Lord, we need all the help You can give us!*

Nobody around him knew his secret, that he and Governor Baker had just helped the scorned Lieutenant-Colonel Robert Lundy to escape the city. At this very moment he was on a ship that was setting out for London.

It was the right thing to do. Apart from the fact that Lundy had begged the governors for their help in leaving, the only way he could have remained safely in Derry was to change his mind and do what Adam Murray had urged him to do: fight. But the lieutenant-colonel was not for turning. He remained adamant that their circumstances were utterly hopeless and he would not be responsible for the bloodshed he believed would surely follow. Furthermore, it made even more sense to help Lundy when he reminded Walker and Baker, 'I'd just be another mouth to feed, should the people allow me to live.'

Whether Governor Walker liked the man or not, he was against allowing Lundy's right to life to be determined by the likes of these smelly, stupid women and their kind, whose brains could be no bigger than a snail's. The mob could not be allowed to take over. After all, Governor Walker was still a man of God. *I've never trusted the man but neither do I desire to have him swing by the neck in front of a baying crowd.*

Now, here he was, watching Adam Murray quite possibly about to accidentally lead a dangerously angry army through the gates of a city that had barely anyone decent to defend it. That certainly was not part of the plan.

The two armies were coming closer and closer. Governor Walker could have painted the scene without looking upon it, using the shouts of the men, the sharp cracks of fired rifles and the thumping of the horses' hooves to fill in the blanks. The defenders were fighting hard but the

Jacobites were closing in. Adam Murray was fending off two men from the back of his horse, swinging his sword one way and then the other.

It was time to act.

Governor Walker released his order,. 'Make ready to fire the cannon!' He had his pistol in one hand and his sword in the other. Tearing down the steps, his coat-tails flapping behind him, the governor brandished his weapons and called for the other guards to follow him. 'Unlock the gate! Follow me outside to help Colonel Murray!' He suddenly remembered what else he meant to say; he looked back, caught Daniel's eye and yelled, 'Start shooting!'

Daniel whisked around, took aim and fired but did not believe he hit anyone.

'Reload! Reload' cried James as he fired his gun. He too could not admit to injuring anyone.

'Should we follow Reverend Walker?' asked Daniel, noticing other boys streaming down the steps toward Butchers' Gate which was being pushed open.

James was busy pouring in more gunpowder but took the time say, 'No. We're better covering them from here!'

Daniel nodded in agreement.

The boys were joined once more by the women, and other friends, who were loaded with rocks and stones. To his surprise, the newcomers looked at him and James, and asked, 'Will we throw now?'

James whooped, 'By all means, ladies. Let them have it!'

The women seemed to relish sending down rocks to bash in the heads of the Jacobites. High pitched shrieks of 'Got him!' were accompanied by bouts of hysterical screaming.

Meanwhile, Governor Walker and his followers had surged out with a triumphant war cry to rescue their neighbours. Adam was still being tormented by two different riders until the governor shot the one on the left. The man fell forward against the neck of his horse, who took this as a signal to make a run for it. How the women cheered his exit and the governor's excellent shooting!

Daniel took aim a second time, making sure to find a target before he pulled the trigger. A soldier on the ground, who seemed to have lost his horse, was attempting to stab as many defenders as he could, including Robert, who had given up reloading his rifle and was using it now as a stick. He waved it about while dodging the swishing sword.

Taking a deep breath, Daniel lined up his rifle, and decided to aim for the space beside the soldier, because he was constantly dancing forwards and backwards. He simply could not allow himself to think about the smallness of the space between the Papist and his brother. An older, more experienced soldier might not have attempted it, which only goes to prove that sometimes ignorance can be a help.

All Daniel knew was that his city had entrusted him to protect her, and – at this moment – it was the only way he could possibly help Robert. He had no choice. Taking aim, he took a breath and sent a brief prayer heavenwards. The gun fired and Daniel, feeling only slightly guilty, saw the man clutch his right shoulder. Nobody else witnessed this marvellous shot. Daniel hugged himself with relief and rubbed beads of stinging sweat from his eyes, wishing his heart would stop its galloping. Robert was still brandishing his rifle, having no idea that his little brother had probably just saved his life.

A woman suddenly shouted, 'Look, they're attacking Pennyburn Hill!'

Several of the women screamed to God above to do something. Daniel was chilled at the sight of two Jacobite regiments riding full-tilt around the back of the hill. *There must be a thousand if not more!*

The Derry soldiers, the second group of infantry, who had snuck out after the first group, were sitting pretty on top of the hill with just musket rifles to defend themselves, not enough against so many men on horseback.

How long would it take for the Derry men to spy the horsemen sneaking around the back? Daniel groaned to himself, *Do something. Run! Anything!*

To his dizzy relief, the Williamites noticed the approaching forces and did just as he'd willed them; they raced down the front of the hill, making fast for the city walls.

While this was wonderful news for Governor Walker and Adam, the same could not be said for the Jacobite attackers, the ones who had foolishly followed Adam and his men. Not only did they have to contend with fresh fighters spewing out the gate to confront them, not to mention being pelted from above by the civilians of Derry, now they were the targets of the retreating Williamite men, from Pennyburn Hill. These men had yet to fire a single shot; their rifles were loaded and ready.

In the midst of all this a cannonball was fired into the city. The Jacobite behind the gun was too busy congratulating himself on his spontaneity to appreciate that he could be seen by the Derry men returning from Pennyburn Hill. They saw him alright, him and his cannon. Three of them ran to the walls and shouted up to Daniel, 'Send cannon fire over there, at that mound!'

Daniel could not see anything but he took their word for it. 'James, the cannon!'

But James had already rolled a ball into the cannon and pushed the women away for their own safety. A match was struck, ears were covered and the gun roared. As the noise of the cannon faded, someone nearby guffawed, 'Sounds just like your Meg!' There was no returning cannon fire, suggesting that 'Meg' had met her mark.

Then, just like that, this particular battle was over.

Rather sensibly, the Jacobites saw that they were in a tight spot. Wounded comrades were picked up, shoved onto the remaining horses and the order to retreat was given. The victors cheered and hugged one another. At long last there was the feeling that they had won something.

Feeling somewhat stunned, Daniel counted almost a hundred bodies on the ground, the ones that lay perfectly still, from both sides. So, it had been a real battle indeed. He couldn't help thinking they had been lucky and then felt a little ashamed of himself.

James thumped his shoulder. 'Are you coming down?'

Daniel shrugged, preferring to stay where he was.

He watched James, Robert and the others peel off into small groups to attend to two important but very different tasks. One was to retrieve the Derry dead for their families while the other was to strip the foreign corpses of coins, ammunition, food, weapons and even boots. Daniel felt strange watching dead men's boots being waved in the air as some sort of prize. However, the truth was that a surprisingly high number of Derry men, including James Morrison, were in dire need of good boots. James whistled up to him to show off his new footwear. Daniel gave him a thumbs up.

Henry Campsie brandished his newly acquired hip flask, generously offering Robert the first sip of the contents which proved to be brandy. It burnt the back of Robert's throat, making him splutter and cough.

Governor Walker could not stop smirking. He patted everyone he passed, saying over and over again, 'Well done!'

Adam allowed himself a smile too, relieved at how the whole community had worked together. However, he cringed at the naivety of his volunteers. He hoped that some lessons were learned today and determined to start training the men properly. Not a single musket ball or an ounce of gunpowder could be wasted from now on. Nevertheless, as he gazed about him, he was pleased to see that out of a hundred dead bodies only ten or so were *not* wearing the tell-tale red jackets of the Jacobite army. His men had done extremely well.

His thoughts were instantly echoed by Governor Walker's words. In preacher mode, the reverend cried out, 'We have with God's help proved ourselves today. Let us give thanks for our victory and ask God to continue to protect us from all harm.'

Adam cheered along with everyone else, wondering how things stood now. The white armbands were everywhere and here was the War Council making their way to Butchers' Gate now that the trouble was over. *Surely those old fogies see that Derry is far from surrendering.*

CHAPTER EIGHTEEN

That was Sunday, 21 April 1689.

This was Monday, the first day of the week and the second of many days of bombardment. Mrs Sherrard thanked God for the rather impressive miracle of Alice falling asleep in spite of the sounds of cannonballs bouncing through houses mere streets away.

Horace had felt obliged to anoint every single crash with much barking, but one look of barely suppressed rage from his mistress was enough to change his mind. Indeed, he thought it best to leave the room entirely and put himself to bed under the kitchen table. He knew when he wasn't wanted.

Things had changed over the last while and he was a bit put out. Daniel had little time for him anymore. Horace could barely remember the last time that the two of them enjoyed a good nose around the streets.

Horace wasn't stupid. Maybe humans don't realise how much a dog senses. He felt the tension vibrate in the house whenever Robert and Mr Sherrard spent too long in one another's company. Indeed he smelled the bewilderment from outside and blamed Robert for bringing it inside the home. Daniel was caught in the middle and Horace sensed the boy's inner turmoil. Sometimes Daniel was in full agreement with his brother but other times he was in full agreement with his father. It was all a bit confusing.

Mrs Sherrard stayed out of it as much as she could. Her job was to mind everyone, keep the house respectable, make sure they all had clean clothes and provide tasty meals. Only in this last matter Horace guessed there was some new trouble and it had to do with food.

The previous day Mr Sherrard called his sons to him. It was a rare enough occasion to have both of them inside at the same time, although Robert was wearing his coat and anxious to be back at the walls. His father knew not to waste time and said, 'If this siege persists, if it runs into months, we will have to consider the possible consequences.' His expression and tone made Robert forget his impatience to be elsewhere. Mr Sherrard continued, 'I don't want your mother and sister left alone. When the people on the streets get hungry enough they may start raiding houses for food.'

Daniel felt icy fingers tip-tap across his shoulders. This was something that he had not considered, that they could be attacked not just in their city, but in their own homes.

Robert could not resist finding an argument. 'Do you think so badly of our people, Father?'

Daniel felt his shoulders sag with tiredness.

Mr Sherrard was ready for Robert this time. 'Do you claim to know all those who are currently living on our streets? I certainly don't. The city is overrun with scared strangers.' Seeing Robert open his mouth again, Mr Sherrard rushed to end the conversation. 'Please! We are talking about your mother's and sister's safe-keeping and nothing else. I'm too busy for a political debate.'

To his credit, Robert looked mortified. He mumbled something which sounded like, 'Yes, Father!'

In any case, Daniel said his words loud and clear, just to be sure. 'Yes, Father!'

Horace, for his part, was relieved to see Robert head out the door. The atmosphere vastly improved in his absence.

Over the following days the guards on the walls found themselves under attack from the actual streets of Derry. The Jacobite cannonballs that were being continually pumped into the city were smashing up the pavements, sending jagged shards of polished stones shooting in all directions.

After two of the guards were soundly walloped on the backs of their heads, an order was given to erect a screen which would act as a shield from the city side of the walls. Plenty chuckled at the irony.

A heavy responsibility sat on the soldiers who manned the walls and gates. Defending the city was no small task now that the big cannons were trained upon them. Civilians were told to keep their distance from the walls. Women, and children under the age of sixteen years were sent to spend their days on the streets that no cannonball could reach.

In the beginning a few of the younger recruits might have admitted their terror. The boom of the cannon gun was all the warning they received with absolutely no hint of where the killer ball would land. Once the gun sounded, birds would take fright, flinging out their wings and rising together like dust from rooftops or trees. Barking dogs would not let up for hours after. But this is what the Jacobites hoped to do: cause unrest in the city.

Things were about to get worse. A contingent of Jacobites had settled themselves into Stronge's Orchard, from where they began to fire mortars straight into the city. In other words, apart from cannonballs that could shatter entire houses, now the people of Derry had to deal with exploding bombs. Not that the guards were always impressed. You see, the bombs came in all sorts of sizes and some were no bigger than pocket watches, doing nothing more than spitting out the tiniest puffs of smoke.

Of course the larger ones were deadly. One killed old Mrs Stewart. Some soldiers had recently taken up residence in her small house and she had just put out their dinner, made up of their daily army rations (2 pounds of flour, 2 pounds of oats and 2 pounds of salted meat). Thick beef soup it was, which the four soldiers claimed later to be thoroughly enjoying, before they were cruelly interrupted by a large bomb that dropped through the ceiling – so quickly that they had no time to move before it left the room, via the floor, to plunge below atop Mrs Stewart as she mended their uniforms.

At least she would have felt no pain. Luckily for her tenants the blast blew out the entire side of her house, giving them an easy escape route. The four of them returned later to pull the poor woman's bruised and bloodied body from the rubble. She had been a good landlady. Her hands still gripped her darning needle and spool of thread. It was judged kinder to leave them where they were, to be buried with her.

Both Daniel and Robert quickly learned to hide their army rations as they walked the streets, otherwise they invited the pleading of despairing women who had no idea how to feed their children. Daniel might have felt more guilt about this, but there was hardly enough to feed his own family, even with two rations. Only soldiers were eligible for the rations that were doled out by Governor Walker.

As James Morrison said, 'If we're too weak to defend the city, then we might as well open the gates.'

Daniel did think to ask, 'But what about everyone else?

What will they eat?'

James had no answer to this apart from a wistful, 'Oh, it should be all over before we run out of food!'

And then James said something else, but Daniel didn't hear it so he asked James to repeat what he just said. His friend blushed as he offered, 'Anyone who tries to get food from a soldier should be locked up for treason. We're too important to go without food. That's my opinion anyway!'

Daniel felt certain that James was not allowing himself to notice the children sitting on the ground, wherever you looked, crying from hunger.

Please God, prayed Daniel in silence, *please let this be over soon!*

Mr Sherrard was also concerned about the rations and wondered if he should say something to Adam Murray. Perhaps it would be best if there were two different church leaders dealing out the rations from Governor Walker's stores. He had heard rumours of the Anglican reverend skimping on rations for the members of Reverend Gordon's Presbyterian flock.

Saint Columb's Cathedral was becoming something of a battlefield itself. Rationing of food was one thing but now there was a rationing of hours of worship. The Presbyterians were feeling hard done by the rambunctious Governor Walker who would keep reminding people of how he had saved Adam Murray's skin that day. Rather wisely, Adam kept his distance, preferring to do his praying in the saddle.

Of course it was Governor Walker who had allotted the times of worship on Sundays, giving himself and his Anglican parishioners the morning service. Sometimes his sermons ran over, leaving the Presbyterians to wait outside in the rain with a fuming Reverend Gordon.

After experiencing this one Sunday, Mr Sherrard exclaimed to his wife, in the safety of his own home, 'As if there weren't enough divisions already!'

Henry and Robert came face to face with the hornet's nest that Governor Walker was – accidentally or otherwise – creating. As they walked through the Diamond a sulky group of soldiers approached them, asking if they had received their rations. Henry was defensive. 'Well, what of it? We're entitled to them.'

Robert didn't know the men. Their uniforms were in foul condition and none of them were wearing shoes, not that this was unusual in itself. Their faces were pale and Robert felt they probably hadn't had a decent meal in a while. He let Henry be the impatient one while he kept an eye on the men's hands.

Sounding like his father, Henry demanded, 'State your business!'

There was surprise at his cheekiness; after all, the two boys were facing five soldiers.

'State my business?' echoed the ringleader in disbelief.

'Who do you think you're talking to, lad, a Papist?'

His friends tittered. Then one of their bellies growled in protest which seemed to embarrass them.

Robert asked them, 'What do you want?'

One of the men asked him a question in turn, 'Is it true that you get money as well as food?'

His friends waited for the answer. Seeing Henry's lips curl with impatience, Robert spoke quickly, 'Well, yes, just a couple of shillings a week.'

The men glanced at one another, hardly believing their ears.

Robert couldn't ignore their response. 'But aren't you receiving the same as us?'

The ringleader shook his head. 'We're living in the same city as you. We're fighting the same enemy as you but … ' Here, he raised his eyebrows while Henry repeated his last word. 'But?'

Choosing to look at Robert instead, the soldier said, 'But we are not receiving any food or money, not from the city anyway. It is our own people, our fellow Presbyterians that give us whatever they can spare which is not much.'

Henry showed them little sympathy. 'What do you expect us to do about it?'

Robert wished his friend would lose his voice for the next few minutes. He rushed out a solution to compensate for Henry's rudeness. 'Have you brought your grievance to Governor Walker? He's in charge of the rations.'

The ringleader smirked. 'Unfortunately your reverend is always busy when one of *us* needs to speak to him.'

The encounter might have ended there as the five soldiers did seem slightly relieved at having explained their woes to Governor Walker's soldiers. Alas, Henry Campsie could not walk away in silence. Instead, he committed a dreadful crime in accusing the men and their ilk of cowardice. 'You lot have been one step behind us since we closed the gates. Wasn't it your ministers who wished them to be unlocked again?'

It was a lie and an ill-timed one. Within the blink of an eye Henry was on his back, blood streaming from his nose. Nobody had seen that coming, including the ringleader, the one who had thrown the punch. He looked as stunned as his victim.

Robert kept quiet, longing for the men to leave. And surely they would if only Henry did not attempt to antagonise them further.

However, instead of shuffling off, the men regrouped, while the ringleader balled up his fist and, at a nod from his companions, issued a demand. 'Hand over your food and coin, the pair of you.'

Robert sighed. It was all so predictable. Hadn't his father warned about hunger driving men to do dreadful things?

Worse yet was the fact that their little tussle was starting to draw attention from the poor unfortunates that lived in, around and on the Diamond; more hungry people who had no rations to speak of. Food was still being sold but only if you had the money to buy it.

As Robert discreetly studied the onlookers who were all barefoot and grimy, he reckoned there was not much coin between the lot of them. There was no doubt in his mind; his and Henry's situation was growing trickier by the second. How he wished it was his cautious brother who was with him instead of the fiery Henry. Immediately he knew this was stupid as it would only mean the Sherrards were about to be robbed of two precious lots of rations.

The crowd pressed ever closer. Among them were elderly men and women, who looked as desperate as cornered rats.

Robert stuck out a sweaty hand and pulled Henry from the ground. He squeezed his friend's hand hard, hoping he'd stay quiet. Poor Robert! As soon as he let go of Henry's hand, Henry squared up to the men. 'How dare you hit me!'

Had it not dawned on Henry yet that he had absolutely no control over the situation?

Two of the men yawned and looked away.

Robert felt keenly that they were only pretending to be bored, that they were waiting for a magic word to jump on the two boys and give them both a right thrashing.

'Shut your mouth, boy, or I'll put you on your backside again!' The ringleader then took a deep breath and said, 'I'm only going to say this one more time. Empty your pockets!'

'No!' replied Henry. 'I'll do no such thing!' He even laughed though his eyes showed no mirth.

Robert longed to sit down. In the old days the two lads might simply have made a run for it.

Then Henry's next words surprised them all. 'I must get home to Mother!'

One of the men was so taken aback he actually said, 'Pardon?'

Henry obliged him. 'I need to get home to Mother now that Father is dead.'

A couple of onlookers nodded sagely while someone explained, 'He's Mayor Campsie's lad; he was a good man!'

Robert was fairly astonished to see genuine pity in some of the expressions.

A second person felt it appropriate to add, 'And the other one's the physician's son.'

Robert was obliged to bow his head to acknowledge a woman who said, 'Aye. Mr Sherrard, he's another fine gentleman!'

Robert was wondering should he say something like, 'My thanks to you, Madam!' when there was a squeal,

'Ooh, look, here is he now! Mr Sherrard, sir, over here!'

The soldiers looked as uncomfortable as Robert when the physician was welcomed into the centre of the disorderly circle. Mr Sherrard hid his surprise at finding his son and Henry Campsie standing in front of him. Guessing that he had arrived at a good time, Robert's father ignored the scruffy soldiers and greeted the two boys. 'There you are. I was looking for you.'

It didn't occur to Henry that this was his cue to play along, so he just looked surprised and asked, 'Why?'

Mr Sherrard just turned and asked a general question of the gathering. 'Well, what is the news today?'

One of the women answered, 'The walls need repairing at Bishop's Gate!'

The physician stroked his chin thoughtfully. 'Indeed!'

Meanwhile, four of the five soldiers were making faces at one another, all suggesting that they should leave without any further ado. However, the ringleader was stubborn, believing they had been seconds away from getting their hands on the boys' rations and coin. But he found himself at a loss when Mr Sherrard addressed him directly. 'So, what are you men up to?'

Instead of being grateful for his father's timely arrival, Robert wanted to stamp his feet and bawl, 'Leave me alone! I'm not a child. I can handle this!'

The ringleader glanced at Robert and seemed to

sympathise with him. We all have parents at the end of the day, and he was not much older than the Sherrard boy. He went on to affect a swagger. 'We were just conversing soldier to soldier!'

Mr Sherrard nodded agreeably while hinting the opposite. 'Don't you mean five soldiers to two?'

Robert hardly knew why but he felt he had to explain for the five soldiers. 'They told us that only Governor Walker's soldiers are receiving daily rations.' This statement was a sort of challenge. Robert waited for his father to make a perfect reply. It would seem that the people here already believed he was some sort of saint. *Well, then, let him prove himself.*

Mr Sherrard issued his own challenge in return. 'And you five gentlemen thought you'd repair your situation by lightening the load of my son and his friend.'

Henry nodded his agreement at the polite but accurate summing up of the situation. *How clever of Mr Sherrard to guess as much!*

Robert stared at the sky over the Markethouse, wishing he was a million miles away.

The ringleader shrugged. 'Well, yes. What else are we to do? We're carrying out the same work in defending the city.'

Mr Sherrard sighed. 'Go and plead your case with Governor Walker.'

Robert sniffed. 'We've already had that conversation!'

The five soldiers finally turned to leave.

'What about us?' asked one of the women.

'Yes,' said a man, who might have been her husband. 'We're hungry too!'

Mr Sherrard looked around the crowd and took in the troubling signs: greyness of pallor, dry and cracked lips, laboured breathing, while some were coughing every few seconds. Suddenly he understood what would happen. The old would succumb first, along with those of imperfect health. Chills would be nurtured by the cold and wet weather; they would spread like fire and quickly wheedle out the weak for certain death. Lack of food would go hand in hand with disease. The physician knew it as sure as he knew what day it was. Derry was going to lose hundreds, if not more. And there wouldn't be a thing he could do about it.

Well, the only thing he could do now was reach into his pockets for his loose change. He chose one of the healthier looking women. 'I want you to take this money and get what you can with it.' It was a tiny amount but it was all he had on him. 'Look for milk and oats, stuff you can stretch out amongst as many as possible.'

The woman bared her broken teeth in gratitude, informing him, 'You're a good man, sir!' Before she could waste another second she was duly escorted away in search of food.

The sound of shooting and cannon fire dominated once more as the square cleared. The Sherrards didn't even notice Henry leaving.

Father looked at son, waiting for something.

'You didn't need to do that!' was Robert's response, followed immediately by 'Will you come back tomorrow to hand out more money?'

His father sighed to himself. Perhaps he had been foolish, passing himself off as the kindly physician who could fix everything.

They started walking towards Bishop Gate Street. It was this part of the wall, between Bishop's Gate and Butchers' Gate, that always received the worst of the attack. *How peculiar it is*, thought Mr Sherrard, *to stand here in the middle of a city that is being bombed*. He said aloud, 'I suppose the walls can take it?'

Robert was still annoyed. 'I was taking care of the situation before you arrived.'

Mr Sherrard took a moment to stamp down his own irritation, before asking, 'And what were you going to do?'

Robert answered, 'Give them everything I had … just like you did.'

His father could make no reply to this.

CHAPTER NINETEEN

Gabriel Murray stood in his doorway, a mug of ale in his hand, to observe a summer's torrential downpour. This was not typical weather for this time of the year. The navy clouds appeared swollen with still darker clouds. They hung so low in the sky that Gabriel felt he might touch them if only he had the strength to climb up onto his roof.

His dog sat down beside him, letting it be known that he would not be crossing the threshold until it stopped raining.

'Wonder how Adam is,' said Gabriel. The dog yawned, but this didn't deter the old man from trying to get a conversation going. 'The fields will be sodden all the way through.' Taking a sip of ale, he added, 'Well, no matter, at least we have a roof to shelter us. Those poor Jacobites camped out in this weather.'

The dog whined, possibly begging his master to be quiet so he could sleep. What else was there to do on such a morning as this?

The rain was heavy and loud so neither Gabriel nor his

dog heard the soldiers approach. Both animal and owner glanced at one another in surprise at the sight of four Jacobite soldiers on horseback, doing their best to ignore the inclement weather. Gabriel only just had time to put his mug down on the stool behind the door. It was uncharitable, he knew, but he felt he shouldn't have to share his home-made ale with anyone he didn't expressly invite to do so. Neither would he invite them in, if he could help it.

He called out a cheery greeting. 'Good morning, gentlemen!'

Only one of the men answered him.

Gabriel saw how the group peered into his cottage, probably thinking about dismounting and going inside to dry off. The old man's stubbornness was legendary. Filling his own doorway, to block their view, Gabriel waited for an explanation. Were they just passing through or were they paying a visit?

'Am I speaking with Gabriel Murray?' The soldier was obliged to repeat himself as the old man struggled to hear him over the sweeping sheets of rain.

Gabriel nodded. 'You have the pleasure!'

Pushing his drenched hair from his face, the soldier asked a second question. 'Are you the father of Adam Murray?'

Gabriel experienced a sudden pinch in his gut. Determined not to reveal his anxiety to the Jacobites, he merely answered, 'Yes, that's right!' *What has the boy done now?*

Have they taken him … or worse?

'Mr Murray,' said the soldier, 'my orders are to bring you to Colonel Hamilton. He wishes to speak with you right away.'

Gabriel shrugged as if he had been expecting this imposition for some time.

'Certainly,' he said. 'Just let me get my coat. Would one of you boys care to lead that old mare to my cart?'

Two of the soldiers jumped to the ground, obviously thinking the faster they got the old man to Hamilton, the faster they could get back inside their tents.

The dog reluctantly climbed to his feet, presuming he was going to have to come along too.

'No,' said Gabriel. 'You stay here and look after things.'

The dog made no complaint beyond a dutiful whine.

Gabriel moved slower than usual, unable to dodge the worry that Adam might be hurt or even killed. He had been half expecting to be told he didn't need his cart, just his horse, but there were the two soldiers backing old Sally into the cart's reins. *Am I collecting my son's body?*

The old man's dog-eared bible was on the shelf. He picked it up and shoved it into his bag, just in case. Next, he grabbed the freshly baked loaf that was cooling on the table and lastly he filled his pouch with the rest of the ale from the jug.

'Mr Murray, are you coming?'

'Yes, yes, I'm coming now!'

As he pulled his door closed, he decided it was pointless to mourn until he was given a reason to.

One of the men roughly helped him up into his cart, having first checked to see he wasn't carrying any weapons in his bag.

Gabriel bent to fetch the reins and succumbed to a moment of panic. Could an ominous fate be awaiting him in the Jacobite camp? *Am I coming back? Am I to be murdered or taken hostage? The dog will starve. Maybe I should put the bread back?*

The soldiers had run out of patience. 'Mr Murray, move your horse, now!'

The old man waved and lightly flicked the reins against Sally's broad back. He did, however, make a quick inspection of his home. It had never looked so precious to him. He tossed his head in an effort to lose fearful thoughts. Then he could have almost sworn he heard his wife say, 'Don't worry. What will be, will be.' Gabriel had no choice but to take comfort in this.

The rain had petered off by the time Gabriel and the soldiers reached the Jacobite camp. Derry was just a few short miles away. Gabriel's back and neck were stiff from sitting absolutely still for the entire journey. He kept watch for his son, hoping he might spot him in the distance, alive and well, perched on Pegasus's back. But neither Adam nor his white steed was to be seen. Gabriel was surprised at the depth of his anxiety. How naïve he had been to think he was beyond worry, just because he was old. He was still a father, whether he was in his forties or in his eighties.

The Jacobite camp was as miserable as he had pictured it. Hundreds of mucky tents sucked into the saturated ground. None of the inhabitants looked particularly cheerful. For the most part, the soldiers were a sorry-looking bunch. Some of them seemed far too young to be this far from their mother's skirts.

Uniforms were tatty and torn. Not everyone had the luxury of good boots, and Gabriel was surprised by the lack of rifles and swords. Maybe the weapons were in the tents to keep them dry or maybe the truth was that some of these soldiers didn't possess so much as a carving knife.

As far as Gabriel was concerned, the tumbledown appearance of the Jacobites only made their presence here even more ridiculous. *What was the point of all of this?*

One of his escorts stood next to Sally. Gabriel asked him, 'Is King James here?'

The soldier forgot himself and snorted, 'You're joking, aren't you? King James here?'

This was interesting. The man's disdain for his supposed king must be a common enough attitude. Why else was it so immediate in reply to an innocent question?

A disturbance behind the old man caused both him and

the guard to turn around. A figure moved through the Jacobite soldiers, a most pathetic figure indeed. Her hair was grey and filthy with stray strands plastered across her face. Her waist was no wider than the scrawny trunk of a sapling tree, while her clothes were mud-coloured rags that barely covered her. Every part of her suggested a terrible hunger.

Gabriel recognised the woman but he didn't know her name; nobody actually did. She was just part of the area for as long as anyone could remember. She lived off whatever she could scrounge, and from the state of her she clearly hadn't had much luck lately. On a dark night she could have passed for a ghost. Rumour had it she once fought a starving dog for a chicken bone, not that Gabriel believed everything he heard. Still, looking at her now, it wasn't hard to be convinced. She had no home and no family that he knew of.

The soldiers were irritated by her presence. That much was clear to him. The old woman was begging for food, making the strangest noises and gestures with her claw-like hands. She only wanted some food, that's all. Her eyes constantly searched for something edible. Gabriel imagined she could be related to a cat. She seemed hardly human at all. But she could have found a friendlier place than this.

The bad weather, the constant rain and biting winds,

had sanded down the soldiers' optimism and curiosity about their surroundings and task. Most of them wished they had never heard of Derry. How much longer would they be kept here, with poor rations and the constant threat of being ambushed by the rebels? And now this mewing old crone was annoying them and getting in their way. It was too much.

At first, they just turned their backs on her, pretending they could neither see nor hear her. She kept moving, all the while, not giving up on her belief that one of them would give her a crust of bread.

Hunger is a fierce taskmaster. It will not let you rest while there is the flimsiest of possibilities that there is food to be had.

Gabriel wished the old woman would give up and take herself out of the camp. But she didn't. Instead, he saw her stop sharply and sniff the air before shuffling towards a pile of horse manure. Bending down, she flattened out the dung, picking out what Gabriel guessed to be seeds. In any case, it was food even if it was sitting in dung, and the smell was making the woman's eyes water.

Adam's father shook his head and glanced at his escort as if to say, *Has it really come to this?*

Suddenly there was an angry shout, followed by roars of outrage. Bewildered, Gabriel looked back again. What was wrong? Surely, they would allow her to eat in peace. And then he heard the accusations.

One soldier bawled, 'Witch!' Others spat at the woman.

You see, it was believed that if a witch took the dung of an animal and burned it, the animal would sicken and die. The paranoid and stressed soldiers did not see a harmless, starving woman wanting only to feed herself. No, indeed. They saw a Williamite who intended to infect their horses with her sorcery so that their army would be left in chaos. In other words, they believed they were under attack.

Even as they surrounded her, she kept on shoving her 'treasure' into her mouth, oblivious to the danger she was in. Gabriel felt powerless to help her. All he could do was bear witness to her comeuppance.

It happened so fast.

Gabriel had seen little evidence of guns, but now, here were three or four soldiers pointing their pistols at her. Unable to understand why she had been dragged to her feet, away from her squalid meal, the woman screamed in protest. The sheer pitch of her scream confirmed for the soldiers that they were right in identifying her. 'She's a witch, a demon of some kind!'

Without further delay, one of the men shot her. Blood spurted from her shoulder and she flung her head backwards in fright. Gabriel didn't believe that she understood what had happened. Perhaps it was nervousness that made the soldiers laugh. It was awful to watch, awful to hear. The first shooting triggered a second one and then another. Three bullets, at close range, tore into her flesh and still she stood, accidentally baring her teeth as she tried to contain the pain and confusion.

The fact that she hadn't fallen prompted a terrible idea as, one by one, the men took up the chant. 'See! She won't die! She's truly a witch!'

One young soldier took a run at her. He didn't have a gun only a knife that he used to slash at her raggedy excuse of a dress. That, at least, fell to the ground, exposing a shrivelled and far too skinny body covered in shiny sores. Perhaps it was her ugliness that spurred the final outrage. A soldier marched right up to her. Calling for his comrades to be quiet, he blessed himself before pressing the tip of his pistol against the woman's throat. She spluttered and tried to get away. One final shot and she was dead. Released by her captors, her body folded over into the muck.

The soldiers stared. No longer was she an object of fear. Now they just saw a dead old woman. But it was too late.

Gabriel sent a prayer heavenwards for the safe delivery of her soul.

His escort felt obliged to offer some explanation for what had happened. 'Look, Mr Murray, we are in a foreign land surrounded by foreign people. We haven't seen our families in months.'

Gabriel felt impatient. 'Why are you here?'

The soldier smirked. 'For God and King, same as your son no doubt!'

Gabriel wished he had the courage to punch the man. *How dare he compare himself to Adam!* Shivering in his damp clothes, the old man said, 'My son would never be scared of an old woman.'

Before the soldier could make a blustering reply to this, Colonel Hamilton sent for his visitor.

CHAPTER TWENTY

Colonel Hamilton did not exactly welcome Gabriel into his tent with open arms. However, Gabriel was surprised at the clipped courtesy he was shown.

'Would you like some refreshment after your journey, Mr Murray?'

'No,' said Gabriel, adding after a pause, 'thank you, sir.'

There was no time for small talk. As soon as Gabriel refused the colonel's second offer – this time of a seat – Hamilton began, 'The reason I've had you brought here is to ask you to speak to your son.'

Gabriel looked around, expecting to see Adam that very minute.

'No. No, he's not here,' said the colonel impatiently. 'I want you to go and visit him in Derry.'

He couldn't help himself. Gabriel smiled in heady relief. *So, Adam was still safe and still free.*

Annoyed by the delight in the old man's expression, Colonel Hamilton rushed to squash it. 'Sir, this is a grave matter. Your son is in open rebellion against His Majesty

King James. I have been informed that he is now residing in Derry where he is inciting the citizens to join him in a revolution.'

How Gabriel longed to say something to show his pride in his son. But he didn't dare. This man had the capacity to hurt Adam so he held his tongue.

Colonel Hamilton sighed. This was not going to be easy. Furthermore, he knew that if the situation was reversed, his own father would probably respond with the same degree of stubbornness. Gabriel stared politely as the colonel stated, 'Resistance is just delaying the inevitable. We are still offering favourable terms. If Derry submits, she will not be punished. Her leaders have actually agreed to this, therefore your son is causing trouble for them as well as for us.'

Still Gabriel said not a word.

Colonel Hamilton wondered how to break through. 'King James does not want to see any civilians harmed in his name. He does not want violence.' He paused to study the old man in front of him and then asked, 'Mr Murray, do you hear what I am saying? Do you understand the words I am using?'

Gabriel blinked. 'Why, yes, sir!'

'And?' enquired the colonel.

'And,' said Gabriel, 'I will go and see my son.'

There was something about the way that Gabriel said

this that prompted the colonel to say what he had hoped to avoid mentioning. 'You will inform your son that if he does not desist, he leaves me with no option but to hang his father from the nearest tree.'

Gabriel looked fascinated by this new piece of information. Then he thought of something. 'If it comes to *that*, perhaps you might be kind enough to have someone see to my animals.'

Colonel Hamilton was puzzled. 'Animals?'

Gabriel explained, 'I left my old dog in the cottage.' He stopped, thought of something, wondered whether to say it and then did. 'No creature should be starved to death for showing loyalty.'

The room seemed to vibrate as the two men gazed at one another.

And then, just like that, the meeting was over. The colonel shuffled papers around his desk. Gabriel turned to go but paused. 'Sir?' Colonel Hamilton glanced up. 'I wonder if I could make a second request. There is a dead woman in the camp; she was shot by your soldiers just now.' The colonel tried not to show his surprise. Gabriel kept talking. 'If I make it back, could I take her away in my cart and give her a Christian burial?' He received a curt nod for a reply.

Gabriel stepped outside again, back into the muddy field with its brooding atmosphere.

At Butchers' Gate, the guards asked Gabriel if he would prefer to come inside, but he replied that, no, he would wait for Adam to come out to him. He hadn't much love for cities, much preferring mountains and rivers – nature's boundaries – to walls and steel gates. Gabriel also did not care for too many neighbours and Derry, as far as he could make out, was full to the brim. The stench was a dead giveaway, making Gabriel wonder if the city herself was rotting away.

Adam appeared after a couple of minutes. 'I couldn't believe it when they said you were here. What's wrong?'

Gabriel gestured to his Jacobite companions who were waiting a few feet away, pretending that they weren't watching his every move. 'No, yes, I'm fine!' He allowed Adam to help him out of the cart and they took some steps away. Adam's face was quite a picture.

Gabriel chuckled. 'I've been given a mission by Colonel Hamilton.'

Adam waited, refusing to smile. His father sighed. 'I've to tell you to stop what you're doing and agree to his terms!'

Adam felt himself sizzle and freeze. His throat dried up as he checked that his father's words hadn't been heard by the guards at the gate. Eventually, he said, 'I don't understand. You have been with Hamilton?'

His father patted him on the arm. They both looked

over the land in front of them, allowing themselves a moment to forget about the crammed city behind them.

Gabriel said, 'You know, I never expected to become a father. Your arrival was quite a surprise and, to be honest, I was more than a little anxious.'

Adam had never heard his father talk like this before. The back of his neck felt like someone had placed a hot coal against it.

Gabriel nodded. 'It was your mother who assured me I'd be fine. Then, when she died, I thought I might die too.' He sniffed. 'Maybe I even wanted to. But, of course, I couldn't, because of this child depending on me. I had to trust in God that I wouldn't accidentally harm you in some way. So I hardly had time to notice that you had become the most important thing in my life.'

Adam held his breath.

'I'm an old, old man and, perhaps, I don't fully understand what you are doing here.' Gazing at his son, he raised an eyebrow. 'You do know you are bringing a whole lot of trouble down upon your head.'

Adam shrugged.

His father continued, 'In any case, I believe you are following your heart and I accept that, no matter what happens next.'

Here, he might've added the threat to his own life but he didn't. However, if Colonel Hamilton followed through and had him swinging from one of the trees in the distance, because of his rebel son, Adam should have his blessing right now.

Fumbling in his bag, he found the family bible.

Thrilled to see something so familiar to him, Adam asked, 'You've brought me something to read?'

His father rubbed the book's worn cover, his fond farewell, and said, 'Perhaps! I had always planned to give it to you and today seems like as good a day as any.'

Still not fully understanding what was going on, Adam was both surprised and touched. Trust Gabriel to choose such an unpredictable time to present him with such a gift as this.

'I'm proud of you, son, and I want you to remember that every time you look at this!' Gabriel wiped something from his eye and said loud enough for the two escorts to hear, 'That city owes you a very great debt! Keep up the good work!'

With that he stepped back to the cart, leaving Adam to stare after him.

Gabriel's mischief-making was relayed to Colonel Hamilton by an irate captain. 'Sir, I beg you, let me arrest him. The old man disobeyed you, telling his devil of a son to do as he pleased!'

'Where is he now?' asked the colonel. 'Is he on his way back here?'

The captain was puzzled. 'But of course he is, sir. You

ordered him to return here.'

'Yes,' said the colonel. 'But I also ordered him to have his son give himself up, and that didn't happen, now did it?'

The officer bristled, longing to say rudely: 'Eh, yes, and that's my bloody point!'

Colonel Hamilton began to write. There was silence, and the captain wondered if he was dismissed. He might have left the tent, but his colonel stunned him by asking, 'What do you know about the old woman who was killed this morning?'

The best the captain could manage was 'I beg your pardon, sir?'

The colonel didn't look up from his sheet of paper. 'Oh, you must have heard about it, Captain. After all, it is not every day that a harmless old woman is stripped and murdered in our camp.'

It was the colonel's tone that confused the captain. It was icy cold, hinting at the presence of utter rage. Swallowing, the officer began to defend himself immediately, 'They … that is, the men … well, they thought her a witch. She was scrabbling around in the manure and they feared she was casting a spell, sir.'

The colonel had a dangerous glint in his eye. 'A witch you say? Tell me, Captain, have you ever met a witch?'

'No, sir,' the captain answered sadly.

'And do you actually believe in witches?'

The young captain felt bound to think about this. True, he had never met one, but that didn't mean they did not exist. Deciding that honesty was the best way to go, he answered, 'I'm not sure, sir. I mean, it's difficult to say, one way or the other.' There, he had told the truth at least.

'I see,' said the colonel.

The soldier didn't feel that he did somehow.

'Let me put it like this, Captain: the next time one of the locals, in particular an elderly, defenceless, starving one, finds their way into my camp, perhaps you would be so good as to see that they are not killed by soldiers representing King James. Instead, you might just have them sent on their way. Do you think you could possibly manage this?'

Wasn't it lucky for the captain that Gabriel presented himself at this particular moment? All he was required to do was repeat another 'Yes, sir' and then make himself scarce, as fast as he could.

'Well, Mr Murray, I hear you met with your son.'

Gabriel nodded graciously. 'I did!'

Colonel Hamilton nodded too as he said, 'And you told him what we discussed, about him surrendering himself in order to save his father's life, if for no other reason?'

'Ah …' said Gabriel, his eyes crinkling like paper. 'Not exactly.'

The colonel didn't pretend to be surprised. 'By which

you mean, sir, you did no such thing. In actual fact, you performed the opposite, encouraging him to keep up the good work while failing to mention the possible consequences for yourself.'

Gabriel relaxed a little. 'Possible' was an important word in that sentence. He was also impressed that Colonel Hamilton knew so much already. Feeling that he owed the Jacobite commander an explanation, he said, 'It's not that I didn't take your words seriously. For all I know I may not see the end to this day. However, I thought that my boy should be free to do what he felt was important.' He rubbed his chin. 'I've had over eighty good years, Colonel. Even if you don't hang me today, I have no guarantee that I will wake up tomorrow.'

While he spoke he realised something that the colonel may well already have known, that if he had Gabriel killed, it would only spur Adam on to do his very worst. Killing Gabriel made no sense at all.

Colonel Hamilton didn't bother to comment on Gabriel's explanation. Instead, he handed him a sheet of paper, without a smile. 'This gives you permission to collect that woman's body.' Gabriel had almost forgotten about her. The colonel was not finished yet. 'You will be escorted back to your house and there you will remain, under my protection, until the situation with Derry has been resolved.'

Before Gabriel could respond with thanks – what else

could he say – the colonel concluded their meeting with, 'Good day to you, Mr Murray.'

For the second time, that day, Gabriel Murray exited the colonel's tent but, this time, the scene that greeted him didn't look so gloomy. It was quite a relief to have his life back, plus Adam was happy and now he was free to go home. Wasn't that all that mattered, when all was said and done? Even the sight of the dirty corpse being loaded into the cart could not dampen his spirits.

CHAPTER TWENTY-ONE

Daniel stopped to pat Horace on his broad head and overheard his parents talking in the next room. 'Little Catherine Williams passed away this morning,' said his father.

'Oh my goodness!' exclaimed Mrs Sherrard. 'Was it the lack of food?'

Mr Sherrard admitted he wasn't exactly sure, saying, 'Possibly, although the child's mother said they had managed to eat meat over the last couple days.' He sighed. 'All the same, she weighed no more than the sheet that covered her. I could plainly see the bones in her cheeks, her jaw, her ribs. The family gathered around her cot, the parents and three older sisters. The eldest read a passage from the bible. All I could do was stand there and watch.'

Daniel heard a tremble in his father's voice. Neither he nor Horace moved a muscle.

'I saw her very last breath leave her body and take her spirit with it. A light mist, or something like that, swirled from within her and just the empty shell was left behind. I … I can't really describe it, but I saw the same thing when my mother died. Anyway, I reached down to close her eyes but Mrs Williams bid me to wait. One of the girls fetched a brush and they all took turns to brush Catherine's hair, giving thanks that she was no longer in pain, no longer hungry.'

David imagined his mother stroking his father's arm. After a moment, he heard her say, 'You predicted this would happen, that the children would suffer.'

Daniel felt something press against his heart. Neither parent mentioned Alice but he felt the walls vibrate with her name.

His mother wanted to change the subject. 'What did they have to eat?'

Mr Sherrard sounded dazed. 'What do you mean?'

His wife answered, 'You said they had recently eaten meat. I'm just curious.'

His father hesitated, making Daniel lean in closer. 'Well, that's the thing. They were forced to eat their dog who was a great favourite of Catherine's. So, on top of grieving for her, they are racked with guilt that the child may have died of a broken heart.'

Daniel's mother said softly, 'What else could they do? They had to feed their children. Choice is a luxury these days.'

As fast and as quietly as he could, Daniel left the house, retreating into the streets that could not provide an escape.

He was breathless but refused to acknowledge the fear thumping through his veins. Fortunately, on his walk to the wall there was plenty to distract him. Misery was everywhere he looked.

On Sundays, Governor Walker and the other church leaders did their utmost to convince the desperate not to attack one another. It was explained, week after week, why the defenders of the city had to be given priority when it came to food. 'We must stand together,' said the governor. 'The enemy is at our gates and that is enough. We cannot turn on each other or it weakens us as a community.'

Daniel noticed a shocking rise in the number of invalids lying, stretched out on the ground, their relatives hopeless to do anything for them. Thanks to his browsing through his father's books, Daniel understood that the crowds of homeless people were succumbing to disease as much as to starvation. As he hurried by he could plainly see that some of the sick were in agony. Here and there individuals clutched at their aching, fevered heads in a pathetic attempt to soothe them while others moaned about the pain in their bodies. Some complained that the drab daylight was hurting their eyes.

Two days earlier he thought he spied Samuel Hunt in the distance, or at least what was left of him. The boy had lost his bulkiness which made him look a lot older. He was on his haunches, completely absorbed in searching through the shrubbery until he found a wriggly worm. Tears pricked at Daniel's eyes as he saw Samuel lick his lips and swallow the worm in one gulp. Daniel had no urge to approach him. He hadn't seen much of him since they closed the gates and, to be honest, the stark change in the boy's appearance scared him. He quickly turned down another street, trying to convince himself that it must have been someone who just looked like Samuel.

Daniel imagined that his father curtailed his own walks through the city, making himself quietly available only to neighbours. There was little a physician could do for the sick and the dying. What they needed was food and that was getting harder and harder to come by.

Adam Murray and his men were doing their best. After every clash with the enemy, the hope was that some of their horses would be left behind. Jacobite horses provided a solid meal for the defenders. The screams of these horses, as their throats were cut, were met with relief behind the walls. 'Ah, meat tonight. Thank God!'

At the wall, James greeted him first, as usual. 'About time!'

Daniel only nodded. It had become a challenge to try to sneak up on James and surprise him before his friend spotted him. However, with all his worries, Daniel forgot to make an attempt today.

'You look awful!' pronounced James.

Daniel made a face and asked if there was any news.

'Adam will be launching another excursion for water later on, so we have that to look forward to.'

Daniel stepped up to look out over the wall, near Bishop's Gate, across the river Foyle. The Jacobite camps were inching closer to the city, while the river remained the one true barrier. One consequence of the constant bombing by the Jacobites was that all of Derry's wells were either broken or full of dirt so that the water could not be consumed. The only well left in use was St Columb's Well. That was the good news. The bad news, however, was that this last source of clean water was outside the city, just beyond Windmill Hill. This was the piece of raised ground that sat behind the busy mill which gave the place its name, about five hundred yards away from Bishop's Gate, to the south-west of the city. There is where the city had built its gibbet, the gallows where criminals were hung until they were dead.

Naturally this bit of information was known to the Jacobites which explains why they built a trench from where they could supervise the well – in other words shoot any Derry people trying to avail of it. It was proving to be a daily battle. Men were sent out to get water, and if they were shot there was real concern that their bodies might fall into the well and contaminate it.

Daniel had thought it cruel to have to spend the day

staring at a river made up of water that was also undrinkable. What was the point of it? Yet, he was reminded of its importance when a boy was sent around, one afternoon, to order all residents to keep pails of water handy in case of fire. It was another worry for Governors Walker and Baker, that a fire would start and spread through the city, wiping out one building after another until nothing was left but burning ash. London, that mighty city, was almost lost in her great fire of 1666. At least the river's waters would be a perfect help in that situation. In its own way the river Foyle was as capable of defending the city as well as any man guarding the wall.

The next hour passed peacefully enough except that James would keep talking about food. Already two other soldiers had told him to shut up before stomping off to another spot.

'Potato cakes, you know, with flour and salt. Now, they can be a bit dry, I'll warrant …' James was oblivious to the torture he was inflicting on his reluctant listener. Then he surprised Daniel by suddenly asking, 'Am I terribly thin?'

Daniel almost laughed. 'What?'

James was serious. 'My mother keeps telling me that I'm skin and bone. It's hard to see it myself, though.'

Daniel looked his friend over. Of course he had lost weight; everyone had. His features were sharper than ever, even his nose seemed longer, but Daniel refused to answer such a silly question. Instead, he issued a gruff, 'You still have your health.'

James took no offence to this; in fact he agreed, 'Yes, we're luckier than most! Sure, the graveyards are full now.'

Daniel focused on the land of plenty – as far as grass and dirty water were concerned – in front of them. Nevertheless, he had to ask, 'What does that mean when people are still dying?'

James hadn't expected a question. 'Oh, well, I don't really know. I suppose the dead will just have to wait …'

Daniel shivered. 'You mean, just leave them rotting in the streets?'

James shrugged. 'Where else can they be kept?'

His friend's casual acceptance of the situation irritated Daniel who snapped, 'So you wouldn't mind having to step over your mother's body if she dies before this is over?'

James looked horrified and Daniel was instantly ashamed, hardly believing the words that had leapt from him. 'I'm so sorry, James. Truly I am. I'm just hungry and it's making me mad.'

His friend nodded.

Hearing James sniff, Daniel stole a glance at him and was mortified to see tears sliding down the older boy's face. He looked away, but James knew he had been caught and offered, 'It's just that Mother doesn't look good. She refuses to eat her share of my rations, saying it's more important that I have the strength to fight.'

Daniel scraped at some stones on the wall with his dirty fingernails, feeling thoroughly gloomy.

Emboldened, James wiped his eyes, muttering quietly, 'I didn't know it was going to be like this.'

Daniel actually felt some sort of relief as James continued, 'I don't want a Papist king, but I can't help it; I don't want my mother to starve to death either.'

Both boys glanced around to make sure he hadn't been heard while Daniel whispered, 'I know exactly what you mean.'

James flashed him a wobbly grin of gratitude.

'HALT!'

It was Robert's voice. Daniel and James spied him down at the gate, approaching a family of walking skeletons. Daniel marvelled at the fact they were able to walk at all. It was a most forlorn group; their rags were dark with rain and muck. The grandparents were tipping forward as if they hoped to kiss the ground while the two women were hardly recognisable as females. The two children didn't talk, didn't laugh; they were far too quiet for their age. Their eyes were like two sunken holes in the middle of their faces. Daniel thought they looked like little old people who had lost the will to live.

In studying them he had the sense that he had seen them before. Weren't they part of the crowd that were living on cold, bare ground around the Diamond? He was almost sure the old man was familiar to him. And he then remembered. *My goodness!* This was the poor fellow that Henry had virtually accused of being a traitor, the morning that the bombing began. The man who seemed to know a lot about being under siege and had stumbled away in embarrassment and confusion.

Daniel was glad that Henry was nowhere in sight. Yes, he was relieved there was only Robert who did not torment strangers nor shove them roughly for no reason at all.

He watched his brother stand between the man and his relatives and the gate, asking sternly, 'Where are you going?'

The old man spoke. 'We're going home, Master!'

Robert was not satisfied with the answer. 'Explain yourself!'

Daniel found that he did not like his brother's manner.

The man did not seem surprised at the interrogation. 'We came into the city to escape the Jacobites but we've run out of food. My grandchildren are getting weak. There is nothing for us here so we're going back home. I've no choice, sir.'

Daniel blinked; there was that word again, 'choice'. *Why is Robert giving them such evil looks?*

'So, you are choosing to give up hope and abandon the

city that has sheltered you. Just like that!'

The family bowed their heads, unable to defend themselves from Robert's accusation.

Seeing their guilt, Daniel's brother pressed on. 'Did you
stop to think how this will look to the enemy; that Derry's
population prefers to be elsewhere?'

Indeed, this had not occurred to the dejected refugees.
Daniel saw them sneak glances at one another, unsure
what to do next. Finally, the old man shook his head; he
would not be thwarted. 'Begging your pardon, sir. We have
been sleeping on the streets. My son gave his life in battle.
We have done our duty to Derry.' He held Robert's gaze.
'I have no more to give!'

As if to demonstrate his grandfather's point, one of the
children, a scraggily little bundle of four or five, began to
cough, and cough, and cough. Exhausted, the small boy
was obliged to sink down on the wet ground. Not one of
the adults took any notice of him.

Daniel found himself wishing that Henry was nearby
after all, to see how he had wrongly accused the man of
treachery. But now, much to his disbelief, he heard his own
brother make the very same accusation.

'This is treason!' Robert declared, though he didn't
seem half as definite as the statement he made.

Daniel rolled his eyes, and wondered if his brother could
possibly be referring to the sick child.

The old man made no response. Instead, he swayed a little, as if he was going to have to sit down too.

Perhaps in search of inspiration, Robert looked upwards and met Daniel's eyes. Something passed between the brothers. Eventually, Robert barked at the guard on the gate, 'Open the gate for them!'

Out they shuffled, in a solitary line, too wet and downcast to bother thanking their benefactor. No doubt they had a long walk in front of them.

Because they had nothing else to do, Daniel and James watched the family's painfully slow walk away from the gates. They appeared to be heading south, bypassing Windmill Hill. From time to time the boys glanced over at them, as they became dots in the distance. It took a while for the two guards to figure out what they were doing and where exactly they were going. But in the end it was obvious. James took off and returned with the telescope so that they could be sure. They passed it back and forth as they watched that poor family deliver themselves into the hands of the Jacobites.

James whistled and said, 'Are you going to tell your brother, or should I?'

Daniel pretended not to hear him. Things were already so confusing without this. *Was Robert wrong to have let them go? Was the family wrong for wanting to save themselves?*

When he realised James was still staring at him, he

shrugged. 'Can't we just not saying anything? It's just one family, who are not even from Derry.' As if in agreement, his stomach croaked pitifully.

James scratched his ear. 'Alright but that doesn't mean that somebody else didn't see them.'

Daniel decided he was willing to take this risk.

As it happened, James was right. Robert was told about the deserters, for that was what the little family were called. However, there was no point in dwelling on that particular bunch of grandparents, parents and children because they were only the first of many, many more. Other families, starving and diseased, began to sneak out from behind the walls to throw themselves at the mercy of Colonel Hamilton who had let it be known that they would not be harmed if they surrendered.

Paranoia gripped the remaining population. Were they insane to stay put and stay hungry? Dying was in full flow, disease finding the weak and eating them alive, no matter who they were.

Perhaps it was inevitable that rumours struck up like wildfire to stoke the flames of terror. Someone told someone else, who told someone else, that Governor George Walker was hoarding food in his house.

What a delicious piece of news to have in the middle of a famine!

With people longing to believe that there were cupboards

still bulging with wheat, potatoes, salted fish and beef, the little story was bounced along from one empty mouth to the next with wondrous enthusiasm. Well, there was only one way to find out if it was true; an immediate inspection of the property must be launched.

Who knows how many started out for the governor's house, maybe it was only a handful of angry individuals, but once they reached their destination their number and rage had increased considerably. Henry happened across them midway through their journey and, noting the determination in their step, decided to follow them. He held back as the men and women confronted the Walker house.

He was fortunate that his father had been popular, much more popular than Governor Walker. Dead men are popular forever and the crowd were ready to blame someone for their hunger and it did not seem that they especially held the Catholic army to account. No, they wanted to blame someone who was nearer home. The very idea that this man of God, who lectured them at every opportunity, would be stuffing his face while his lowly congregation and the rest of the city were living on candle wax and mice was too much to bear.

Henry briefly considered placing himself between the mob and the governor's house, but even he understood that nobody would be able to calm them down. However, it appeared that God was looking after the governor and his family because the house was empty. *Well, now the jig would be up.* Henry shrugged. *Let them do what they must.* He had the strongest feeling that his father stood beside him, willing him to keep his distance, for now. The young man's nose and cheeks felt as cold as stone as he felt his heart harden against the governor. *Besides, it's only what Walker deserves if he is hoarding.*

There was a crash followed by a boorish roar of triumph. The front door was smashed and the house was invaded. Henry licked his lips as he listened to the sounds of furniture being thrown around.

As the son of a politician, he was equipped to reason that the poor do not altogether mind hardship in order to make a point, to be patriotic in the face of a foreign enemy. However, should the people feel that they are the only ones to endure suffering while those with money and fancy clothes continue enjoying their comforts, benefitting even from their neighbours' hardship, *well, then, this is only to be expected.*

Henry waited but when he heard exclamations of outrage, and joy, his curiosity got the better of him and he hurried through the broken entrance.

A man yelped, 'I don't believe this!' A woman screamed.

In spite of himself, Henry grew excited at the thought of decent food. 'What? What is it? Meat? Fish? Bread?'

He found the gang in the pantry, standing in awe at the sight of a multitude of bottles filled with beer alongside plates of what looked like butter. Nobody said a word.

Henry, taking in the reverent expressions on the faces of the intruders, along with the liquid treasure trove, couldn't help it; he threw back his head and laughed.

To their credit, his companions – most of whom looked to be of a rough sort – waited until he was finished before one of them asked, 'What's so funny, friend?'

Henry beamed at his interrogator. 'Don't you see? Can't you guess? Surely you do!' But they obviously didn't, so he enlightened them. 'All those speeches every Sunday. I thought he was being fired by God above but no ...' Here, he pointed at the beer and laughed again. 'No! That's all it was!'

CHAPTER TWENTY-TWO

The old dog was off his food and Adam Murray's father had no sympathy for him.

'Don't you know that people are starving and here's you turning up your nose at porridge?'

Gabriel shook his head in disgust. His pet stared at him, refusing to be blackmailed into eating his meal. Wagging his finger at him, Gabriel said, 'It's that or nothing!'

The dog whined.

'No,' said Gabriel. 'I'm not making any more biscuits until tomorrow.'

Sitting down, he stirred his own porridge. He couldn't help grinning at the dog. 'You're a stubborn fool and you know it!'

He received a sharp bark by way of reply.

Gabriel made a face and said, 'No, you shut up!' before continuing to eat his breakfast in peace.

In the city Daniel was relieved to reach his front door. There hadn't been a break from the rain in the last couple of hours. How lovely it was to get away from it and remove his sodden clothes. He did his best to ignore the creaking of his empty stomach, wishing that the sun would shine. One's appetite was never as demanding on a hot summer's day.

He peeled his wet coat off himself, trying not to make a puddle on the floor. The fire was lit so he dropped his things over the nearest chair, hoping that they would dry out quickly. So absorbed was he in fussing over his clothes that it took a few minutes for him to sense that there was something different about the house. For one thing he could smell food, hot food. Real food. The fire crackled in the grate and the delicious scent thrilled him, giving him goosebumps – a proper dinner at last. Baby Alice gurgled in her cot, which had been placed to the side of the fire-place. For too long she had either wailed out of hunger or was silent from the effort. Now, she was punching the air in front of her with her little fists, her toothless mouth curved into the shape of a gaping grin.

Daniel cooed at her, 'Are you trying to tell me something, Alice?'

When was the last time that the house had felt like home?

His brother and father appeared. Daniel was pleased to note that they were neither arguing nor pretending the other was absent. Yet, somehow, they did not exactly appear at their ease. He caught them stealing glances at him but was too enthused about dinner to enquire if anything was wrong. So he merely smiled at them as they stood in front of the fire.

'Did you get very wet on watch?' asked his father.

Daniel replied, 'It rained all afternoon. I thought I'd never get home.'

Robert nodded vigorously to this. There was a pause before he then said, 'I was just telling Father about the new leader of the Jacobite army, the French lieutenant-general called de Rosen. Rumour has it that he is appalled at how little Hamilton has achieved.'

Mr Sherrard nodded. 'I think we may expect an increase in pressure from the Jacobites. By all accounts, the French-man shows none of Colonel Hamilton's patience.'

'Yes,' agreed Robert. 'He has already made his presence felt. There are trenches being dug near Windmill Hill while their long cannons, the culverins, are being moved towards Butchers' Gate. It seems he intends to start firing at it.'

Daniel's head dutifully swivelled between his brother and father, as each spoke, while they failed to meet his eye. He put it down to the fact that Robert and his father were out of practice at relaxing in each other's company. That explained their hearty voices and unwillingness to allow even the tiniest pause. He was ready to bridge any gaps in the conversation and was surprised to find that he was not needed in any way.

A crash from the pantry startled him but the other

two made no comment. So, Daniel felt he should ask, 'Is Mother alright?'

His father shrugged. 'She complains of dizziness.'

Rather unnecessarily, Robert explained, 'It's the lack of nourishment. She needs to eat for two or the baby will die.'

Daniel asked, 'Should I go and check on her?'

His father surprised him by saying rather quickly, 'Oh, I'm sure she'd call us if there was a problem.'

His father's casualness regarding his mother was a bit strange but Daniel chose not to dwell on it. At least there was dinner.

It struck him that he had not thought to ask about the smell until now. 'Where did the food come from?' He couldn't understand the confusion on his father's and Robert's faces. Suddenly alarmed that his belly was conjuring up a smell that wasn't real, he asked his father, 'Is it my imagination? Mother *is* cooking something, isn't she? Can't you smell it too?' He failed to see the panicked expression on Robert's face.

Meanwhile, his father ignored Robert and said, 'Yes, of course', which could have meant anything at all.

'I need you boys to keep a proper eye on Alice,' his father quickly added. 'Babies are defenceless against hungry rats. There should be no need to describe the state I found an infant in after a rat got under her blankets.'

In a sudden panic, Daniel immediately pulled back Alice's covers. She squeaked as they flapped in her face.

His father nodded. 'Very good, Daniel. We'll need to remember to do that as often as we can, to be safe.'

Mrs Sherrard appeared with two bowls of steaming stew. 'Right, are we ready to sit down together? Robert, you say grace!' She returned to the kitchen to fetch the last two bowls.

Daniel expected his brother to roll his eyes, but Robert sat down, waiting for the rest of the family to join him. He didn't have long to wait. Daniel's mouth and eyes watered in anticipation. 'Thank you, Mother!' She didn't seem to hear him.

'Now, mind you don't eat too fast,' warned Mr Sherrard. 'Our stomachs need to get used to eating solid food again.'

The family held hands and Robert rushed through a prayer of thanks to God for the food they were about to eat. His voice trembled slightly.

Something bothered Daniel but he chose not to explore it, just yet. He did feel guilty about his dinner, hoping that James Morrison was enjoying a tasty meal such as this. His companion on the walls deserved it just as much as the Sherrards did; indeed, everybody in Derry deserved a meal such as this.

It was difficult to banish all those starving people huddled in the streets from his mind. How they would enjoy this, actual *lumps* of dark meat sitting in their own greasy juice.

Nobody spoke. Four heads hung over their bowls and moved in time together, spooning out the meat, catching the fat, swallowing it whole and returning for more. Mrs Sherrard's face was flushed from the heat of the kitchen. Her hair was askew but she barely allowed herself the time to push it back out of her way.

Daniel smiled in gratitude at his mother, but she was too absorbed to notice. He was looking away from her to focus on his next mouthful when a sliver of a thought – that is, the merest whisper from the depth of his being – nudged him, forcing him to take in his surroundings. He could deny it no longer; his family were definitely avoiding him even as they sat right here at this table.

What is wrong?

Was this how Robert usually felt, always on the outside of the family group; feeling that he had taken a wrong step or misjudged what was understood by his parents and young brother? Well, now it was his younger brother who was feeling left out. And then it was as if the fog dissolved to allow the sun to shine through because, in that instant, Daniel realised what was troubling him. He pronounced it calmly. 'Horace!'

The Sherrards, as a family, stopped chewing and sat frozen as if some wicked enchantress had struck them with her magic wand. Only the clock kept moving, its ticking dominating the unexpected stillness.

A timid voice in Daniel's head tried to tell him something that he did not wish to hear. Nevertheless, he glanced around the table and settled on his father, saying again, 'Horace?'

Out of the three, Mr Sherrard had been the most confident of handling this scene when it finally unfolded. However, now that it was here, he found himself abandoned by his deceitful confidence. He was unable to swallow the morsel in his mouth, clinging to it as a reason for being unable to speak.

In any case, his father's delay told his youngest son all he needed or wanted to know. The spoon spilled from his hand and slid into his bowl with the daintiest splash.

His mother began to cry even as she continued to eat.

Daniel's tone was flat. 'Was it you who killed him? Or you, Father? Or was it you, brother?'

Only his mother answered him. 'I gave him to the butcher to do it because … we … I couldn't …'

Daniel closed his eyes; his head felt as if it was being struck by a heavy object.

Robert spoke. 'I'm so sorry, Daniel. But we had to eat. Mother is getting weaker by the day. Alice is sleeping so much because she hasn't the energy to do anything else. And, Father, well, we didn't like to worry you but he has fallen down on the streets once or twice while making his rounds.'

Daniel opened his eyes and looked around the table once more. This time he saw the greyness in his mother's face, noted how the bones of her cheeks and the line of her jaw protruded; her skin was tightly drawn as if there was barely enough to cover her. My God, the shape of her face had completely changed. Why hadn't he noticed this before now?

Look how his father had aged. Daniel was reminded of his grandmother as she lay dying. Up to this moment, he had forgotten what she looked like; he had been so young when she died. But, see now, here she was again! His father looked like an old, old woman. When did this happen?

Robert was no better. His hands shook while his wrists seemed dwarfed by long and skinny fingers. Goodness, when did those blue veins start showing through, like cold, narrow streams cutting across one another? Daniel stared at his brother's hands for a moment, mesmerised. They reminded him of maps ... or something like that.

It wasn't Robert's fault, but he decided to break the silence, saying something that really, *really* did not need to be said. 'We all have to make sacrifices at times like this!'

Daniel blinked, shook his head and asked, 'What?'

His brother obliged him, which was a mistake. 'I mean, we all have to make sacrifices ... you know ... at times like this.'

Slowly, Daniel pushed back his chair, giving himself over to the roar within, gritting his teeth as he asked, 'Pray tell, what sacrifices have you made?'

Robert gaped, realising he had jumped too soon, far too soon.

Their parents did not attempt to intervene. In any case, what could they have said to make this right? Daniel was free to collect every little anxiety he had accidentally gathered over the last few months. He stood up, wanting to be the tallest in the room, wanting to make them look up to him, for once.

'You,' he spat at his brother, 'you have dragged this city to her knees, ever since we closed those gates on your orders. You – yes, YOU – have caused much more damage than any Catholic.'

Robert was stunned. Who was this stranger?

'Oh?' snorted Daniel, his face blotchy with rage. 'Don't you see the dying on your strolls to the walls? The graveyards are full, or did you not know that? Imagine – not one more body can be buried properly.'

His father laid a heavy hand on his eldest son's arm, preventing him from also standing up; Robert was obliged to gaze up at his younger brother as he fought to respond to these impossible accusations. 'Daniel, you're not thinking straight! You know as well as I do why we keep the gates locked. It's for all our sakes and Derry's too. You know this!

I know you know this!'

He reached out to take Daniel's hand but thought better of it when the boy looked at his limb as if it were a poisonous snake.

'Boys.' Their mother uttered the word feebly, not expecting it to have any real effect. She brought a hand to her forehead, causing her husband to get to his feet and rush to her side. 'My dear, are you alright?'

Daniel's anger would not be quelled just yet. Pointing at the frail couple who all at once seemed overwhelmed by life, he demanded of his brother, 'Do you not see how you have caused this?'

This was too much for Robert. He exploded too, tears pumped out of him – a rare sight – and his face contorted in agony. 'Of course I do, you little fool! What? Do you think I'm made of stone like the walls?'

Ah, so that was it. That quenched Daniel's rage and his father's too for that matter.

Robert felt that his father agreed with everything Daniel had just said. He fell back down onto his chair. His head throbbed while his heart struggled to keep up with him. Almost fascinated by his own admission of guilt, Robert repeated the words, 'Of course I do.'

Mrs Sherrard patted her husband's hand and bid him to return to his seat. 'It was just another dizzy spell but it's gone now.'

And just like that the family returned to their meal. Daniel's was flavoured with his salty tears yet he kept eating because he knew he had to. Not another word was said and no more apologies were given.

As soon as she emptied her bowl, Mrs Sherrard took the baby upstairs to feed her. Somehow Alice had kept quiet throughout the upset. Daniel's mother was sorry about Horace; she truly was. He had gotten in her way for years now, sometimes causing her to lash out at him with her foot so that she could have the kitchen to herself. Only now she realised that she had lost a true companion. No matter how badly she had treated him he always – *always* – wagged his tail at the sight of her the following morning. His love for her had been pure and undeserved.

She was none too surprised at the tears rolling down onto Alice's head. Confiding in the baby, she gasped, 'I can't believe how much I miss him already!'

Alice stirred but did not stop feeding.

The thought of returning to the empty kitchen filled Mrs Sherrard with dread. Nonetheless, she nursed her baby, knowing that she had done what was absolutely necessary. *I chose the lives of my family.*

A few miles away, at some point in the evening Gabriel's old dog relented and ate the cold, lumpy porridge. When he was finished he took his place at the foot of his master's bed, both friends again.

261

CHAPTER TWENTY-THREE

On a cold night in May Daniel and James were keeping watch over Bishop's Gate. Conversation had long dried up as they huddled against the chilled stone of the wall, trying not to think about a hot supper that did not exist. Daniel wondered if he should strive to be a decent companion and find a topic to take their minds off their condition. But what else was there to talk about, beside their incessant hunger, their work of guarding or … or the weather? After sharing hours upon hours of standing side by side there was little enough left to discuss. Daniel even knew rather too much about the wondrous size of the blister on Mrs Morrison's left foot.

However, the sound of a scuffle somewhere below them suddenly freed Daniel from the need to fill the silence. 'What was that?' he whispered as James was already straining over the wall in an effort to peer through the darkness.

'I don't know. I can't see anything,' replied James in frustration.

The two boys stared hard, the sound of their own breathing obscuring all other sounds until a blast of gunfire deafened them. Musket balls spat against the bricks beneath them while James swore in shock and grabbed Daniel by the neck, dragging him to the ground. Now they huddled in panic while James roared in Daniel's ear, 'We have to return fire!'

Too shocked to answer, Daniel could only think how dangerous it would be to stand up and face shooters they could not see. The torches on the wall served to show the guards off to an enemy that remained swathed in darkness. It would be madness, but he could not refuse to put up a defence; otherwise what was he doing here?

James began the countdown and Daniel clutched his rifle, determining to locate the courage required. 'One … two …' James did not bother with three because the shooting ceased. Then he and Daniel clearly heard feet running off into the night. Without another word, they both stood up and fired their rifles, hoping against hope to find their mark.

Not surprisingly, the incident caused huge consternation throughout the city with both James and Daniel obliged to repeat the meagre details for the governors and Colonel Murray.

The following morning Governor Baker made a close inspection of the wall around Bishop's Gate and then he moved his search to the houses nearby, ordering his men to check every single cellar. Naturally the occupants were anxious as to what he expected to find. He wore a grim expression as he sent soldiers here and there to demand entrance to any building he deemed to be a threat.

He had explained himself to his colleague, Governor Walker, saying, 'The fact that the Jacobites came right up to the walls makes me extremely nervous.'

Governor Walker nodded thoughtfully, asking, 'Do you think they will attempt to climb the walls? We don't even know how many there were last night.'

Governor Baker shrugged. 'George, I fear it may be worse than that. For all we know we could have Jacobites in the city who are trying to find a break in the wall to allow their fellow soldiers inside the city.'

'Good God, man!' Reverend Walker was breathing heavily while trying to process this theory, finally saying, 'Yes! Yes, I see what you mean. That is entirely possible. What should we do?'

His friend shrugged and said, 'I think we need to examine all the houses near the wall, concentrating on their cellars for signs of newly dug tunnels. But we should keep it quiet, we don't want to alert our enemies to what we are looking for and give them a chance to cover up their evil work.'

Governor Walker thought this a splendid idea. 'Yes, let's not say a word to anyone. In these dark days it is hard to know who we can trust.'

Even innocent people did not like to see their own soldiers poke about their homes, turning over their belongings.

Governor Baker stood apart purposely to watch the soldiers bang on door after door and make their ways inside the houses. He carefully observed the attitudes of the house-owners, trying to discern any hints of treason in their faces. And it wasn't just house-owners; a lot of these houses had opened up lodgings for the new arrivals into Derry. Governor Baker shivered as he imagined that there could be Papists amongst the population.

'What is all this? What on earth is going on?'

Oh no, groaned Baker to himself. He recognised the voice immediately. It was Colonel John Mitchelburne.

It was not that he didn't like and respect the colonel, he did. The governor had a lot of time for the colonel who had had to sneak away from his position as commander of the Irish army in order to come to Derry's aid. It was a story that the colonel enjoyed telling, how he had dressed himself up as a Scottish highlander and rode away from Dublin, hardly stopping until he reached the besieged city.

No, it was simply that the colonel was the type of man one did not like to offend which was fine except for the fact that he could be sensitive to offence where none had been given.

'Ah, Colonel Mitchelburne, good morning to you.'

'Governor Baker, why is my sister crying in the middle of the street?'

The governor had known that the gentle lady was indeed the colonel's sister, but he and George Walker had both determined that all houses should be searched, no matter who the occupants were.

Gesturing that perhaps they should talk quietly, without being heard by any of the soldiers and concerned citizens, Governor Baker said, 'I'm sure you have heard how the Jacobites reached the walls last night, actually came right up to Bishop's Gate and started firing at the guards.'

The colonel was already impatient. 'Yes but what has that to do with my sister?'

Without meaning to, Governor Baker sighed. He had not slept much after the shooting, although he had not slept much before it either. In truth, he could not remember the last night he had slept soundly and woke feeling refreshed. Governing a city under siege was not a relaxing occupation.

Colonel Mitchelburne's response to the governor's sigh was sour and instant. 'Forgive me for upsetting you, for making you sigh like I am dreadful news. Perhaps I should go knock on your relatives' door and see how you like it.'

It was a ridiculous conversation and both men knew it, but they were stressed, tired and – of course – hungry. Colonel Mitchelburne would only eat what was available to his soldiers, refusing to take advantage of his position. Yesterday his breakfast consisted of a small, flimsy pancake and dinner had been the exact same. This morning he had yet to break his fast. A quiet voice in his mind advocated calm but he was too worked up now to listen to it.

'Yes,' he said excitedly. 'Perhaps I should go and rouse your sister from her bed and make her cry in front of her neighbours.'

Biting his lip to delay his reply, Governor Baker decided to assert himself. 'My dear Mitchelburne, this is a governor matter. George Walker and I believe that someone could be harbouring a Jacobite sympathiser who may well be trying to dig a tunnel, a passage through to the other side.'

'You think my sister is a traitor? How dare you, Baker! I mean, I have not always agreed with you on certain matters, but this … this is preposterous! You are insulting my family and thereby insulting me.'

The governor suddenly felt exhausted and longed to sit down. How he wished that his colleague would appear beside him and handle the irate colonel because he suddenly felt incapable of doing it. People had started to stare and why wouldn't they? The colonel was creating quite a scene. Who would want to miss it? The sight of the governor of Derry being bawled at on the street.

Governor Baker could only think of one solution to end this embarrassment. Calling for two soldiers to approach, he explained to the colonel, 'You need to calm yourself, sir. I am going to have you escorted back to your home where you will remain until my say so.'

However, the colonel was not used to being treated as if he were a mischievous child. To the surprise of the onlookers, including his sister, he drew his sword and commanded the governor to do the same. To his credit, John Mitchelburne was aware of some shame at his dramatic behaviour but felt it was easier to pursue his anger than attempt to reason with it.

'Draw your weapon, Mr Baker!'

The governor snapped with whatever energy he could muster and raised his sword to meet the colonel's which was already swiping at him.

'John, stop. Please, I beg you!' The colonel's sister pleaded with her brother as more and more people gathered to watch. Finally, her voice punctured her brother's temper and he dropped his sword, looking as if he had just arrived and had no idea what was going on.

Governor Baker was sweating heavily and fought to catch his breath. When he could, he berated his attacker. 'Look around you, John. We are checking *all* the houses, not just your kin. Of course she isn't a bloody traitor but someone could be hiding in her cellar. Surely you understand?'

John Mitchelburne immediately offered his hand and his genuine apology. 'I am so sorry for my rudeness. I can't think what came over me. I'll go home now, in accordance with your wishes, and will wait to hear from you.' His cheeks were red and his voice trembled.

Baker grasped his hand and waved his other to disperse the audience. When they were alone again, he assured the colonel, 'No, stay where you are. I could do with your assistance. It is only natural that tempers will burn when we are hungry and locked into the one place for months on end. As much as I love this city, I would very much like to be able to leave it and go elsewhere, just for a couple of days.'

The weeks passed as they do. People grew hungrier and weaker. Is it part of the human condition to get used to a situation no matter how bad it gets? Surely it is a gift and explains how after a certain point the people of Derry simply gave into their circumstances.

No longer was the siege, the stubbornness, questioned. Every day was the same: the gates remained locked to the army outside while the population tried not to think about the emptiness of their bellies.

The number of dead bodies rose hour by hour. Tears were shed but there was no special anger over the loss of the old, the weak and children. It was accepted that this was what was happening now; this was the state of affairs for the time being. Derry would starve for as long as the siege continued.

Adam Murray prayed for relief from his constant anxiety. He did his best to hide his worry from his comrades. It was important he was calm and always looked as if he knew what to do. If he managed to sleep at night, he dreamt that he was in his father's house, where there was neither bombing nor bone-thin corpses, only breakfast and hot soup. Under his father's roof he could relax, be free from responsibility and people who expected him to save the world.

He was only human after all. Surely it was natural if sometimes he wondered when this was going to end. And other times he was scared; there was no other way to put it. He had never ever seen so much death before. Who had planned for that? Certainly not he. His nervousness increased when he patted his horse's scrawny neck and felt hungry eyes upon her. Other horses had been sacrificed to feed the soldiers, but he couldn't – wouldn't – allow Pegasus to be taken. She trusted him with her life. How could he look her in the eye and take her life from her? No, she would not end up on someone's dinner plate, he'd kill himself first.

Even a passing visitor could not fail to notice the absence of animals in the city. Nothing was going to waste. A mouse cost six pence. In exasperation Adam wondered what was next to be consumed: a bowl of spiders, worms, wool, or words of passion? There were days when he believed all that was keeping the people going were Governor Walker's Sunday sermons from the altar of St Columb's Cathedral that were full of begging for strength and faith and making threats against cowardly behaviour. All words.

William of Orange had to send help soon, because how else was this going to end? Their king and queen coming to their rescue was the obvious solution. They had been told about Derry's suffering. There were stories about ships full of men and supplies being sent from London. Where were they?

One June night he found himself wide awake. It was a common enough occurrence by now. In the early days of hunger he could fool his stomach into feeling full by drinking a glass of beer. Nowadays, his body was weaker and wiser and demanded nothing less than good, solid food, such as Gabriel's biscuits and bread. What wouldn't he give to have some now? Wait, was that really true? Could he give up his religion, his king or his freedom for a mouthful of biscuit? No, that was unthinkable.

Yet it was good to think about Gabriel and the world beyond Derry. On nights like this, when sleep just would not come, Adam toured the walls, checking that the gates were locked and the night guards were awake and breathing – so many were dying on duty. It's not that he was in charge of what was left of Derry's army. There were still professional military men – generals and captains – organising the men, but he felt better after personally seeing that all was quiet.

It had rained earlier and Adam kept stepping into puddles, the cold water splashing up his legs. However, there were no bombs or cannonballs to frighten people out of a good night's sleep. Adam breathed a sigh of thanks before instantly worrying that he had been thankful too soon. Just because it was almost midnight did not mean the Jacobites were giving them a night off from terror. Now if he was a Jacobite general that's what he would do: lull the city into thinking there would be no trouble and then let them have it good and proper, when they least expected it.

But he wasn't a Jacobite general. He shuddered at the way his mind could work against him.

These days he carried rocks in his pocket just in case he spied a bird that he could make a meal out of. He had long given up hope of finding a stray cat or dog. Of course he knew that birds did not fly about in the dead of the night and even if they did, it would be impossible to take proper aim in the darkness. In any case it would appear that the birds had warned one another against landing anywhere near the walls of Derry. Only God could know how many hundreds had ended up flat on their backs on various dinner tables across the city.

Just then, he felt the less than stealthy approach of a

dizzy spell and stopped for a moment to deal with it. *How long could a person exist without proper food?* It was a good question but one he could not answer. Leaning against the wall of the nearest house, he closed his eyes in an attempt to absorb the dizziness. So far, no spell had proved strong enough to force him down to the ground and he was quite proud of this small truth. It was a personal challenge to endure the nausea and thundering fog, along with that strange prickling feeling beneath his skin, while he stubbornly remained on his feet.

Another silly habit had developed in recent days. Out of pure absent-mindedness, he had taken to running the palm of his hand over his own stomach, marvelling at how flat it was; in fact, he was quite sure it even dipped inwards now, like a valley on the plains. Where was the bump of extra flesh that had been a part of him for as long as he could remember?

There was also the thinning of his legs. It must have been the layer of fat that made it possible to endure hours in the saddle. Now he suffered from bruising and rubbed raw skin from the more pronounced chaffing against the leather.

Was it vanity that made him lament over the physical changes in the body that had never given him cause for anxiety? If only it was that simple. No, the truth could not be denied. Adam's strength was a fraction of what it had been in the days when he helped Gabriel on the farm. What man would not be affected at the thought that his masculinity, his very identity, was ebbing away like a pool of water drying up in the sun. It occurred to him that perhaps it was flesh that made people human; otherwise they were just a collection of bones.

'Oh, I must stop this brooding. Why is my mind filled with so much nonsense?'

He said the words aloud, desperate to distract his mind by making noise. It was time to head back to his bed. He opened his eyes thinking someone had called his name. It wouldn't do for him, the brave Adam Murray, to be found propped against a wall. Perhaps the inhabitants of the house had been disturbed by the sound of his voice. He paused to listen out for the sound of footsteps, expecting at any second to feel a hand on his shoulder. But no one came.

Blast! There's the rain again. He could not afford to get his clothes wet. It really was time to go back, but his body delayed in making the required movement.

Once more Adam thought of his father, wondering if this was what it was like to be old: your body losing respect for, or even interest in, your commands. Both his knees trembled in protest, refusing to take his weight just yet. He tried pleading with them, bartering with them. Had he no control over anything anymore?

The rain was cruel, blinding him, and soaking him right through, making him feel that he just might be the most miserable and lonely human being in Derry. *God help me!* Then he said the prayer aloud, 'Please, God help me!' because in saying those words he felt something shoot through him. As he pressed against the wall, the air around him seemed to lose the sharpness of the cold night. How peculiar!

What was that? Could he actually feel someone, or something, breathing softly right beside him? His face felt caressed by warmth, by tenderness. Adam begged himself to cease this madness. If he had to lose his strength, he was damned if he'd allow his sanity to go with it.

Nevertheless he didn't feel scared.

He heard his name being called but from where he couldn't decide. *Did I imagine it?* He peered up the street, unable to decide whether he'd actually prefer somebody – anybody – to arrive and give him their arm to lean upon.

Oh! Now he was shivering yet felt perfectly warm, as if he were already home and beneath his blankets. Perhaps he was and this was just a dream. Then he felt his hair lift slightly from the top of his head. That was the best way he could describe it. Was it the breeze at his hair? Well, then maybe it was the breeze calling his name? But would it sound like a woman?

A part of him feared he was losing his mind while

another part felt embraced. 'Mother?' He hadn't realised that he was going to call out. How could he recognise her voice when he had no real memories of her?

He was dying. It was the only sensible explanation. He could hear his mother's voice because she was coming for him. This was it. *Poor Gabriel*! Adam hated the thought of leaving him alone but what could he do? He was going to die here on this mucky path. He waited for his legs to give way.

'No, Adam!'

In the midst of everything he surely had not expected a debate. He repeated what she said. 'No?' He waited and then grew impatient with the throbbing silence. 'I'm not going to die?' Again he heard, 'No.' Was he alone? He couldn't see anyone else. But then he looked up into the night sky.

Did he really expect to see something, his mother's ghost or someone else's? With death all around him there could be any number of spirits walking the streets at night, complaining that they had yet to receive a proper burial. Adam was not entirely sure he believed in ghosts, but as he leaned against that cold wall, in the middle of the night, it occurred to him that if they did exist, they probably belonged to those relatives who wished their bodies to be treated with more respect than being dumped on the street or in a basement.

As usual, the stars blinked away merrily in the sky. Adam was comforted by the familiar sight. He tried to gauge where the moon was. His father was much better at this sort of thing. It was something he had always envied in Gabriel, his being so in tune with nature. As Adam stared a mist began to form, swishing and swirling itself into being. No doubt Gabriel could've explained it to him. It was as bright as the stars, and then it even surpassed them. He had seen spiders' webs that glistened in a certain light, but a mist that glowed in the night sky? Adam had never seen the likes of it before.

When he was a little boy, his father told him about a big, shiny star that looked like a ball of white flames and had a long tail of smoky light trailing after it. Only Gabriel didn't say it was a star; he called it a comet. Of course Adam trusted his father's explanation; that it was a piece of rock from some place the eye couldn't see. Adam fancied his father meant Heaven, although if the rock was aflame, maybe it was from Hell.

'Was it like a shooting star, Father?'

'No,' said Gabriel. 'It was much better than that. Imagine something the size of a big turnip streaking through the night sky, with a long tail like a flashing snake behind it.'

Flashing snake? How Adam had wished and wished he could see a comet for himself. He did his best to. Over the next few weeks he stood for hours each night in front of the window, hoping to see one, until he fell asleep with his elbows propped up on the window sill, and his head in his hands. And every night his father carried him to bed without waking him. How much simpler life had been back then.

So, what was he looking at now? It couldn't be a comet as it wasn't going anywhere.

The mass of mist seemed to be breathing in and out, looking for all the world as if it had a heartbeat. Adam rubbed his eyes, relieved to discover that on moving his hands from the wall he hadn't fallen to the ground. He decided to step away from the house in an effort to see as much of the sky as he could. Perhaps he hoped the immensity of the sky would dwarf the strange sight.

As he continued to watch, he could see that something was beginning to take shape. Yes, look at how the mist thickened here and there, almost pulling itself in until Adam gasped. *Was that actually a head, a face?* The features were blurred but, meanwhile, there was what looked like a neck, shoulders and chest. Arms too.

Adam blessed himself. Was this creation? Was something being born in front of him?

One of the arms seemed to hold aloft something that looked like a sword. Adam blinked heavily to be sure. Yes, it was still there and continuing to grow in size and detail until it was finished, until it just hung in the sky for Adam to see.

Now he did fall to his knees, but not because he felt dizzy; he was awed by the magnificence of this figure. He couldn't deny it: a huge, warrior angel sitting on a white horse. His wings stretched out behind him; they flared in the dark like the mane on his horse's neck.

Adam said the first words that came into his head because they were the truth. 'I don't know what to do!'

Whether he meant he didn't know what to do with this vision, or he was making a confession about matters as they stood, the angel seemed to hear him. Its two arms, sword and all, widened as if to embrace the stricken city. A moment passed, or maybe two or three at the most, and then there was an explosion of dazzling light. Adam shielded his eyes and when he looked up again the angel was gone and the sound he could hear was St Columb's bells ringing out for midnight.

CHAPTER TWENTY-FOUR

A robust discussion was taking place on the walls. King William had finally sent help in the form of ships laden with food and healthy soldiers – only the ships would not present themselves to Derry.

It was an exhilarating sight for the lookouts. Someone excitedly rang the bell of St Columb's, sounding out joy and relief to Derry's population, who all rushed to the walls to drink in the wondrous sight of the Williamite fleet in the far distance.

Over by Ship Quay Gate, Daniel, Robert, James and Henry roared in delight with Daniel gasping, 'But how many ships are there?'

The others were too busy celebrating, so he squinted his eyes and counted as best he could, finally declaring, 'Twenty ships, I think. That's an entire army, surely?'

Beside him, Henry and Robert were waving their arms while singing in unison, 'We're saved; we're saved!'

Three cannons were readied and fired from the walls, in hearty welcome. How everyone cheered when the ships made their answer, sounding like thunder rolling through the distant skies. Whiffs of black smoke sauntered off the ships before disappearing.

Impatience grew alongside excitement; the ships seemed to be hardly moving. Indeed, they remained a long way off. It soon became apparent that the fleet had dropped anchor way out in the bay, much to the confusion and disappointment of the citizens of Derry.

Some hours later, as darkness fell, torches were lit along the walls to guide the ships into the Foyle but the ships remained where they were.

Henry was the first to shed the initial euphoria, muttering, 'I don't like this. Something doesn't feel right.' He stared out at the boom and shook his head.

Robert followed his gaze to an ominous barricade that they could all see snaking its way from one side of the Foyle to the other.

The Jacobites had concocted a boom, specifically to prevent ships coming to Derry's rescue. It was built to withstand the big ships, to halt their approach, allowing the Jacobites to pummel the vessel with cannonballs from the far banks.

A stalemate had been reached. As the days continued to start and end without any sign of relief coming from the fleet, despondency set in behind the walls of Derry.

Daniel was horrified when Henry's sense of foreboding proved to be correct. He had thought it was just the usual showing off, Henry always wanting to lead the response within their group of friends, and – unlike Robert – he had ignored Henry's worried expression, believing it was simply for their benefit.

Finally, after many days, there was movement, but it caused great upset on the walls. The boys and their fellow lookouts stood, ashen faced, as they watched the ships sail *away* from the city.

Daniel could only repeat over and over again, 'But why? Why are they leaving us?'

Nobody could provide an answer. Even Henry Campsie was stumped.

Later, the city learnt that the fleet had made its way into Lough Swilly and set up base about twelve miles away at Inch Island.

Henry declared the ships' captains to be immoral or unworthy men. 'Where are they? Are we all to waste away before they reach us?'

His listeners, Robert, Daniel, James Morrison and a few others, were as mystified as he was.

Robert sighed. 'They are afraid of the boom smashing up their ships. It's no use to us either if all that lovely food ends up at the bottom of the river Foyle.'

Henry spat, refusing to be appeased by this explanation.

Robert persisted. 'And it's not just the danger of the boom. I mean, how many Jacobite cannons are poised on the banks of the Foyle to fire upon any ship that dares to approach us?'

'Ha!' snapped Henry. 'They need not worry about the number of guns since they are clearly too cowardly to act. King William would be furious if he was here!'

The idea of their king standing beside them was a pleasing one. James Morrison nodded and said, 'I bet a lot of things would be different if William was here. Why, he'd thumb his nose at James and say, "I have won! Derry is mine!"'

Completely out of sorts, Henry snarled, 'Derry is his!' He glared at James who refused to cower.

Daniel marvelled at James's cheek as he heard him say clearly, 'Henry Campsie, are you giving me the evil eye? Do you doubt my allegiance now, along with the ships' captains?'

Henry would not make a reply.

Tempers were short these days. The guards were hungry, exhausted and by now every man had lost someone to hunger or disease. The sun had not been seen in some time despite the fact that it was the second of July, while the constant smell of rotting bodies, faeces and urine would wear down anyone's resistance.

Daniel wanted to change the subject or at least move the talk to more positive ground. 'I bet the Jacobites didn't think they'd be here so long.'

Everyone nodded to that. One of the other guards added, 'I've heard they're in a bad way too, thanks to the bad weather and lack of grub.'

Even though he knew it was a silly question, Daniel asked, 'Why don't they just go home then?'

His brother sighed. 'I'm sure they'd love to but they have their orders too.'

The boys stared over at the Jacobite camp that was sprawled behind Windmill Hill. In truth the distance was too great to make out much detail of the foe; nevertheless it was readily agreed that the Catholic soldiers were not doing much on this wretched and gloomy afternoon. As the boys stood together in moody silence, someone's stomach growled pathetically; surely their bellies knew by now that they could growl all they liked, it was not going to make food magically appear.

'What's going on there?' James peered hard to the right, pointing as he appealed to the others, 'See? There!'

A large group of people was moving slowly into sight. Daniel strained his ears to hear any sound of voices but there was none to be heard. The people, whoever they were, trudged in silence. If they were coming to Derry, they still had some ground to cover.

Henry called down for a telescope to be fetched, while Robert asked nobody in particular, 'Are they coming this way?'

James, sounding upset, said, 'I don't think they're wearing any clothes.'

'What?' said Henry. 'Don't be daft!'

A telescope was put in his hands and the others waited for his report. Immediately he cried out, 'They *are* naked. I don't believe this! Someone'd better get Adam Murray.'

Adam arrived to find the boys in quite a state. Not one of them attempted to explain why they had summoned him; instead he was handed the telescope and shown where to direct it. A crowd began to gather below, sensing that something serious was afoot.

Shaking off his wearisome dizziness, Adam put the telescope to his eye. Daniel watched as he clenched his jaw and noted how his knuckles whitened with tension. How many minutes passed before he said anything? And what he said shocked the group. 'Whatever happens, don't let them in.'

The boys glanced at one another, hoping that one of their number understood the peculiar order. Robert determined not to ask for an explanation. Looking at the puzzled faces around him, Adam added grimly, 'You'll probably know some of them but we cannot let them in.'

So, all they did was stand there and watch as that pitiful group got closer and closer. It was a horrible sight. A crowd of maybe two thousand strong, men, women and children, all shivering as they walked, heads bowed in shame at their nakedness and bowed in defeat under the lashes of the cruel wind and rain. Daniel gaped in bewilderment. *How had so many people managed to lose their clothes?*

Here and there he thought he recognised a face, but it was difficult to be sure. Their nakedness obscured vague recollections about having either seen them in church in St Columb's or going about their business around the market stalls in the Diamond.

The women and children were crying, while the men looked desperate and useless. Nobody said a word as the crowd approached the gate. The people of Derry looked as uncomfortable as the newcomers.

One man, who walked in front, called out in a hoarse voice, 'Don't let us in!'

This was unexpected. Indeed, some of those on the cityside were moved to shout out, 'What do you mean? Why are you here?'

A young child, watching from the walls, could be clearly heard asking the obvious question, 'Where are their clothes, Mama?'

The man spoke again, 'Lieutenant-General de Rosen had us stripped and brought here so that you'd pity us enough to bring us in.'

Accordingly, a sudden cry went out from the residents, 'Let them in. Open the gates!'

At that moment, Adam was relieved to see newly

appointed Governor Walker make his way through to the gate. He raised an arm for silence as he stood in front of it. Adam stood by, ready to show his support for the reverend, should he require it.

Governor Walker gave a sombre nod to the people outside the gate before turning back to his own. 'We can't allow these poor souls in because it is part of Lieutenant-General de Rosen's plan that we bring them in, divide our remaining food with them and be left with nothing at all in no time.'

Naturally there were those listeners who understood what he was saying, while the more sensitive individuals could not believe their ears, that the church leader was refusing shelter to their neighbours and relatives.

Seeing the disgusted expressions on some of the faces, Adam took a deep breath and moved to stand beside Reverend Walker. He deliberately kept his back to the outsiders because he did not want to see their misery up close in case he faltered in his belief that they had to be kept at bay. He did his best to deafen his ears against the sound of sobbing and hacking coughs while he said loudly, 'Reverend Walker is right. The Frenchman is trying to trick all of us. This is just a bluff!'

To his mortification he heard a voice behind him say, 'How can that fellow be so unfeeling? Isn't it well for him in his coat and boots?'

Adam called back to the man, who seemed to be the spokesperson for the shivering crowd, 'I am so sorry for your trouble; I truly am!'

The man believed him. 'You haven't inflicted this upon us.' His voice shook with the cold, and it was with an apologetic look that he wrapped his arms around his middle. 'No, this is not your fault, sir. If Derry falls we all fall.'

Adam and Reverend Walker exchanged a glance as they tried to gauge the response of the city's population. They needn't have worried. Adam had hit a nerve when he said the Frenchman was trying to trick them. He could see the realisation in their faces and he felt only scorn for Lieutenant-General de Rosen. *Who did he take them for? Did he not realise that his shameful plan would only make them more determined than ever? What an awful man to put these innocents through such barbaric treatment.*

Now, what? These two words surged from the pit of Adam's being. *Now, what? Are we to stand here gaping at one another?*

However, Governor Walker was already one step ahead of him. He fired out an order. 'Gather the Jacobite prisoners together and bring them to where they can be seen, to the double bastion between Bishop's and Butchers' Gate.' The governor paused – for effect, no doubt – before adding, 'and put up the gallows.'

He gave Adam a questioning look, one that Adam

replied to by nodding his head in agreement. De Rosen had left them with no choice.

The prisoners numbered twenty and had been taken alive during the various skirmishes led by Adam. They were allowed to live because, in a siege situation, it is wise to have hostages for such moments as these.

Reverend Walker called for paper and ink and, using the wall itself, began a letter to the enemy. The reverend fought to keep a tight rein on his emotions yet could not help confessing to Adam, 'I would love to take the opportunity to name them as servants of the Devil, himself. I mean, how else to explain this monstrosity.' He sighed heavily. 'But I suppose I have to be polite and professional.'

Not knowing how to respond to this, Adam stared at the governor's letter. He could not have guessed that it was his personal show of support that boosted the reverend's confidence. Quite honestly, Governor Walker seemed to be relishing his role as the one who knew exactly what to do.

He wrote large, adding twists and curls to letters that did not require them. He read his letter aloud, 'To Whom It May Concern …' To Adam, he said, 'After all, there are so many of them over there now and who is to know who exactly is in charge? Is it the French, the Irish or the English?'

Adam merely shrugged at this, concerned that there

was a little too much casual conversation on display in front of the downtrodden crowd who had nothing to do except watch the governor and the young colonel. How he wished that they would move away to where he didn't feel their sorrowful eyes upon him.

'Wait a minute.' The reverend had thought of something else to write and scribbled hard against the wall. He said to Adam, 'I'm a God-fearing man, as you know, and I've explained that we will hang our prisoners if these refugees are not allowed home. But I've added that we'll allow their priests in to prepare them for death. It shows them that we're serious.'

Adam was impressed but would not admit it to the reverend who seemed to be waiting to be complimented on his wonderful idea. As much as this sort of peacock behaviour grated on him, Adam did envy the reverend for the enormous sense of belief he had in himself.

A messenger was despatched to the Jacobite camp. Now, there was nothing to do except wait.

The people of Derry moved away from the walls but did so slowly in the hope that the ones on the other side wouldn't feel abandoned. Even more rain fell. Adam had hoped that the weather might take pity on the naked crowd and allow the sun to warm them, but no such luck.

He was unsure what to do himself as the good reverend made for the cathedral, in order to pray, he said, for a timely solution to the matter in hand. For a second or two, Adam considered following him, putting space and the walls of St Columb's between him and the poor unfortunates milling about. However, he was his father's son and, therefore, not surprised when his legs refused to take him away from the wall. Instead, he found himself calling down to the spokesman and asking his name.

'Samuel Clebourne,' the man said, adding, 'I'm a school teacher.'

'Nice to meet you, Samuel,' said Adam. 'I'm Adam Murray.'

Samuel smiled. 'Yes, I know who you are, Colonel Murray. We all do. You're the one who is going to save us.'

Adam was stunned by the teacher's words which had been spoken with absolute conviction. Doing his best to mask his confusion and come up with some sort of response, Adam couldn't help noticing quite a few heads bobbing up and down in agreement. He tried, 'I don't … that is, I don't know. I'm not sure …' Adam felt dizzy.

Using his shoulder to flick the raindrops from his nose, Samuel said, 'In the years to come people might well wonder what this was all about.'

As casually as he could, Adam leant the top half of his body against the wall, hoping that it merely looked as if he was interested in what Samuel was saying and not that he feared he was about to fall down at any moment.

'Not just this,' Samuel was saying, gesturing at himself and his soaked neighbours. 'I mean, all of it. Keeping the gates closed when it would be so much easier to let the Jacobites in, especially after James assured us he wouldn't punish anyone.'

Adam couldn't help himself; he whispered, 'I cannot imagine that it will make much sense at all.' It was the first time he had admitted this.

Samuel shook his head dolefully. 'No, probably not. But I generally find that the big things that really matter – things like love, duty and truth – don't always make sense. In the end, you just do what you feel is right.'

Samuel might have said more except he succumbed to a coughing fit, reminding himself and Adam of the horrible position he was in. Adam couldn't imagine what it would be like to be naked in this weather, not knowing how long they would have to wait until they could go home again.

They probably expect me to do something and here I am, just talking away like it's an ordinary day and I've nothing better to be doing.

He was relieved to have his attention diverted by his guards and the Jacobite prisoners. No doubt Samuel meant well, but on this wet Tuesday afternoon the responsibility and expectation that Adam felt was too heavy for his thin shoulders.

Nodding a curt salute to Samuel, who had managed to

catch his breath and stop coughing, Adam followed the others to the bastion while his thoughts crashed about inside his head. He was pleased at the shock and bafflement on the Jacobite prisoners' faces on seeing the vast crowd of freezing men, women and children huddled in front of the city walls. One of the more senior officers didn't have any qualms about voicing his surprise, 'What on earth is going on? Why are they naked?'

Adam answered him, 'They are our Protestant neighbours. Your Lieutenant-General de Rosen rounded them up from nearby villages, stripped them and marched them here in the belief that we'd have to take them in, all these extra mouths, to finish the last of our food but ...' Here, Adam experienced a surge of pride. 'But they won't come in.'

The officer scowled. 'That fool, de Rosen! King James will have his head for this!' The man went on to study the crowd and muttered, 'No, this isn't right at all!'

Adam shrugged and said, 'You should know that we have sent a message threatening to hang all of you if these people are not sent home.'

The prisoners glanced at one another and then out beyond to their fellow soldiers in the distance. Not one of them showed the slightest hint of fear.

'Governor Walker has asked for your priests to come over. They'll be allowed to see you and make the necessary preparations.'

The officer made no comment on this; he was more concerned about something else. He said, 'We are soldiers of King James.' He was obliged to ignore the rude sounds of grunting and spitting from the large crowd of onlookers in order to continue. 'What I mean is, we should die by the pistol not be hung like common criminals.'

'Or,' offered Adam, 'Lieutenant-General de Rosen could allow these people go free and you and your men can go back to jail?'

The officer conceded, 'Well, yes, that would be the best outcome. No denying that.'

For those few minutes Adam and the Jacobite officer could have been any men, any place in the world – two acquaintances gadding about the day's work. Instead, they were on the walls of Derry, a Jacobite and a Williamite, drenched from the rain and yearning for a hot dinner that wasn't to be had. They looked out at the hill across from them, each thinking the same thing. *Where, in God's name, is this going to end?*

Neither Lieutenant-General de Rosen nor his Irish counterpart Colonel Hamilton were impressed by Derry's threat to hang the prisoners. This was war after all and the death of soldiers was only to be expected.

Governor Walker scoffed at the fact that not one priest had turned up to administer the last rites to the Jacobites. He had them write to their immediate superior, Colonel

Hamilton, not to plead for their lives – they were happy to give their lives for King James – but that they didn't want to die like common criminals. They wrote:

Driving the prisoners to the wall has enraged the garrison. We are to be killed unless they are withdrawn immediately. We should die with our swords in our hands. We beg you to speak on our behalf to Marshal de Rosen.

Like his king, Colonel Hamilton was known for his dislike of killing civilians. However, his reply was a short note stating that the naked Protestants had only themselves to blame. They should have begged Derry to take them in. Meanwhile, the only comfort he offered his own men was that their deaths would be avenged, which was truly no comfort at all.

In other words, everyone was at a standstill for the rest of that miserable day. Nobody was to sleep much as darkness fell. Of course it rained and the wind howled throughout the night.

Adam tossed and turned, wondering how many of the crowd would be dead before the morning. He swore he could hear their moans beneath the wind, and the hopelessness of it all burned in his empty stomach. *What kind of men make hundreds and hundreds of ordinary folk spend a night out in that without a blessed stitch between them?*

There had been an attempt to scrounge some food to smuggle out to the desperate crowd, but there really wasn't much to give. Also, Adam knew that refusing their fellow Protestants entry into the city hadn't been a popular decision but it was a necessary one for Derry's sake.

Nevertheless, the physical appearance of the pathetic crowd, which was all too obvious, did provoke some jealousy amongst the hungry population. For instance, Adam had clearly heard one woman loudly proclaiming, 'Them folk had their breakfast before they got here. Look at the plumpness of them! It's plain to see *they've* not gone without food.'

Adam had gritted his teeth and taken a deep breath. Food wasn't the only thing in short supply at this stage: mercy and kindness were becoming scarce too. The worst of it was that Adam had found he could not ignore her words. To his mortification he had realised he agreed with her. They did look well-fed, though he knew that at least he and the rest of his fellow citizens still had their clothes. *We're all prisoners, no matter what side of the gate we're on.*

As he lay sleepless on his mattress, his hunger assailed him again. 'Oh my God!' He said this aloud but it wasn't a prayer. An idea had sprung out of the darkness of his mind. 'We're all prisoners? So be it!'

He left his bed and made his way to the bastion wall in search of Reverend Walker and found him up by the Jacobite prisoners who all seemed in dire need of a wash. The churchman looked up at the young officer's arrival. Adam greeted him. 'I was just looking for you, sir. I've thought of something we can do with the group!' He spoke quietly so that only the reverend could hear him.

After the previous long, long evening, Governor Walker was open to ideas about anything at all. This waiting for something to happen was bad for his nerves. There had been no positive response to his letter yet, aside from Colonel Hamilton's snippiness, which he had convinced himself was only a temporary response. Surely the man would not allow this situation to continue much longer. The governor found it hard to concentrate on much else as he waited, and hoped, to hear from Colonel Hamilton a second time.

He stepped forward to meet Adam and they moved farther away from the Jacobite soldiers and their own guards.

'Let's make a secret exchange!' Adam's eyes shone as he spoke. 'We sneak out some of our sickest people to join the crowd and take in some of their healthy men to boost our army.'

Expecting to have to explain himself further, Adam opened his mouth to say more but there was no need. Governor Walker actually punched him in the arm, by way of thanks, and called the two Sherrard boys over, only telling them: 'Colonel Murray needs your help. Do whatever he asks of you!'

Adam's first order was an easy one. 'Follow me!'

CHAPTER TWENTY-FIVE

Some of the older soldiers did not want to leave Derry. They had stood guard on the wall from the very beginning. It was up to Robert and Daniel to find them, wake them up if necessary and tell them that Adam Murray needed them to go.

Robert found the guard, who all those months ago had taken a chance and handed him the keys of the gate. He was in a bad way; his mouth was a curve of open sores and Robert wasn't entirely sure that the man could see him because his eyes looked like they had been dipped in milk. Assuming that the man probably had gone blind, Robert felt free to take a step back from him. The guard's breath was dreadful, and a second smell, that caused Robert's own eyes to water, told him that the poor fellow was no longer in charge of his bodily functions. Yet, despite all this, the guard wanted to stay and fight.

'But I can't go now. It wouldn't be right, I'm no coward!'

Robert shook his head, forgetting about the man's possible blindness. 'It's nothing to do with being a coward. Actually, it's the opposite.'

How many times more would he have to say this today?

Adam wanted a hundred men at the very least. It was proving difficult to keep count, especially when men like this guard, who felt that Derry was expelling them as failures, required more than a few words of coaxing.

The guard persisted. 'Let some other man take my place. I can still hold my sword.'

Robert doubted if the man could stand by himself, never mind swing a heavy sword. 'You're right,' he said. 'Some other man will take your place.' He paused to allow his listener to think about this. Then he said, 'We're going to switch you for one of the fellows outside the gate, a fresh fighter. They haven't been starving like we have.'

Tears rolled down the guard's face as he accepted what Robert was saying.

Robert bid himself to be kind. 'There's no need to feel shame. You have given your all and now you are being asked to go one step further. I warn you, what you are being asked to do is not easy.'

At this the guard forgot his sadness and sat up a little straighter.

Robert knew he was winning this little battle. 'Do you hear that wind and rain? Well, Derry needs you to remove your clothes and spend the rest of the day outside.'

The boy could see the guard running through all this in his mind and added, 'It is of great personal risk. Really, you would be risking your life in these wet conditions, particularly after months of reduced rations.'

The guard began to smile and now he nodded his head, saying, 'Yes, yes, I understand. And you say that Colonel Murray has expressly ordered me to do this?'

Before Robert could answer him, the guard stretched out a scrawny arm. 'Begging your pardon, sir, but if you would be so kind as to help me up and out of my shirt. It's just I get a little dizzy.'

Robert offered, 'You can leave it on until we reach the gate.'

The guard, however, wouldn't hear of this. This was his chance to take command of himself. 'No, sir. Best I take it off now, for the colonel and for Derry.'

On the other side of the city Daniel led a group of grumbling ancient warriors towards Bishop's Gate. Thoroughly frustrated, he felt that snails could crawl faster than the men were walking.

'Of course, you're young!' One of the men kept muttering this as if that fact was Daniel's fault.

Fortunately it was too dark, and the soldiers were too caught up in their ailing bodies to notice the black looks that Daniel fired at them. *Did they have to be so slow? Did that fool Scarrow have to keep coughing like that; it was disgusting. Why was this taking so long?*

His thoughts weren't exactly charitable. Since Horace's

death he hardly recognised himself. There were days where he felt he had been cruelly tricked into taking part in something that he should never have got involved with. He knew it did not make a whit of sense because if he somehow was given the opportunity to do it all over again, he knew he would do the exact same thing again, that is follow Robert and the others and help close the gates. *But nobody told me that my dog would have to die.*

He had said as much to his father who upset him deeply by asking if he would have preferred his baby sister or his mother to die in Horace's place. It was a horrible question and also, Daniel felt, an unfair one. *Is my father actually criticising me for mourning my pet?*

These had been his waking thoughts and, thus, explained his appalling bad mood.

This miserable lot are being handed their freedom. Why can't they move faster?

Scarrow started whining again, in between creaking gasps for air, 'Oh, why won't he slow down?'

Daniel bit his lip but ended up saying anyway, 'Just be glad you're getting out of here. How can you want to delay a moment more, for God's sake?'

His three followers were too exhausted to form a reply to this so Daniel was free to continue berating them. 'You get to go somewhere else, where they don't eat dogs or people's pets!'

His anger, however, wasn't strong enough to carry him when his own strength dwindled. Therefore, it was with great bitterness that he had to slow down, accidentally giving in to the useless Scarrow.

Because he had time to think, the most outrageous thought formed in his mind. He could strip off and slip out with the sick soldiers or – even better – he could hit one of these fools over the head with a rock and take their place. He could do it; he really could. And go somewhere else where they don't make you eat your best friend.

He yelped out a word, a bad word, one he had never dared to say aloud before, but now he sent it bouncing off the walls and the stones beneath his feet. It summed up everything, all his frustrations and his mixed-up feelings about Derry and even his family.

The men didn't chastise him; words like that were part of their daily conversation. They merely shrugged their bony shoulders in agreement, not that Daniel noticed.

At Bishop's Gate, Adam was busy. As the Sherrard brothers delivered their charges, and then returned for more, it was Adam who held the gate open, just enough to allow the sick to squeeze through and then have their substitute come through from the other side.

The bad weather was both a hindrance and a help. On the one side it was not pleasant to be out in it but, on the other side, the Jacobites preferred to be out of it too and kept to their camp.

Each naked body that came in was quickly given clothes and told to take their place on the walls. The new men were glad to be of service and glad to be wearing clothes again, although they could have done with a bowl of soup after their ordeal. However, they quickly understood the city's plight; there really was little food to be had, other than small tallow pancakes that were flavoured with ginger.

Samuel Clebourne was among the new men. He shook Adam's hand warmly. 'Thank you, sir. I won't let you down!'

A couple of hours later, Adam decided that enough people had been swapped. He told the Sherrard boys to return to their posts, noting how exhausted they looked. He had forgotten which one was older and younger; they were both so thin and pale. *Of course*, he reminded himself, *I probably look as bad as they do*.

The new men stood out as if they had a light shining on them. It inspired confidence in him that there was plenty of fight left in Derry.

So, now, we wait once more, he told himself.

The following day the naked crowd outside the walls was shepherded over to Windmill Hill, to wait yet again for what, nobody was sure.

Throughout all this the bombs continued to fall. Bishop's Gate was taking a right battering and the walls either side of it needed constant attention and the reapplying of mud and stone. Fortunately these were two items that were still plentiful in the city.

Governor Walker was adamant that any able-bodied soldier must now stay on the wall. He walked about with his notebook and pencil, constantly counting things like musket balls while also making lists of what foodstuffs were left, along with the number of soldiers who had died that day. He didn't share with anyone else that he was keeping a daily record of events.

It had started accidentally. One day he busied himself listing out the food measurements, for he was in charge of doling out the soldiers' rations. Next, he thought he should list the prices of the foods that were available to buy, along with their prices: 2*s* 6*d* for a dog's head; 1*s* for a rat and 4*s* 6*d* for a cat. Gradually it occurred to him that he should write everything down. For one thing it gave him something to do and it reminded him that there would come a time when the siege would be over – nothing lasts forever – and people might like to understand how it had been for him and his parishioners, what they had gone through for God and for King William.

He blotted his paper, one evening, after describing how a certain citizen of ample proportions had not left his house in days because he felt his neighbours might wish to kill him in order to make a meal of his wobbly belly.

Oh, he wasn't entirely sure if it was true or not but it made a good story.

He smiled and nodded his head, looking for his cat to share his excitement with. However, the poor creature had gone the way of other pets. After all, just the same as everyone else, the reverend had had to make sacrifices, including parting with his collection of beer and butter, but that was a long time ago now and best forgotten. He wouldn't be writing that particular story down.

Yet, his ambition was being realised: *I will write about everything and then, when this is all finally over, I will publish it as a book. My own book!*

He puffed out his chest and continued aloud, 'My book will be known as the one and true account. Yes, yes, the king and queen themselves will read it.'

The reverend took a clean sheet of paper, dipped his pen in ink and, with a worthy sniff, wrote in large, confident letters:

A TRUE ACCOUNT OF THE SIEGE OF DERRY

BY

REVEREND GEORGE WALKER

He peered over what he had written, holding the page up to the flame of the candle, turning it this way and that, highlighting one letter at a time. Who would doubt the written word?

From the city walls a shout went up. 'Look! They're leaving.'

James Morrison, Robert and Daniel followed the sound of the voice, just in time to see the crowd of naked parishioners being led off in the direction they had come from.

James took a guess. 'They must be bringing them home.'

The brothers felt he must be right. Daniel also felt relieved but he wasn't sure why. Something niggled at him. What was it? As they watched the sprawling crowd recede into the distance, he realised what it was. Now, he had to decide whether to keep it to himself or not. After all it was only his opinion and what did he know?

Still, at the heart of his understanding beat his rage over what had happened to Horace. The world was a different place since 'that' day, or maybe it was just that he had changed. He made sure to say the words as casually and lightly as he could. The last thing he wanted to do was provoke a heated debate that he didn't have the energy for.

''Tis strange that!' he sighed.

Robert glanced at James, leaving him to be the cooperative one.

'What do you mean?' asked James. 'What's strange?'

Daniel looked at him and looked away again as if he were embarrassed.

The reliable James was intrigued. 'What is it, Daniel?'

How he hated to be left out of anything.

Daniel ignored his brother's obvious growing discomfort, while poor James was oblivious to all.

Meanwhile, Robert sensed a tingle of his brother's attitude. He stared hard at the multitude in the distance, prepared for just about anything. Daniel was so moody and peculiar these days. His father said he was grieving for Horace, and that grief affected different people in different ways.

Daniel leant against the wall and lied, 'Well, it has only just struck me that no massacre ever occurred.'

James scrunched up his face to make sense of this but he needn't have bothered. Daniel didn't want his conversation side-tracked and continued, 'All those hundreds and hundreds of people out there with no clothes and no weapons. The Papists could have slaughtered them all but they didn't. It would have been so easy … but, they didn't hurt them at all.'

Against his better judgement, Robert queried quietly, 'So?'

By now James had figured out that he wasn't required to make a contribution.

Daniel repeated his brother's word, 'So? Oh, nothing. I was just thinking out loud.'

Robert wiped his nose with the back of his hand. 'I'm glad they are being allowed home, but that doesn't mean that we are out of danger yet. Those people didn't close the gates on the Jacobite army or fire on a king. We may still be made to pay for all of that.'

James wanted to add something else. 'Have you forgotten that the ships William sent are somewhere out there?'

He was surprised at the scowls on the brothers' faces and added, 'Why would we give up now that help is almost here?'

Robert replied before Daniel could name his own feelings. 'He doesn't know what he means.'

It wasn't kind, but then again it wasn't meant to be.

Robert felt as prickly as if it was his father standing in front of him. He felt keenly that his younger brother was trying to provoke him, wanting to make the point that everything they had gone through, everything they were going through and everyone they had lost had been for nothing. Well, Robert was not prepared to play along or act the least bit guilty. After all, he missed Horace too.

In any case, it was James who persisted with Daniel. 'Have you lost your faith in us?'

Daniel hesitated. His head hurt, and the questions in his mind were too big and too many.

Both brothers were startled when James suddenly leapt to the front of the bastion, collected as much spit as he could inside his mouth and spat it over the wall, watching it fall, fall until he could no longer see it. James breathed heavily, with the effort, and bent over slightly to steady himself. Hunger had reduced his strength considerably. He glanced from one Sherrard to the other. When he was able, he said, 'It's easier to just make a decision and stick with it, no matter what.' He thought for a moment before saying, 'This whole thing will be something to tell our grand-children!'

Robert smirked, not unkindly. 'You do know that you have to find a girl who will marry you before you can start dreaming about having grandchildren.'

In spite of everything, Robert and Daniel laughed at the expression on James's face.

Their friend just winked and tapped his index finger against his nose. 'Oh, don't you worry about me, boys. I just have to decide which one I want.'

Daniel added, 'You mean which one will have you.'

James shrugged. 'Ach, same thing!'

CHAPTER TWENTY-SIX

Robert and Daniel were on the wall when they heard shouting from the Jacobite camp. To their horror they could see that the Jacobites had hastily constructed a gallows from which a sodden body dangled. The enemy soldiers were doing their damnedest to get the attention of the city's guards, hollering and pointing at the corpse, while also taking the opportunity to make coarse, rude signs with their fingers. They put on quite a show complete with lots of laughter, as if mocking the dead man.

Appalled, Daniel barely waited for Robert to focus the telescope on the scene, before demanding to know, 'Who is it? Do we know him?'

Meanwhile, Henry Campsie had raced to their side and lifted his rifle to fire at the soldiers. It was Robert who snarled at him not to waste time or precious bullets. Despite the state of the body, Robert recognised him as the plucky McGimpsey, a Derry man who had bravely volunteered to swim up the Foyle, past the Jacobites, all the way to the Williamite fleet, carrying letters from the governors describing the state of Derry and urging Major-General Kirke to come to their rescue before it was too late. Robert shook his head in sorrow. McGimpsey had been a favourite of his; he'd always had a joke ready to cheer up his fellow guardsmen.

'Oh my God!' was Henry's response. 'Do you mean to say that they have actually murdered him?'

Robert passed him the telescope saying slowly, 'No. I think the poor fellow drowned, judging from his pallor. They must have found his body and decided to have their fun by taunting us.'

'Fun,' gasped Daniel.

Robert shrugged an apology while Henry growled, 'Yes, the curs are signalling that he drowned. They keep pointing at the river.' He offered Daniel the telescope but he refused it.

The Sherrard boys alerted both governors and Adam Murray. The mood on the wall was sombre.

Adam Murray offered, 'It would have been a hard swim for any man under any circumstances.'

He longed to say more, to curse Kirke for his stubbornness and stupid fear. *Derry is dying and still that fool will not come. What does he imagine the city to be living on at this point?*

Governor Baker stated the obvious. 'Well, now the enemy has our letters they know how badly off we are, just how little food and bullets we possess to get us through the next few weeks, if even that.'

The situation was alarming and depressing to say the least. Even as the miserable group stood there, the bombs began to fly over the walls once more.

A few nights later about two hundred Jacobite soldiers followed their commander to the outskirts of Butchers' Gate and proceeded to throw bombs into the trenches built by the Williamites.

Governor Baker, who was suffering from shortness of breath and overwhelming fatigue, determined to lead the counter-attack. 'They are daring to do this because they know how vulnerable we are. We must put up a fight as a show of strength, if nothing else.'

Even as his soldiers began to prepare to exit Derry, they could hear, much to their horror, Jacobites just outside Butchers' Gate; one man was clearly heard calling for a torch. 'Let's set fire to the gate!'

Meanwhile, someone on the wall shouted out that there were Jacobites approaching the Gunner's Bastion, mere yards from Butchers' Gate, with spades and picks in their hands.

Governor Baker was appalled. 'They're going to try to collapse the wall!'

With every breath in his feeble body, he summoned his soldiers back to the wall. 'Take your position and fire on my command!'

Fear was no longer an option. There was no time to think so the various leaders spurred their soldiers into action.

Adam Murray led about sixty men out of Bishop's Gate, ignoring the weakness in his legs as he kept up a tremendous pace, praying to God for help and strength. As soon as he and his men got close enough to the Jacobite party that was posted to protect the diggers at Gunner's Bastion, they fired on them, sending them running.

'Re-load! Re-load,' roared Adam needlessly since his men were already doing just that. No one was going to allow a single moment to pass without attempting to blast a hole through a Jacobite soldier.

Shots rained down from the walls as the two governors and the rest of the soldiers, as well as civilians who could use a rifle, fired at the Jacobite soldiers. The noise was tremendous, while Governor Walker forbade himself to think about all the musket balls that were being used up.

He saw his co-governor sprint along the wall, urging everyone to keep firing as fast as possible.

To the city's immense relief, the Jacobites fled, the volume of rifle fire being unexpected. Once the danger was removed, the Williamites' adrenalin evaporated, leaving a lot of men quite literally leaning against the wall to stop themselves folding to the ground from the exertion and stress.

It had been so close, so close. Women who had once cheered their men now cried openly in shock. Children were too stunned to do much other than cling to their mothers.

Governor Baker found it necessary to bend forward, willing his heart to return to normal. His face was covered in sweat and his vision was blurred. He realised now just how ill he was but, nevertheless, he congratulated those around him, in between painful gulps of breath, saying, 'Well done, well done!'

It was this generosity and determination that George Walker alluded to in his homily, just two days later, on Sunday, 30 June, at Governor Baker's funeral, saying 'His death is a terrible loss for Derry. His courage and good humour will be missed.'

Mr Sherrard had done all he could for the governor, but they both knew it was useless though, typically, even as he was dying, Baker had thought to thank the physician for his attention and care.

Furthermore the governor wanted to leave Derry in good hands and had, therefore, nominated Colonel John Mitchelburne to be his successor. And so Mitchelburne's first sad task as co-governor, with George Walker, was to help to carry his predecessor's coffin, not at all embarrassed by the tears that ran down his face.

The second thing he did was to have a red flag flown

from the tower at St Columb's, which served both to show the city's defiance in the face of the Jacobites and to signal to Major-General Kirke and the Williamite fleet just how perilous the city's state was.

CHAPTER TWENTY-SEVEN

Mrs Sherrard made her way to the cathedral. It had recently become a habit of hers to spend ten or fifteen minutes a day praying to God that all this would come to an end.

She had become used to stepping over the bodies in the street. The trick was not to look too closely. If it was dark enough some of them looked like bundles or clothes or logs. Of course she had heard the stories of bodies being cut up for food. She was quite sure she couldn't eat a human body; oh yes, quite, quite sure.

God must have meant this to happen. There was no other way to explain it. 'No other way!' Sometimes she spoke out loud to herself, taking comfort from the sound of her own voice. There were fewer and fewer people left to talk to. So many of her friends and neighbours were lying dead in the basements of their houses. Their families couldn't squeeze them into the graveyards and wouldn't have them out on the streets, so into the basements they went, accidentally infecting the atmosphere with the poisonous stench that would not go away.

She was forced to stop every few steps to catch her breath. Her heart thumped in her chest from the least bit of movement and she had to keep catching the front of her dress so that she wouldn't trip herself up. Now that she was so thin her dresses were too long. She put a hand to her mouth to try and stop the smell. What kept her going was the fright that she might fall down here and not be found. What if she fainted and somebody looking for a tasty morsel thought she was dead? No, she mustn't think about that. She simply mustn't fall down.

The dirt was everywhere. Filth clung to her shoes, while sludgy puddles splashed up her calves. It was too much. *No, I can't think about that either. I'm only one person. God can't mean for me to clean up this whole mess. It's absurd.*

Meanwhile her own house was spotless. Well, what else was there for her to do? If she couldn't make meals for her family, she could scrub the furniture, brush the floors and wash the walls. The house was her domain, her world, no matter what king sat on the throne.

Dirt was evil. She believed that more than ever. Dirt represented the city's misfortunes, a city in peril. Oh, she knew that Derry had been built out of the earth. What city hasn't?

Her lips curled as she turned a corner and the onslaught of urine and vomit made her gag. She imagined the air was thick with bitterness and this is what caught at her throat.

When the city was born back then, well, it was only a mound, covered with lots of oak trees. That's what attracted St Colmcille's attention. When he looked at those trees he saw a home. So, he gave birth to a settlement which was to become the city she was today.

Mrs Sherrard was mortified to discover that she could not remember the name Colmcille had bestowed on the city. *How could I have forgotten it? Can the lack of food rid my head of knowledge, and such basic knowledge as this?*

She struggled to focus her mind on the problem. Derry's other name, it was something to do with the trees; yes, it was the Irish for oak tree. Oak trees. The answer was nearby if she could only forget about being hungry and feeling weak. Half-closing her eyes in order to concentrate, she suddenly seized upon it and yelped the name aloud in triumph: '*Doire.*' She blushed as she walked, *Oh, thank goodness, I will not forget that again in a hurry. How foolish of me! Doire* begot Derry.

Years later, her grandfather arrived from London to help build the cathedral, the very cathedral she was heading towards. Derry was the only home she knew. Everything that had ever happened to her had happened within the city's walls. For instance, this path with the broken stones, still wet from the morning's rain, she remembered bursting her lip in a fall here when she was about six years old. How funny that she should think of that now.

'Mrs Sherrard? Good morning to you.'

She hadn't noticed the soldier until he addressed her which was peculiar since he was directly in front of her, sitting on a grubby white horse whose ribs she could plainly see.

'Oh, Mr Murray. You've still got your horse; I thought they had all been eaten.'

There was no malice in the woman's words yet they shocked Adam just the same. He patted Pegasus as if to make up for her tactlessness.

Forcing a smile through, he said, 'Yes, I've still got her. There are a few more about the city. It's mostly the Jacobite horses we've been eating.'

Mrs Sherrard nodded but seemed distracted already.

He offered her another titbit of information. 'There are still some cattle left too, though I think they will be slaughtered soon.'

She thought about this. 'That will mean an end to the milk supply.'

Adam blushed a little, feeling awkward. 'The Jacobites have some cattle. I hope to make an attempt to grab them.'

'An attempt?' Mrs Sherrard repeated carefully.

He couldn't think of what to say to this. She reminded him of his old teacher who never allowed him to be vague in answer to her questions. Her response to any ambiguity, on his part, was to immediately follow with a second question, usually repeating his words back to him, just as Mrs Sherrard had done.

He was doing his best to provide conversation but was quite unable to affect determination and positivity at this particular moment. Some days his confidence was strong and then there were days like this when he dithered about, unable to convince himself of anything.

'I'm going to the cathedral.' Adam hadn't actually asked her where she was going but Mrs Sherrard thought he should know.

There was an explosion somewhere behind them; not even Pegasus bothered to be frightened by it. The Jacobite cannons were fired day and night; the only option was to become used to them. Adam was perplexed at how the guns were aimed to fire over the walls instead of being used to blast a hole through them. It was such a waste of their artillery. He found himself wondering if the Jacobites had not, in fact, lost some of their determination, or else their leaders were lacking in basic military intelligence. He became aware that Mrs Sherrard had fixed her gaze on him.

How long had she been staring at his face? For the want of something to say he exclaimed, 'But, where are my manners? Please allow me to accompany you to the cathedral.'

He was half-hoping that she might refuse his offer since

he felt a little shy in her presence and briefly wondered what on earth they might talk about as they walked to St Columb's. He was unused to being alone with a married woman – or any other woman for that matter.

As if to confirm his own awkwardness, she misunderstood his intention. 'No, I'm not getting up on your horse. It doesn't have the strength to take two.'

Adam got down from Pegasus and followed the woman's sharp glance at his horse's flank; he could see the ribs too. Sounding both defensive and guilty, he said, 'She has a strong heart.'

He had only climbed into the saddle to prove that Pegasus was still a working horse that was needed for skirmishes with the enemy. Although there was another reason too, something he hadn't told anyone else. For some reason he decided to confide in Mrs Sherrard, despite the fact that her eyes bore no warmth. He struggled to find, in her pinched face, the kind and gentle woman he remembered from previous meetings, before all this trouble began. She scared him a little now; she seemed so shrunken, inside and out.

'Some weeks ago, I had, I think, a vision.'

To his relief, she tipped her head to one side as she considered his confession. 'A vision? Whatever do you mean?'

A smirk played upon her lips. He hadn't expected that. Would she think he had lost his mind? In any case it was too late to stop and he hadn't the imagination to make up anything else.

So, he continued, 'It was the middle of the night. No, wait, it was just before midnight ...'

But it was too late, the woman's attention had wandered, and she started her own confession. 'Sometimes I cannot remember why we're doing this.'

To their right were bodies, some wrapped in blankets and some with just a couple of dried-up flowers on their chests. She focused on the smaller ones as they walked by. 'Do you think that King William and King James would agree with those children dying for them?' Her voice was strained. 'I'm sure they would have preferred to live. After all, children don't decide to be martyrs, do they? They probably didn't even understand why they had to be hungry.'

Adam swallowed and felt the by now familiar trembling in his legs.

They continued to walk although perhaps it would be more accurate to describe it as shuffling. From a distance you would be forgiven for believing they were an elderly couple as they bent forward to protect themselves from the sharpness of the summer breeze.

Paying little heed to the explosions, the dead, the dying and the begging of the homeless, they eventually arrived at the cathedral which continued to stand strong, just like the walls, the red flag of defiance waving gaily at their approach.

'What time is it?' Mrs Sherrard asked. 'Though I don't know why I should care. Time means nothing nowadays; it marches forward, leaving us behind, reminding us how stuck we are here.'

Adam took out his pocket watch. Mrs Sherrard peered at it, saying, 'What an unusual piece.'

Adam found himself holding it up for her to inspect, turning it upside down so that she could see the engraving on its back, in black and red, of a bare-backed rider, on a horse, with his bow and arrow.

Mrs Sherrard asked, 'Is that you?'

'No, ma'am,' he said, wondering how she could think that. The watch had belonged to Gabriel who had made a present of it to him, explaining that he no longer cared what time of the day it was.

Adam told Mrs Sherrard it was almost ten o'clock, showing her the clock's face with its dainty hands and roman numerals as if afraid she might doubt him.

They were still some distance from the cathedral and, needing to fill the uncomfortable silence that threatened, Adam tried to return to their earlier conversation. 'My vision, it … well, it looked like … an angel.' He found himself unable to say more than that.

'An angel?' Mrs Sherrard stared at the sky as if searching

for one of her own. 'They are God's messengers. Maybe it was telling you that we're about to win … or we're all going to die. I should imagine it's too late for anything else.'

Adam knew she was referring to the cannonball that had recently been fired into the city. The massive ball of lead had landed in the middle of the street, inflicting no damage or wounds. Closer inspection revealed that it had been hollowed out to carry a sheet of paper with yet more terms of surrender penned by the Jacobites: if the city reopened her gates, nobody would be punished. Quite reasonable really, all things considered. Nevertheless, the cry of the people remained solid: NO SURRENDER!

Perhaps in an attempt to instil some positivity before she left him, Mrs Sherrard gestured to the cathedral. 'Either way, I'm sure this will continue to stand here whether we survive or not.'

Adam smiled politely and watched her go through the door into the darkness beyond.

The very next day it was Henry Campsie's turn to deliver shocking news. 'Adam Murray has been shot!'

Robert gasped, 'Is he dead?'

Henry shrugged. 'No, I don't think so. Last I heard the surgeon was working on him. It's his legs, I think, both of them.'

Mr Sherrard went to visit Adam as soon as he heard.

He found him in bed, in his aunt's house, looking frail and forlorn. His aunt was crying. It was Adam who explained her tears. James Murray, his cousin, had been killed.

'I'm so very sorry for your loss, Mrs Murray, and you too, Adam.'

When the tearful woman left them alone, Adam whispered, 'I think she blames me.'

Mr Sherrard checked the young colonel's wounds; the surgeon had done a good job as usual. 'Well, you're looking a lot better than I expected. I feared we had lost you. Someone must have been watching over you.'

Adam shrugged. 'It was my idea but I felt it was worth it, to make another attack on the trenches near Butchers' Gate.'

Mr Sherrard sat down heavily on the side of the bed. Adam took this to mean he wished to hear more and obliged. 'There were twelve of us, all armed. We got as close to the Jacobites as I am to you and we just kept firing our rifles until we had no more bullets left.' He paused, to catch his breath.

'Are you in much pain?' asked Mr Sherrard.

Adam shook his head, but Mr Sherrard knew better than that. He also knew better than to air his opinion about what he thought of the whole adventure. Twelve men running out to attack goodness knows how many enemy soldiers. *What was he thinking? It was suicidal and a miracle that more of them weren't killed!*

Oblivious to the physician's thoughts, Adam spoke slowly now, exhaustion beginning to claim him. 'I didn't see who shot James. I didn't even see who shot me. It happened when we were falling back toward the wall.'

Mr Sherrard just nodded and listened, waiting for his patient to drift off to sleep. When the physician stood up and prepared to go, Adam stirred and murmured, 'Tell your wife I'm sorry I didn't get the cows for her.'

CHAPTER TWENTY-EIGHT

Yes, there were cattle to be got. The Jacobites had put them to graze on the grass just behind their lines, not too far from Pennyburn.

Daniel and James reckoned they had been put there, in full view of the hungry guards on the walls, to taunt them.

Robert warned both of them, 'Keep your rations on you, in your pockets, at all times.'

The two boys nodded at this. Food was number one on everyone's list and some guards had learned the hard way that it wasn't wise to leave anything edible lying around.

The three of them and Henry Campsie were standing beside Ship Quay Gate in order to volunteer their services, along with five hundred other men and boys, for the planned big cattle raid.

Despite the tiredness and lack of strength, the atmosphere was one of good cheer.

The last of Derry's cows had indeed been butchered for meat, all except one. So, as Mrs Sherrard rightly predicted, this precious source of milk – not to mention butter, cream and cheese – was coming to an end.

Something had to be done.

A couple of short streets away, Adam Murray lay awake, bitterly disappointed that he couldn't join in the raid. He tried to distract himself by reading his bible, but when he came across the words 'lowing cattle' he felt too upset to continue. At least he had managed to get word to Gabriel that he was alive and as well as could be expected.

Daniel wondered why one cow had been kept alive, although it did mean that his father could continue to get a little milk for his sister.

So, here they all were, at three o'clock on the morning of Thursday, 25 July – and it wasn't raining. That in itself was a good enough reason to be cheerful.

As usual, Henry had all the information. 'Our job is to herd the cattle back here, which sounds easy enough except for the ditches and trenches full of Jacobites that stand between us and the cows.'

James Morrison got so excited at the thought of a hot meal that it triggered a coughing fit. The others stood by, useless to help him catch his breath, as he wheezed and spluttered.

In fact, Daniel was growing more and more concerned about his friend. He had confided in Robert that James was doing poorly these days. His mother had taken to her bed and James was sorely torn between duty to his king and duty to his mother. The stress was taking its toll on him.

Thanks to his father's profession, and teaching, Daniel could spot the worrying signs. James was constantly trembling with the cold and complaining about strange pains in his bones. His breathing always sounded forced, and once or twice he had actually fallen asleep on his feet. It was hard to believe this was the same boy who had boasted of catching the fastest rodents with his bare hands.

Poor James suddenly found himself the centre of attention when the captain in charge appeared in front of him and said, 'We can't have you coughing like that when we go outside. If we can't surprise the enemy we're done for! I'm afraid you'll have to stay here.'

Even if James had managed to speak, he wouldn't have bothered to argue. He just hoped it was too dark to see the tears in his eyes. As soon as he could, he wished his friends the best of luck and turned away, meaning to climb the walls, to watch the proceedings from there.

Governor Walker called for silence. 'I just want to say a few words before you go. Keep up your hearts, my dear fellow-soldiers, if you care about your families, your homes, your freedom and, above all, your religion. Take courage. It's because of our courage and religion that we are persecuted. And it's for that we shall be glad to suffer for and defend until our last breath. So help us God!'

Every one of those five hundred officers and soldiers made a hearty reply. 'Amen!'

They were split into three groups: the first would go out by Bishop's Gate, and the second would go through Butchers' Gate, to the north-west of the city, while the last group would stand by Bishop's Gate in case of attack.

Daniel filed out through Butchers' Gate, following his brother and Henry. Because so many of their guards had died from hunger and disease, there were now enough rifles to go around. Daniel clutched his to his chest, determined neither to look nor be scared. He would have preferred to have James with them and experienced a wrench at leaving him behind. But he had to concentrate on the job at hand.

Right at that moment he found himself missing poor old Horace. His dog would have loved this, going for a walk in the dead of night with all these comrades in arms. Also, Daniel knew that Horace would not have allowed any harm to come to him.

In those few minutes Daniel missed his dog more than he had ever missed anyone in his entire life.

Robert checked his brother was right behind him but he wasn't making any promises to look after him. Well, he would do his best to protect him, but Robert intended to be busy dealing with the enemy. How wonderful it was to get out of the city, to take control and make something happen. It was now that Robert truly understood why Adam Murray had done what he did, risking lives to shoot up one trench in the hope of sending men scattering to the winds. Glancing back at the walls, he appreciated their protection but they did make him feel like he was locked up and hidden away from the world.

It was too early for birdsong, too early for that fresh smell of morning that includes every blade of grass, every leaf on the trees and clods of earth. Nothing had a distinctive scent at this hour, although maybe that was because the Williamites' noses were too full of the city's stench.

Henry's thoughts were of death – not his, but of the Jacobites he was about to kill. He smiled to himself as he thought of how he was going to waken them from one sleep in order to put them to sleep again forever. They wouldn't even have time to realise that those waking moments were the last they would ever have.

The captain, one of Adam's friends, instructed his group to stop when they were about twenty feet from the walls, in order to load their rifles. Those with flintlock rifles moved to the front to use their bodies as walls for their comrades with the old-fashioned matchlock rifle so that the telltale glow of the burning rope that would light the gunpowder could not be seen.

How loud their footfall sounded in Daniel's ears, though he could hear something else – snoring. Nobody knew exactly how many Jacobites were asleep in the trench or how many would be keeping watch. Therefore, it was important to act fast once they were in firing range. Of course Henry and Robert claimed the newer flintlocks, obliging Daniel to take his usual spot behind them.

Making sure his brother blocked him, Daniel shook out his burning rope from beneath his cloak and, pulling back the small hammer of his musket rifle, he set the rope into it, relieved to see the gunpowder spark.

There was a shout from the trench. 'Halt! Who goes there?'

It was the signal to go, and the front line did, sprinting hard. Daniel ran too, keeping behind Robert. He hardly knew where he was and was almost deafened by his own breathing and thumping heart. The heavy gun suddenly felt like butter in his hand. *Please God, don't let me drop it!* As if he hadn't enough to worry about.

He narrowly missed crashing into Robert when the front line came to a sudden stop, raised their muskets and took aim at the dense mass in front of them. This was the plan; they would fire first, and then those with the match-locks would step out from behind them and shoot. By the time they had finished the front line's flintlocks would be ready to fire again.

Daniel forgot the one thing that Robert had told him. 'Remember to close your eyes when you pull the trigger!'

You see, because it was so dark, his old rifle was going to light up like a torch for just a second or two before the musket ball shot out in search of something soft to plough into.

But Daniel had so much to think about and, furthermore, he found he was not prepared for the confusion.

Over a hundred Williamites bellowed their arrival and their guns sounded out like firecrackers, exploding every few seconds. Once they had been fired, the guns smouldered like campfires.

Daniel couldn't make out the smoke in the darkness but it caught the back of his throat and made his eyes water. It didn't matter if he coughed now.

Not surprisingly, the Jacobites were in complete chaos. Hundreds of men were shouting in real panic as they woke up to find themselves in the most dangerous situation: packed close in rows, in a deep trench and now having to find their rifles and try to load them in the dark. There were already plenty of screams, suggesting the success of Derry's front line in finding targets.

Now that Robert and Henry were behind him, the way was clear for Daniel to shoot. He raised his heavy rifle, pulled the trigger and was immediately blinded.

'AAGH,' he shrieked. *No, no, how could I have been so stupid?* Half-blind, he stumbled backwards, knowing that he had to start preparing to shoot once more.

Bodies pushed by him, presumably Robert and Henry. Sure enough, he heard Henry snarl, 'You little fool!'

Daniel didn't need his sight to know that this was directed at him.

I can do this! I can do this! He reached down with a shaking hand, to feel for the bag of gunpowder that was tied to his belt, vaguely aware that he was drenched in sweat. The constant shouting and shooting assailed his ears. Another round of bullets soared into the trench, adding to the mayhem. Men could be heard crying out, 'I'm hit! I'm hit!'

Daniel dropped the bag and reached for it again, wondering if it was really dark or if he was still blinded from the first gunshot. Somebody tripped over him. 'Sorry!' Daniel gasped as the man grunted something appalling.

Again, Henry was in his ear. 'Forget it. Just move. Charge!'

The running began again and ended just as abruptly. Daniel and the others jumped into the trench, landing on the bodies of Jacobite soldiers, who had, in some cases at least, managed to find swords, pikes or empty guns to hit out with. He lost sight of the other two and, just for a solitary second, was unsure what to do next. Nothing had prepared him for this, but he couldn't just stand there, hoping to live.

There was a movement to his right; a voice, foreign, exclaimed as something swiped the air just in front of Daniel's nose. Before he could engage the Jacobite officer, a figure pushed by him, knocking him over on top of someone else. Daniel peered and recognised the man's attacker – and his saviour – as Henry, who swung hard with his rifle, cracking it against the officer's skull.

Where was Robert?

Daniel couldn't see his brother and now he too had to lash out at whoever he had fallen onto. Somehow he found the room to lift his gun over his head and bring it down on the back of the soldier who was having difficulty finding his own feet in all the turmoil. He hit him as hard as he could; only thinking that if he paused he'd be killed.

Meanwhile, Henry was swallowed up in the rage he had barely contained behind the walls. It all tumbled out now, onto the Jacobite officer's head, again and again, long after the man stopped begging for mercy and the air around tasted of his blood.

'Run! Run!'

Well, they all understood those words, Williamites and Jacobites.

Daniel wondered who they were for until he saw who proved obedient with their response.

But what else could the Jacobites do? There was no time to collect themselves and put up a decent fight. If they stayed put, they were going to be bludgeoned, stabbed or – if they were lucky – shot at point blank range. There was nothing the Jacobites could do except climb the hell out of the trench and retreat as fast as they could.

The Jacobite officer responsible for screaming 'Run!' probably did not realise what a terrific idea that was. Run! It was brilliant, perfect even. Because once the initial rush wore off those underfed Williamites, their slender bodies reminded them that they were lacking in their normal strength and speed. The one thing they could not do was give chase. It was impossible.

Undoubtedly the Derrymen had won the battle for this particular trench; within minutes it was theirs, leaving only wounded, dying and dead Jacobites, but perhaps they could have won so much more if only they had been able to pursue the fleeing enemy all the way back to their cattle.

But they couldn't; they simply couldn't.

As it was, most of the Williamite men were forced to take a rest amongst the blood and the corpses in order to be able to get back to the city. As they struggled to recover some strength they could hear the cattle in the distance, but they were too far away for the soldiers' tired limbs.

When the raiding party was ready, they slowly collected what they could: weapons, prisoners, clothing and bits of food. Once the bodies had been stripped of anything that might be useful, they were used as stepping stones to get back out of the trench.

Just like the rest of his fellow soldiers, Daniel stood on heads, shoulders and legs and didn't allow it to bother him in the slightest.

He led Henry by the arm or else he would have been left behind. Henry never said a word or made an attempt to wipe the blood from his eyes. The soldier he had attacked no longer resembled a human being, such were his horrific injuries. Daniel looked away in distaste. As far as he was concerned, Henry, for those few moments, had gone quite mad. There was no other explanation for it. The man was dead long before Henry stopped hitting him. In any case, there wasn't a sound out of him as Daniel roughly pushed and pulled him until they reached the top of the trench. On the one hand Daniel hated him for sneering at him for forgetting to close his eyes, but on the other hand Henry had probably saved his life.

The gust of wind was a delicious treat. Daniel would have preferred to stand there for a bit and allow it to cool him down. Robert appeared beside him, shaming Daniel into admitting to himself that he had completely forgotten about him.

Robert whispered, 'Is he okay?' – meaning Henry.

Daniel shrugged. He was too exhausted for conversation.

Nobody spoke on the walk back. Daniel felt like he had left Derry hours ago. The warriors trudged through Ship Quay Gate to be met by a crowd hopeful for spoils. They had watched the action from the walls though the darkness had made it difficult to see much. Still, they knew that their men had proved victorious.

There was just the small matter of the herd of Jacobite cows still out there, tucked away from all harm.

Nevertheless, the atmosphere was almost jolly. Rumours flew about that between one and two hundred enemy soldiers had been killed. Meanwhile, the Jacobite prisoners were locked up and told they could look forward to being hungry for the foreseeable future.

Mr Sherrard came out to see his sons. He didn't recognise them immediately, which shook him, yet he managed to hide his dismay at the changes in them, reminding himself that hunger alone would make them look older and wilder.

He greeted them with an explanation. 'Your mother was worried.'

Robert sneaked him some biscuits he had liberated from a dead red coat. All food was to be handed into the authorities for them to share out again.

James Morrison found them too. The four of them – three Sherrards and James – instinctively formed a protective circle around Henry who seemed unable to understand he was home.

As they stood there, a discussion erupted about the Jacobite cows. For some, the dream of beef stew was not extinguished just yet.

Someone said, 'If only the stupid beasts would approach

us themselves, without us having to go and fetch them.'

A spluttering of guffawing and name-calling greeted this unhelpful observation.

To his companions' surprise, James had an idea. He had missed out on the fighting but he hadn't given up on contributing to the night's work. 'Wait a minute!'

Daniel felt less than hopeful about whatever his friend might be about to propose.

James held up a skinny arm. 'We still have one cow left, don't we? What if we make it call out, you know, hurt it in some way? Mightn't the others come running to help it?'

The thing was that everyone was desperate for a proper meal so when they heard this plan, instead of denouncing it as the most foolish plan they had ever heard, they slowly and gradually decided that it was better than no plan at all.

The Sherrards weren't farmers and really hadn't had much contact with cows but even they were not convinced that cows grazing several miles away would pay the slightest bit of attention to the cries of a stranger cow in distress.

James looked at the brothers, expecting to be complimented on his idea. Daniel was tongue-tied, while Robert sighed, muttering, 'Well, I suppose it's worth a try.' He was only being polite but it was enough to encourage James to shout out again, 'We'll set our cow on fire. That should do it!'

Daniel couldn't see the expression on his father's face. He felt giddy as if he had stepped into some fantastic fairytale. Furthermore, he did experience a vague guilt for the poor animal that had helped sustain Derry's infants, but what could he do? It seemed to him that, in times like these, animals had to die like soldiers. Besides, no one else seemed to doubt that James was making sense.

And so the cow was rudely woken up and led into the middle of the Diamond, where some fellows had hastily put together twigs and rags. She was positioned over the bundle and a post was knocked into ground, tying her into place. Sensing trouble, her ears were pointed as she looked warily about her, trying to sort out why she was nervous. Robert scratched his chin, while his father seemed surprised to find he was still standing there.

The fire was lit and the crowd waited. A few seconds passed before the animal realised that she was in trouble. She tried her best to step off the bundle, swishing her tail in alarm. Several impatient people turned towards the gate, hoping to see Jacobite cows demanding to be allowed through.

The flames flicked the cow's belly, and she did start to bawl as it became increasingly impossible to keep her four legs out of the fire at the same time. She strained against the rope, trying to work out how to stop the pain. There was a strong smell of singed hair but still no thunderous roar of hooves from outside. In any case, the cow was not going to wait to be rescued. With an almighty shudder, she flung her head back and leapt into the air, ripping the post out of the ground, and made a run for it.

Not even James suggested a second attempt. People looked away from one another as if suddenly embarrassed for ever believing in such a foolish idea.

A peculiar sound punctured the awkwardness. Daniel saw Henry bend over, his entire body shaking as he appeared to be gulping for air. Was he choking? Mr Sherrard rushed to see if the boy was alright. There was a loud snort ... of laughter. Henry could not catch his breath because he was laughing so hard. Tears rolled down his face and his shoulders heaved with the effort.

James Morrison suspected he was the cause of this undignified display and was much put out, pouting in such a way as to make Daniel and Robert join Henry. Even Mr Sherrard seemed to lose his anxiousness for those precious minutes as he watch the boys – minus James – laugh as if they were never going to stop.

Three evenings later, on 28 July 1689, a young Williamite was standing guard at the top of the St Columb's tower, idly staring out over the Foyle, hardly remembering why he was there or what he was looking out for. His empty belly croaked miserably while his head ached from lack of sustenance, both liquid and solid.

That afternoon Governor George Walker had preached in the cathedral, telling the people, 'God won't let us down. He hasn't kept us safe thus far to allow victory to be taken by the Papists. All He needs is for us to remain strong and devoted.'

A variety of parishioners sat before him, wanting desperately to believe his words.

Where were the ships? Why didn't they come now?

This was the question on everyone's lips. Despite the governor's sermon, the population, or what remained of it, recognised that the end was near. Soldiers were dying in their hundreds every single day and nobody knew this better than Governor Walker. He was keeping count of the army deaths but had no idea how many civilians were succumbing to the rampant diseases and starvation.

Daniel and James were on the wall, with Daniel doing his best to hide his terror from his friend. James refused to go home and refused to lie down on the ground. Daniel offered his coat for a pillow. 'But why won't you just rest? I can keep watch alone. If anything happens I'll wake you. I promise.'

James was in a bad way. He had lost teeth while his face was drawn and a deathly grey. Daniel could clearly see his jawline. It made his chin jut out as if it had been carved from a sharp rock. Also he wheezed instead of breathing normally. 'I'm fine,' he gasped.

Daniel wanted to shake him. 'No, you are not fine. Nobody is going to think any less of you for taking a break. We're all suffering, you know, and you're no different from anyone else.'

James looked hurt and shivered.

'You see,' pounced Daniel. 'You are shivering but it is not that cold. That means you're not well!'

He had to wait for James to stop coughing in order to issue a threat. 'James Morrison, if you do not lie down for a few minutes I will never talk to you again. I promise you that much!'

Resting a thin hand on Daniel's arm, James whispered, 'Yes, Mother!'

Daniel laughed in spite of himself before removing his coat and bundling it on the ground, just a few feet from where he stood. 'Go on, lie down there like a good boy. I'll wake you up in a bit.'

He had to help James to lie down and then stepped quickly back to the wall.

'Daniel?'

'Oh, God! What now? Will you just go to sleep?' He was pretending to be annoyed.

'Thanks!'

Daniel glanced around. 'For what? For lending you my coat or for having to put up with you?'

He couldn't see James's face properly but he heard him

murmur, 'For everything!'

There was gunshot in the distance, but it was impossible for Daniel to see where it was coming from. He expected to be grilled by his friend on its origins but James had fallen into a sound sleep.

The wind stepped up, alternating between dancing with and pummelling Governor Mitchelburne's flag.

The young guard at the top of St Columb's tower could hear the guns but could see no smoke. *What's going on? They had to be Jacobite guns, didn't they?*

Looking down, he could see people in the city slowly looking up at him or at the sky above, all engaged in listening to what sounded like a gun battle being carried by the wind. Perhaps it was even cannon fire. Over the next few minutes he watched as crowds of people made their way to the walls to peer out across the Foyle in expectation and in trepidation. The guard shrugged his shoulders, to show he knew as little as they did and then he looked again, and stared … and stared.

He saw them, mere seconds before everyone else: ships. Was he dreaming? No, the wind prevented him from sleeping on his feet. So, this was it, the ships, King William's ships appeared like golden swans out of the gloom. The Jacobite cannon along the Foyle did its utmost to puncture holes in the vessels that looked so proud and dignified. One sailed ahead of the others and it was obvious that it had the dreaded boom in its sights.

On the walls Daniel shouted at people not to step on James. The crowd quickly spread down along the walls, blocking his view of his friend. Daniel reckoned that James would have had to get up, with all the noise and bustle, and had probably been carried farther down the ramparts by the sheer force of all the bodies pressed together. As the first ship sailed closer and closer Daniel trained his eyes to watch her progress.

The gunfire was deafening. The Jacobites on the banks were giving all they had while the sailors onboard returned fire. Black smoke hung in the evening air and the wind died down, as if it too wanted to watch the scene unfold.

Robert and Henry fought to move in beside Daniel as he did his best to make room for them. He allowed himself to look for James, noting that just about everybody must be gathered around him, all watching and praying for that good ship to blast through the Jacobite barricade in *their* river.

Daniel saw her name and read it aloud, the *Mountjoy*, in case anyone else needed to know it. Nobody thanked him because they were fixated on the sight of the *Mountjoy* charging that boom. She hit the chain but it did not break; instead it curved towards her with such force that it flung her back towards the east bank of the Foyle where she got stuck in shallow water. Women screamed while cheering could be heard from the Jacobites.

Robert gasped in horror at the sight of Jacobite soldiers running into the water, heading for the ship. 'Oh no, they're going to board her!'

The people of Derry could do nothing except watch and pray. Someone in the crowd began quietly to recite 'Our Father who art in Heaven, Hallowed be Thy Name', and people all over the walls joined in. Men, women and children. 'Give us this day our daily bread.'

Some were overcome and wept openly. They were starving, weary civilians who, along with their soldiers, had faced hunger and violence, bombs and disease for one hundred and five days and, by now, all had lost someone dear to them. They leant against their city's walls and watched those Jacobites gleefully tramp through the water, already calling out their threats to the sailors.

The captain onboard could be seen, sword in hand, cheering on his men. His arm was raised until the enemy soldiers were mere yards from his ship and then his arm slammed down, the signal to fire three cannons right into the centre of them. Derry watched as the bulk of those Jacobites fell back into the water, hardly knowing they were dead. This captain, whoever he was, was mourned by the stricken population as he too was caught by fire and toppled to the ground.

Now Mother Nature stepped in, the rising tide tipping

the ship out of the shallow water and towards the boom once more. Not one person on the walls could release a cheer; instead there was a frozen silence as the *Mountjoy* made her approach again and, this time, she passed through, thanks to her first attempt which had weakened the chains. She was closely followed by the second ship, the *Phoenix*. Sometime later the third ship, the *Darmouth*, would make her appearance.

As soon as the guard on St Columb's tower saw that the boom had been smashed, he fired his cannon in celebration, announcing to all and sundry that the siege was over.

Only then did the crowd give voice to their joy and relief. People wept in happiness, clasping one another, looking for their relatives and friends. The soldiers hugged one another and then turned to rush down to open Ship Quay Gate, ignoring the Jacobites who still continued to shoot because what else could they do?

Robert and Henry thumped each other and dragged Daniel in between them, tousling his hair and pushing him back and forth until he begged them to let him be. They couldn't stop laughing and shouting and then Henry cried, 'Come on, let's go down to the river!'

They turned to run with Daniel following them until he remembered James. Where was he? Over the last few months, Daniel had had to listen to James over and over again, moaning about the fact that he had not helped to close the gates that day back in December. So he knew better than to run off and forget about him now.

'James? James Morrison, where are you?'

Daniel looked all around him, expecting at any moment to see his familiar face. Other people made their way down to greet the sailors, who were still a while off yet. Daniel grew impatient as he remembered that the ships were bringing food, real food. He could hardly believe it. *Oh, where is he? Maybe he has gone ahead and is already down by the Foyle.*

No, there he was, exactly where he had left him.

'James?' Daniel burst out laughing; surely he had not slept through all the fun. *Oh dear! I'm in trouble now after promising to wake him if anything happened.*

'James, you fool, wake up. It's all over. We're saved!'

Bending over him, Daniel saw the smile on his friend's face, but although his eyes were open, they were completely still.

CHAPTER TWENTY-NINE

Having repaired his father's trousers for the umpteenth time and stuffed himself on biscuits, Adam Murray got back on his horse, setting him off at a smart trot for Derry. It was a pleasant afternoon, the type that made one truly grateful to be alive. Adam breathed in the smell of the countryside, enjoying the sun's warmth, and the wondrous peace. Birds twittered and sang, bees hummed and the multitudes of flies were their usual irritating selves.

All was as it should be.

It had taken a while to reach this point, but as Gabriel had assured him, 'You'll appreciate everything all the more now!' As usual his father was right.

He visited Gabriel more than ever since the old dog died. His father wouldn't hear of getting another one, sure that he wouldn't be around himself for much longer. Adam didn't bother to argue, suggesting that he could get a kitten instead. His father sniffed and said he'd think about it.

Adam waved to the farmers working in their fields.

His horse sneezed and shook his head. He was a young horse, black with a white stripe on his snout. Gabriel had insisted on buying him after Pegasus was confiscated from his son by Major-General Kirke who had finally arrived with his ships of food and soldiers on 28 July, three days after the infamous 'Battle of the Cows'. That was certainly a day to remember, with plenty of rejoicing and merriment. However, the celebration didn't last too long as the major-general took charge, stamping out all opposition to his new rules and regulations, and thanking just about nobody for what they had done for the city.

Gabriel refused to indulge his son, merely asking him, 'But what did you expect? Were you looking for glory?'

Adam shrugged. 'I didn't expect him to cut the army in half, leave us without wages, thus forcing our sick soldiers to have to beg for food and take my horse because he didn't like me.'

His father was blunt. 'You were too popular with too many followers.'

Adam stiffened. 'Was that my fault?'

His father only smiled at this.

Of course the walls had been repaired and now looked the exact same as ever. Perhaps the only change was that the gates were always open these days. There were rumblings elsewhere now, thanks to the French King Louis XIV pushing King James to try again for the English throne. But Derry was safe from trouble and that was the important thing.

Adam sought his father's understanding if not his sympathy, saying: 'It feels like I'm being punished for what I did. Surely you can understand that. I fought to keep the city free from the Papists, and so we did, enduring starvation until Kirke finally found the courage to break through the boom.'

Gabriel nodded. 'Then just be happy with that. You know what you did, I know what you did and God above knows what you did.'

Adam smiled in response to various greetings, a much quieter entrance than the one he made over a year ago now, when people chanted his name and prepared to follow him to war. He had had his chance for more, of course. He could have been a governor of Derry but he had no interest in that. He still didn't.

Then there was Reverend Walker's book. His father had merely laughed when Adam told him that the reverend's book made no mention of him, hardly describing anyone else's achievements aside from his own and his parishioners'.

Adam fumed, 'I hear it's selling by the hundreds in England – his version of the truth about what happened.'

'Write your own book!' was Gabriel's unhelpful response.

It was market day and the place was buzzing with all

sorts. Young children ran about, getting in everyone's way while cheerfully ignoring their mothers' threats. The smell of fresh manure was strong, but it didn't bother Adam in the slightest. He liked to see it and hear the mooing of the cows, bleating of goats and lambs and the excited barking of the dogs that ran riot, here, there and everywhere.

The butcher was sharpening his knives and calling out his wares to the housewives whose attention were caught by the fishmonger and the candle-maker.

In the distance Adam spied Mr Sherrard and quickened his pace to catch up with the physician. As usual, Mr Sherrard produced some sugar from his pocket for Adam's horse who nuzzled him in gratitude.

'Well, Adam, how are you on this fine day?'

Adam grasped his hand warmly. 'As well as can be. It is really busy today, isn't it?'

Mr Sherrard shrugged. 'Isn't it always? How is Gabriel?'

'Oh, the same as ever. He's like these walls, he'll never change!'

Mr Sherrard laughed. 'But you wouldn't want him to change, would you?'

Adam said nothing to this and searched for another topic. Mrs Sherrard had never been the same since the trouble though Mr Sherrard had confided that he did expect her to get better when she was ready: 'All that hunger and worry took its toll on her system.' She never left the house now, not even to go to church. There were dark days when she didn't leave her bed. From time to time Adam called in to see how she was but only when she asked for him.

'How are the boys?'

'You mean, the men,' corrected Mr Sherrard with a smile. He sighed.

Adam waited politely.

'Ah, they're fine, don't mind me. They are set on army life and this morning told us that they will be leaving shortly to fight for King William.'

'Father, Mr Murray!'

Adam turned and joked, 'I think you've gotten even taller. What are they feeding you?'

Daniel blushed. He was still his father's youngest son though he looked and felt a lot older since the day he helped closed the gates against the Redshanks.

'Father, you've to buy more candles. Alice ate another one and Mother is beside herself.'

Mr Sherrard tutted, 'Oh dear, not again. I'd best be off, Adam. If I don't act now, I'll forget all about it and then I'll really be in trouble!'

Adam and Daniel watched him hurry away, the tail of his coat flapping behind him.

Daniel said, 'He's more afraid of Mother than of anyone else.'

Adam asked, 'I hear you and Robert are leaving Derry?'

'Father told you!' said Daniel. 'Yes, there are a few of us going. My brother Robert, Henry Campsie and some other friends of ours. We owe that much to King William and, well, it's important to take a stand … as you know yourself, sir.'

Adam was surprised when Daniel blushed some more and admitted, 'The truth is you have inspired me to do this. I never saw myself as a soldier before last year, but I learned from you that it can be a noble and even holy calling. You taught me to care about what's important.'

Adam bowed his head in thanks, and Daniel shyly asked, 'Do you wish you could come with us?'

'Oh,' said Adam, 'I don't know. My legs don't work as well as they used to and, to be honest, I think I gave all the fight I had in me during the siege. I have other things to focus on now.'

Daniel nodded. 'Of course, sir. I hear you're about to be married. May I offer my congratulations?'

'Of course you may!' said Adam. 'So, last I heard, James and his cousin's army are stopping off in Dublin for a bit. Do you know where King William wishes to confront him?'

Daniel scrunched up his face to think. 'Some place near the town of Drogheda.'

Adam nodded. 'And you are sure this is what you want to do?'

He wondered if the young boy was just blindly following

his older brother. Daniel had seemed a world apart from Robert; at least that's what Adam had always felt.

And, for a moment, Daniel did look slightly unsure of the question and how to answer it. 'I am scared, if that's what you mean.'

Adam was going to protest but Daniel continued, 'A lot of people died during the siege, including one of my best friends, James Morrison, I don't know if you remember him, but I'm still here and I can't help thinking that James would relish joining William's army. So, I'm doing it because he can't.'

Daniel stopped to collect his thoughts. This was a conversation he hadn't been able to have with anyone else.

'It's just that if the Jacobites win it will all have been for nothing: all those deaths, all that starvation, it would be forgotten about and judged to have been a waste of time.' He swallowed and reached out to pat Adam's horse. 'We lost so much, all of us, but as long as King William rules, there is a point to it.'

Adam gazed at the boy in earnest, saying, 'My word, Daniel. You're absolutely right. All that trouble with Major-General Kirke after he took over Derry, I don't mind telling you that I questioned why I ever got involved in the first place. But now I remember, thanks to you.'

Daniel glowed under the unexpected praise. 'Well, thank you, sir. I … I'd better be going, now. I promised to visit

James's mother today and tell her all the news. She doesn't like me to be late.'

Adam shook the boy's hand and prayed that God would keep him safe, watching him until he disappeared around the corner.

He stood for a while longer, thinking that he really should be getting on with his own business too; he had plenty to do before he visited his fiancée's house. Gabriel's new trousers would be ready for collection. Ignoring his father's lack of interest in this particular topic, Adam had determined to buy him new clothes for the wedding.

The city was pumping with life and colour and Adam enjoyed the bedlam around him. It was difficult to remember how things had been last summer, when everything seemed to be dying, including Derry herself. But here she was, still standing and stronger than ever: the walls, the gates, St Columb's Cathedral, the river Foyle – and, of course, the people too, who hadn't surrendered in the most horrible of situations. They had all proved themselves immovable in the fantastic storms of 1688–89. Most of the streets had been repaired while there was yet work to be done to replace the broken houses, but it would be done in its own good time. There would always be work needing to be done which was a comforting thought in itself.

It would seem that the angel in the sky that night had been a positive message. Even Mrs Sherrard, on a good day, agreed with him on that matter though he suspected she had never believed in his vision. She went so far as to say, 'I think we see what we want to see, what we need to see. Maybe that's how God answers our prayers.'

Adam thought about that for ages after. Was it the angel who helped him find the hero or courage within himself? After all, he had only ever been a farmer and a dutiful son. And all Derry had been was a small town behind a big wall. The eyes of the world had watched her defy a royal army – one that was superior in number and experience – in her own peculiar way. It was a fantastic achievement.

'So,' his father had finally asked him, his eyes twinkling with mischief, 'was it worth it then? Would you do it all over again if you had to?

Adam's answer was absolute. 'Yes. Yes, I would! Of course I would.'

That evening, at the Sherrards' house, Robert asked, 'Well, are you ready? You know you take longer than a woman to pack a bag.'

Daniel stuck out this tongue and gave his rifle a last spit and polish. 'I met Adam Murray this afternoon. He says he's not sure whether he'd come with us or not.'

Robert shrugged and studied his brother's face, pretending he hadn't seen Horace's collar being shoved into the bag. He also recognised James Morrison's old and battered rifle that was being scrubbed within an inch of its life. He felt his heart dip and said quietly, 'And what about you, Dan, are you sure?'

Daniel wouldn't look at him, not until he was sure that his face showed no doubt. He nodded eventually, adding, 'I'm doing this for lots of different reasons. Don't worry, I've thought long and hard about it. And I don't like leaving Father to cope with everything but ...'

Robert smiled. 'But?'

Daniel continued, 'But you'll be with me and that makes it alright.'

When Robert said nothing to this Daniel looked up just in time to see the emotion in his brother's expression. They both shrugged in defeat, each wiping the tears from their eyes and then grinning, just like they did when they were mischievous little boys running in circles around their mother who could never catch them.

'Where is it we're going anyway? Adam asked and I couldn't remember.'

His brother replied, 'Some place called the Boyne. It's a river, I think.'

THE END

GLOSSARY

Alderman: a member of the governing body of a city.

Bastion: a tower that sticks out from a wall or castle.

Jacobite: a follower of King James.

Magazine: a room where ammunition is stored.

Master of Ordnance: a military man who is responsible for the city's
army and weapons.

Papist: a Catholic (follower of the pope in Rome).

Rampart: a wall for defence purposes.

Ravelin: a separate barrier to defend a wall or gate.

Redshank: a Highlander or an Irishman.

Williamite: a follower of William of Orange.

WRITER'S NOTES

I did not set out to describe every single episode that took place in and around the Siege of Derry. Believe me, there was lots of drama and this could have been a much longer book. When I research a story I read as much as I can about it, waiting for certain people and certain situations to jump off the page of the history book and into my novel.

The Apprentice Boys of Derry was only founded in 1814 and has its base in Derry. The aim of the society was to commemorate the Siege of Derry and keep the memories of its heroes alive. In the book I do not use the term 'Apprentice' to describe the boys primarily because I could not find out what sort of apprentices they were and I am unsure if this is what they would have been called back in 1688.

Fortunately, however, we do have their names which were as follows: William Cairnes, Henry Campsie, William Crookshanks, Alexander Cunningham, John Cunningham, Samuel Harvey, Samuel Hunt, Alexander Irwin, Robert Morrison, Daniel Sherrard, Robert Sherrard, James Spike and James Steward.

Also the thirteen boys, alongside James Morrison and Adam Murray, might have been a bit older than how I presented them in my story.

From the beginning I was drawn to the fact that two of the thirteen boys who slammed Derry's gates closed, in the faces of the Redshanks, were brothers. How interesting! What if one brother was more confident than the other about holding out against King James's army, when the population began to starve and then die around them.

I knew nothing about the Sherrard family and resorted to imagination in order to bring them alive in the novel. I 'made' Mr Sherrard a physician because that's how he presented himself in my mind.

Another person who attracted my immediate attention was Adam Murray and his father Gabriel. They might well turn in their graves if they could read my portraits of them, but I must say I became extremely fond of both of them and hope that shines through.

Thanks to the kindly and proud men who look after Derry's St Columb's Cathedral today I was allowed to hold Adam's sword and his pocket watch. It was exhilarating to touch something that Adam actually carried around with him over three hundred years ago.

At some point, it struck me that I was focusing on fathers and sons in this story. To me, it was a real strand, or theme, of the Siege of Derry. Religion is generally passed on from generation to generation and, over centuries, plenty have thought it necessary to fight and die for their father's beliefs, beliefs which are also their own. And, of course, God is the ultimate father.

I have moved some things around, time-wise, to fit the timeline of my narrative, primarily the 'hanging' of McGimpsey and the governors' (Baker and Mitchelburne) sword fight. Nobody appears to know what the sword fight was about so I have come up with my own explanation.

Many of the people that appear in the story were 'real', alongside most of the episodes – including the sightings of an angel on horseback, sword in hand; the murder of the old woman who was believed to be a witch; the naked parishioners; the Battle of the Cows and the bizarre attempt to have Derry's last cow call out for help to the Jacobite cattle.

Both contemporary and modern histories on the siege vary regarding dates and consequences. Ultimately I chose what suited my story.

Some readers may disagree with my portraits of several characters, notably Robert Lundy or George Walker. All I can offer is that I was writing a novel. The characters weaved themselves in and around the facts I gathered, but since they had been dead for so long I was allowed to interpret what I learned about the individuals to fit the tale I was interested in telling.

In other words, I was frequently making things up as I went along, as writers do.

BIOGRAPHIES

Major-General Percy Kirke: It seems that, once he finally braved the boom and rescued the stricken population, Kirke's behaviour and attitude was unexpectedly harsh. He set about demobilising the city's men, taking guns and ammunition from them, and replacing officers with his own men. When a captain complained, Kirke threatened to hang him. Thanks to Kirke, most of the men who had followed Adam Murray left the city in droves. They had expected to be paid or, at least, thanked for their hard work. Instead, Kirke seemed to treat them as some sort of threat.

Lieutenant-Colonel Robert Lundy: He was suspected of treason and imprisoned in the Tower of London, where he knew he would be hanged if he did not clear his name. So he began a campaign to do just that, writing to important friends and acquaintances, pointing out that if he were a traitor he would have joined the Jacobites, on leaving Derry. Instead, he sailed for London, proof that he was innocent of all charges. He succeeded in being cleared and returned to his military career.

However, he has long been widely judged to have been a traitor to Derry and, every year, his effigy is hung and burned during the celebrations in the city to mark the anniversary of the closing of the gates in 1688.

Colonel John Mitchelburne: The colonel lost his wife and children during the siege. Nevertheless, he did marry again and chose to stay on in Derry. It was he who demanded, in vain, that the government pay the soldiers who had protected the city. On his death, 1 October 1721, he left a sum of money to allow his red flag to be flown from St Columb's Cathedral, just as it did during the siege. He is buried in Old Glendermott churchyard.

Lord Mountjoy: Lord Lieutenant Richard Talbot sent Mountjoy to France and had him imprisoned there, telling King James he was a traitor. He could have been hanged, but luckily James had no interest in killing him. On his release, Lord Mountjoy returned to army life and was killed in 1692, at the Battle of Steenkirk in the Netherlands during the Nine Years' War.

Colonel Adam Murray: Adam is pretty much everyone's hero of the siege. He never received any reward for his tireless effort in protecting the city. There are accounts that his horse died in the clash against Maumont. However, I have also read that he managed to keep his horse alive throughout the entire siege only to have it taken from him by Captain Kirke after Derry was relieved.

He is buried alongside Mitchelburne in Old Glendermott churchyard and his memory is cherished by a club of the Apprentice Boys of Derry.

Lord Lieutenant Richard Talbot: Possibly Talbot's arrogance can be blamed for the siege and the ensuing battles that followed. In any case, he died of a stroke in 1691, soon after which the Treaty of Limerick was signed.

Governor George Walker: He left the city a few days after the ships arrived and his book about the siege became an instant bestseller. However, it also became a sore point for Derry's Presbyterians when it was discovered that they had received scant mention in the Anglican reverend's book. Governor Walker was appointed Bishop of Derry but never got to enjoy this promotion because he was killed on 1 July 1690 at the Battle of the Boyne.

BIBLIOGRAPHY

Doherty, Richard: *The Siege of Derry 1689: The Military History*.
Gébler, Carlo: *The Siege of Derry: A History*.
Lacey, Brian: *The Siege of Derry* (pamphlet for Irish Heritage Series)
Simms, JG: *Jacobite Ireland*
Walker, Rev George: *A True Account of the Siege of London-derry*
Windrow, Martin: *Not One Step Back: History's Great Sieges*

The BBC website provides a detailed timeline of the siege: www.bbc.co.uk/northernireland/siege

Carlo Gébler also presents a documentary based on his book and this can be accessed from Youtube.